Children
of the
Mersey

George Horsman

MARGERY

Chapter 1
1928

In the beginning God created the heaven and the earth. And the earth was without form and void. And darkness was upon the face of the deep.

But under that dark face in the warm, amniotic fluid moved things that seemed not outside, but part of, herself, that moved to her will: a stubby finger, a tuberous arm, a foot. There were movements beyond these, too, huge and powerful movements which erupted and swirled the vast cataracts of the deep, making the waters surge like seismic tides.

And there were reverberations that drummed on muffled ears. Sometimes as if chords from outside the water-filled medicine ball in which she swam beat or pattered upon its enfolding membrane; sometimes as if reedy notes from something attached to the membrane trilled through the quivering fluid. There were moments when the notes brought excitement, making her shoot out arms and fists or kick her legs. They unclasped her fingers. The whole sealed universe spoke only with two languages: feeling and hearing. The rest was darkness.

But in the darkness some other being moved. Margery was not alone. In the enclosed, watery gloom limbs collided, fingers prodded at head, arm, leg, eye. Bellies and chests entangled in submarine logjam; two beings barely found room in this abyssal cavern.

Yet two was company. Whatever shock might kick the bladder they inhabited, whatever pale distaste might pollute the waters, there was someone else there. The rescue from loneliness redeemed all. Nothing gave love and warmth like this, nothing security so deep. Two beings were living as one.

So that when, after eternity in the ocean trench, that other one hung limp and inert, no longing fumbling, entwining, playing the game, no longer there when danger sounded, when there were, instead, only floating disjointed limbs in the chemical water, terror and loss entered to fill the void from which life had fled. And from then on until the end of her life Margery was incomplete, not whole, living out an endless, irredeemable loss, Rachel weeping for her children because they are not.

Chapter 2
1939

'As we all know, this is a very special day. And since the person for whom it's most special is going to be joined by some of her school friends this afternoon, we're holding the family celebration this morning.'

Arthur beamed round the Great Hall. It was as full an assembly of Munnerlys as Margery had ever seen. Arthur raised a glass. The family followed suit.

'I propose a toast to the lady of the hour. Ladies and gentlemen, here's wishing health and long life and happiness to our birthday girl, Margery.'

'Margery!'

There was a general melee of glass-clinking, an outbreak of excited conversation. Margery twirled round in her new frock, delighted to be the focus of attention. Arthur, proud head of the family and always one for a good tune, struck up *Happy Birthday to You* and in a performance which compensated in vigour for a gradual sliding of pitch, the others joined in.

'How old are you, then?'

'Eleven, Mother!' Trust Nancy, as the grown-ups called her, to have forgotten. And to nod like that, as if eleven was all right but only just. Why did she have to act as the household's high and mighty judge of things, the one you had to satisfy whenever you did anything?

'Before we go on to the most important event of the party, the opening of presents, may I say thank you to everyone for coming, even though it has meant missing morning service for those who would have gone and a round on the golf course for others. At least this happy event takes our minds off more worrying ones. And in that connection I think we should drink a second toast, to the two family members who're not with us today: one who's in an Army training camp of unknown location and a second who's at sea, possibly somewhere off Gibraltar, helping to defend our country.' Arthur raised his glass more gravely this time. 'To Tom and Edward.'

'Tom and Edward.'

Conforming with a small pout of impatience, Margery sipped some more of her lemonade. She didn't know what they were all worrying about and wished they would stop it; it was a bad habit. When Tom had called in on a weekend's leave he'd seemed perfectly happy. And as for her other brother, Edward, it must be fun sailing round the world and wearing one of those floppy navy-blue uniforms with a sort of little square apron at the back of your neck? There was no need to go all solemn about it. She kept her eyes glued on Arthur, a runner waiting for the starter's gun.

'And now the presents.'

She burst into a sprint down the Great Hall. Parcelled up with string and brown paper and set out in a row under the round-topped, church-like window at the far end, the presents had been kept hidden until now. She knelt, undeterred by the cracking sensation of her new patent leather shoes or the strain on their button fastenings. With deft fingers she tore off the wrappings of by far the biggest present.

'A Fairy cycle!' She clasped it to her chest. Light blue with silver handlebars and pedals, it was what she'd been longing for. She'd be able to ride round the garden – the 'grounds' as Nancy called them – pretending she was one of those men on the advertising billboards for Speedway Racing. She could use a plank propped on bricks as a kind of jump. 'It's lovely! Just what I wanted!'

'Who do you thank, then?'

'Oh, er –'

It took some minutes to extricate the little card from the shreddings of brown paper.

> *To Margery from Mother and Father*
> *on her eleventh birthday*
> *with love*

'Oh, thank you. It's super!'

It wouldn't be from Mother, of course. Dad had written the card. He would have thought of it and bought it. And you could tell from her face that Nancy didn't approve of *super*. An Americanism. Ugh!

One by one the other presents burst into daylight. A hockey stick and greetings telegram from Tom; she'd need the stick now she was starting at St Teresa's. It could lead on to great things, seeing how well she'd done even with old, borrowed sticks at Rock Ferry Elementary. A new frock from Georgina, all fresh and light in pastel green and red. An educationally improving terrestrial globe from Flo. And a Bible with flimsy pages and lots of coloured pictures - Elijah ascending into heaven and the waves of the Red Sea dividing

6

and Moses coming down from the mountain and telling the children of Israel to take the tablets. The handwriting on the card was Nancy's this time. Margery thanked her with downcast eyes, hoping it would make up for saying things were super.

'So what does it feel like to be eleven, Margery?'

She pondered her elder sister Georgina's question. She did feel different. Partly, it was being in this big, rather gloomy, old-fashioned hall with lots of grown-ups. She would rather be out in the garden, speedway racing. Partly, though, she felt annoyed at the way people kept on refilling their glasses and talking instead of paying attention to her.

And yet that still wasn't all. There was some sort of apprehension – was that the word – about the whole house.

'It feels one tenth older than being ten. And when I'm twelve I shall only feel one eleventh older still. And so on. The fractions get smaller. Is that why they say time goes faster when you grow really old?'

There was general laughter. Flo took up the questioning. 'What are you going to do when you grow up, little sister? What job?'

Another puzzler. Did they have women speedway riders? Perhaps she could join the Navy, like Edward, disguised as a man if necessary, and then they'd all drink her toast, except that she wouldn't know, at least not till their letters arrived months later in Gibraltar or somewhere.

'I shall be a dancer.'

'Oho, a dancer!'

'Yes.'

She'd said it out of nowhere, it wasn't something she'd ever thought about; but having said it, she felt it was all right, rather a good idea. There were all sorts of dancers, weren't there – tango and ballet and professional ballroom dancers and belly dancers and women who danced wearing pythons and not much else wrapped round them in night clubs... Something like that was sure to turn up.

'And who will you marry?'

'Do they let you marry if you went to St Teresa's?'

The laughter was a gale this time. And yet you could tell: they still weren't sure. None of the teachers, the nuns at St T's, was married. Perhaps it was sinful. Did that mean the nuns' parents must have been sinful? Not too good, that. Unless they were born by – what was that long word for not needing a husband -?

'Marry a rich man, Margery.'

7

'No, Georgina, I shall marry for love.'

'My, we've a romantic girl here.'

'In fact I may not marry at all. I may just have affairs.'

An awkwardness descended, moderated but not eliminated by some patronising half-laughs and one or two Oohs..

'Why should I bother with a minister and a marriage licence? If you do it that way there's a lot of trouble if you want to change your mind. That's right, isn't it, Flo?'

She only mentioned Flo because she seemed the most likely source of support. But the silence that followed, like sudden darkness, told her she'd said something wrong. It really was bizarre, the way grownups pretended to be so rational and yet all the time they were not talking about things, sort of hiding them away, not even letting themselves think about them. What a benighted, superstitious world they all lived in. Silly people!

Arthur cut short further questioning.

'Well, this has been a very happy occasion. But I'm afraid I have to end it now because, as we all' – he looked towards Margery – 'or most of us know, there's a broadcast we all have to hear. So, if everyone would like to sit down I'll tune in.'

But no one sat. As he moved towards the bakelite wireless set, they gathered round. A weird silence, the silence of fear, dampened the room. Arthur turned the knob.

It took time for the broadcast to emerge from a medley of tapping and piping sounds. When at last it did the talk or speech seemed to have started. It was made in an old, rather enfeebled voice, as if the speaker was upset by what he was saying.

...This morning the British Ambassador in Berlin...
(more interference drowned the next words)*...to withdraw their troops from Poland. I have to tell you now that no such undertaking has been given, and that consequently this country is at war with Germany...*

No one spoke. And when, after a silence like the sort they had at funerals, low words were uttered no one seemed able to take them in. A weird, tingling strain which at the same time came close to relief, even happiness, expanded the room.

Annoyance gripped Margery. Neglecting her again! Just like they always did! It was as if everyone – Mother, Father, her sisters, the family, the whole world – were determined to spoil things, forgetting altogether that today, the third of September 1939, was, for Heaven's sake, an important day!

Chapter 3
1928-46

To grow up in Havana House was an immersion.

Built with the thrusting severity of the Victorian middle classes, the house's character had survived the changes of the years. The exterior doors and window frames, though repainted many times, still wore their original black. The front door with its mosaic of stained glass lozenges in purple and maroon still blocked from the hall all but the feeblest filterings of sunlight. No modern curtain seemed right for the high sash windows, so that heavy velvet drapes still hung there, voluminous, a blackout in place long before and after the falling of the bombs.

Inside, imposing high ceilings and moulded plaster friezes vetoed all prospect of homeliness. But some rooms reached further towards it than others. The nursery was bright, wallpapered with cartoon-like flowers and trees in blue and green. In the thin band of time when their childhoods overlapped and the eight- and ten-year differences in their ages could be forgotten, Margery and her sisters, Flo and Georgina, at times played together on the carpeted floor. There were armchairs which, with a little imagination, could become beds for sick dolls, to be visited by lady doctors with cotton reels on strings masquerading as stethoscopes or by nurses with handkerchiefs made into caps. By the time she reached five Margery's sisters had grown into a far bigger part of her life than her mother, Nancy, ever did.

But as Flo and Georgina outgrew the nursery Margery found herself alone more and more. There were times – at Christmas or during summer holidays when they stayed in superior guest houses along the North Wales coast at Colwyn Bay or Conway – when her father, Arthur, seemed momentarily to fill the gap. He would help her build castles against the advancing tide, attracting other urchins, Pied-Piper-like, to join in and add their bucketfuls to a rising Camelot of sand. Then she felt huge pride in her father as if he were one of her possessions, a thoroughbred far stronger than herself but subject to her orders: 'Put a flag in this tower, Daddy. We need more pebbles for this sea-wall.'

One summer, newly possessed of a secondhand Humber car, Arthur drove the family to Scarborough where for two weeks they lorded it at what seemed to Margery a hotel of Babylonian luxury, with deep-pile carpets and spotless damask tablecloths. They rented a beach hut, called a 'bungalow', where they ate sandwiches prepared by their housekeeper and general help, Annie Smith, who'd been allowed to come with them. For years afterwards Margery remembered the salt smell of the hut's woodwork, damp from drying bathing costumes, and the crunch of sand in the lettuce. When the drama of sandcastles palled they walked along the clifftop or swam in the oncoming waves; and at low tide Arthur led them on to the rocks to peer into pools for tiny fish, winkles and baby crabs.

Then, as soon as they reached home again, Arthur disappeared back to the office. Shortly afterwards – for reasons dimly to do with his work or the family business or something – the Humber likewise vanished. In a way it was a relief. Sitting in the back had afforded no view and on a long drive car-sickness was a constant risk. All the same, without father or the sociability of car rides Margery was alone once more.

It only troubled her in a way. The habit of solitude made companionship hard to imagine; and even after the older girls had moved on to secondary school Flo would still slip into Margery's room at night after her sister's earlier bedtime and tell her about the things they did and learnt there. French, for example, the language, it seemed, of bohemian artists and can-can dancers in a place called Montmartre and little moustached men in suits who presided over unbelievable soarings in the prices of things you bought and who couldn't keep their country in order. William the Conqueror – a Frenchman of sorts though he didn't seem to have the ambience of bohemian artists in Montmartre or can-can girls - had invaded England on a cock-and-bull excuse and started History. There was hockey and netball and the unheard-of game of lacrosse played on huge, open playing fields. And Geography where you learnt that they made coffee in Brazil and what the capitals of different countries were.

There was even a booklet about something called Lillets which Nancy had thrust into Flo's hand and told her to read but which meant nothing at all to Margery. That was the thing about Flo. She came into your room at night and was nice and talked to you almost as if she was your mum, but only if you didn't ask questions. If you didn't understand you had to sort it out for yourself. You were on your own, yet again.

Looked back on later, isolation grew most when Georgina married and Flo left school and learnt shorthand-typing to start work in the family business. At about that time she had a follower, Margery remembered, but he seemed to disappear without explanation; and there was no one to ask for reasons. At that time,

11

too, Flo herself vanished for several months, going to stay with Georgina, and came back in a muted mood, not the old, sociable sister Margery remembered and treasured as a secret nocturnal informant. In retrospect the whole episode seemed odd: Georgina wanting Flo to stay with her at exactly the time when she must have been heavily pregnant with the twins, Hazel and Caroline. Somewhere hereabouts, Margery felt, lurked a mystery, a problem to be sorted out. She would have buckled down and completed the task if only she'd had the time and concentration.

Throughout it all, though, one solace was Margery's constant companion. Poetry was always there in the dusty bookshelves of a room still called the Library though no one else ever seemed to use it as such, offering the magic of poets' feelings, always willing to speak, always bristling the hairs on the nape of her neck or swelling delicious grief in the depths of her solar plexus. Here, deep as the Kraken's cave under the hackneyed tides of the Mersey, lay a hidden world of passion and heroism. Here were sand-strewn caverns cool and deep, here a dais of purple and gold, here winter promising a spring not far behind, here the golden apples of the sun. With this store, what else mattered?

Even the shreds of family history that came to her, caught in her hair by the action of an idle wind more than by any attempt to listen to Nancy's odd, oracular utterances, re-formed and wove themselves into a romance of knights and ladies. There'd been George Munnerly from Ireland, the founder of the family and builder of Havana House. Margery thought of him as a sort of Abraham figure who led the chidren of Israel through the desert into the Promised Land. How he made his fortune was never clear: whenever conversation trembled on the brink of the question a sudden silence would fall, Nancy would cough and like the passing of a storm cloud the subject would change. Something to do with slaves, Margery guessed. Had the Queen given him money for speaking up in their defence? Or had he freed thousands out in the West Indies and been rewarded? Probably. At any rate, it was what Margery decided to believe.

There'd been someone called Caspar, too, a bad lot by all accounts, though again in no clearly expressed way, who in the end took to his heels and disappeared. A bit like Flo's boyfriend only more sinister. Not that vanishing was all that bad. Not bad at all. In a way it was quite romantic. Margery might like to do it herself one day; just vanish and travel round the world like a medieval minstrel, earning one's keep by singing ballads or reciting epics round the baronial fire. At any rate it was a card up her sleeve.

After Caspar the business seemed to have fallen into poor shape but was saved, magnificently, by one of his sisters - Margery thought it might be the one called Chloe – who heroically, for the sake of the family, married well (Margery was sure she didn't love the man, just gave her body as a sacrifice for the Munnerly line) and so brought new funds in. Margery imagined it. Marrying a horrid old man with no sex appeal and body odour as an act of pure oblation – a word that had come up in a hymn at church -, a sort of Aztec virgin throwing herself on the flames. The image was tremendously exciting. The troubling doubt was whether Margery herself had what it took to do such a thing should the need arise.

It seemed to be at about that time that the firm changed its name (Margery was never too precise about dates despite being clued up on William the Conqueror) and became the Atlantic Finance and Shipping and when things looked up they were able to restore Havana House to its former glory. Well, to stop if falling down. Which was just as well, because Georgina was not only widowed in the war but bombed out in the blitz and had to bring the girls, Caroline and Hazel, back to live here. All a bit like that long saga by that man – what was his name – to do with property? – whose books Margery had once tried to read. Why couldn't he be less longwinded?

Then, at long last, she herself disappeared - to St Teresa's and after that to what Mother called 'higher things'. Leaving Havana House was like coming out of a funeral, or like a caterpillar shedding its skin and becoming a butterfly. Margery always thought of it, *felt* it, as an outburst of light blazing through the stitches of a heavy, dark cloak. Those years at Cambridge had been a liberation, a spring. And had enabled her to eke out a living ever since by lecturing, free-lance, on the writers she'd studied. They were a source of money she could save up for travel, as well as of hope and joy.

Her only regret, looking back, was that it left her, as she'd always been and perhaps because of her own nature would always be, alone.

Chapter 4
1943

St Teresa's Girls' High School,
BickensteadRoad,
Wirral,Cheshire

18 August 1943

Dear Mr Munnerly,

I am writing further to our recent conversation. May I express my thanks to you for sparing the time to call and discuss the matter in hand.

Following the lines of our agreement during your visit I have recommended to the Board of Governors that the School should adopt a lenient attitude towards Margery's behaviour at the end of term. This would not normally have been the School's policy; several years ago a girl was asked to leave for engaging in a lesser escapade. The placing of potassium permanganate in the School's water supply, in particular, drew strong demands for her expulsion from a number of parents who felt, despite my reassurances, that their daughters might have been permanently damaged by the prank. It was the publicity which this outcry attracted which unfortunately brought the matter to the attention of the Governors and indeed the wider public.

However, in view of Margery's undoubted ability and our reluctance to waste her talents, I have submitted a request that she should merely be punished by a series of detentions and a severe warning and happily the Board has acceded.

As to the matter of the so-called 'apple-pie' practical joke in the prefects' room of the neighbouring Boys' Grammar School, I have dealt with the matter by appropriate disciplinary measures. The detritus of empty gin bottles, stockings, cigarette stubs and lipstick-stained playing cards irresponsibly placed there has been destroyed, a warning against any attempt at retaliation issued to the Grammar School boys, and the matter kept from public notice.

There is, however, one further matter. Margery drew deserved praise for her portrayal of Cleopatra in the School's summer production of Shakespeare but a number of parents have complained that her display of bosom went beyond what was necessary for the application of the asp and was not in keeping with

14

the School's Catholic tradition and standards. I would be grateful if, bearing in mind the confidential nature of these comments on a sensitive matter, you would kindly pass them on to Margery in reinforcement of what I have already said to her, and see that behaviour of this kind is never repeated.

Thank you again for calling. I hope that this will draw a veil over our recent tribulations.

Yours sincerely,

Edith Meade, Headmistress

*

Margery surveyed the sheet of paper in her hand. Nearby, the kettle whose steam had curled open the school's soggy envelope still whistled faintly. She turned out the gas and sat to study the document.

St Teresa's Girls' High School
Terminal Report: Winter 1943

Name   Margery Rosalind Munnerly
Age   15 years 3 months
Form   5A
Art: Margery shows promise and even a certain artistic flair but must learn greater perseverance and attention to detail.

French: Has a gift for mimicry which stands her in good stead in French conversation but is weak on grammar

History: It is important for Margery to learn that imaginative writing is no substitute for a knowledge of the facts.

Geography: Has gained good marks on the Caribbean and the Himalayan Kingdoms but appeared to lose interest when the class turned to the United Kingdom.

Physical Education: Played well for the school's second eleven. Higher things next year?

English: Margery shows a real appreciation of the Romantic poets and the Elizabethan period. Her prose, however, tends to be excessively flowery and verbose. She should try to cultivate a clear, precise and succinct style. If she can achieve this, she could become university material.

Conduct: When interested in the subject, Margery behaves well. She should not, however, allow a certain perversity in her character, or perhaps a dislike of some of her colleagues and teachers, to lure her into acts of mutiny.

Form Mistress's Comments: Margery's record is rather mixed. She should learn to behave with greater decorum and not allow her language and mode of dress to be inappropriately influenced by popular magazines and films.

Margery reached for her school bag under the kitchen table. She took out a small bottle, opened it and sniffed. Mm! Chlorine! What a lovely, acrid whiff it gave off. A deadly poison, the chemistry books said. Best taken only minutely in tap water.

But applied generously. With deft strokes, using the brush inside the cap, she dabbed the fluid on the paper. What a thrill to delete the past. It gave a sense of altering history such as she'd imagined only dictators had.

She halted only when the report lay damp and crumpled on the table, emasculated and harmless under the softening tears of W.H.Smith's best ink eradicator.

*

St Teresa'sHigh School,
Bickenstead Road,
Wirral,Cheshire

15 September1945

Dear Mr Munnerly,
  Thank you for your recent visit.
  The School appreciates that you are naturally anxious for Margery to take the entrance examinations for Cambridge, especially in view of the aptitude she has shown in some areas of her academic work. You will, I hope, in turn understand that it would be impossible for the School to recommend her for University entrance if at the same time her repeatedly poor conduct obliged us to suspend her from her studies here.
  Fortunately, at a meeting I held yesterday with her form mistress and house mistress I succeeded in persuading my colleagues that that, despite our considerable distress at her recent conduct, suspension would be too severe a penalty and that the School should therefore be willing to allow her to complete this academic year and with it her school career. I shall be grateful if

you will kindly convey this decision to Margery while at the same time impressing upon her the full extent of the concession being made and urge her to act with restraint in all matters during the coming months.

I trust that this outcome will proved satisfactory to you.

Yours sincerely,

Edith Meade, Headmistress

Chapter 5
1946

Havana House, which the family still seemed to regard as an emblem of wealth and success, for Margery symbolised loneliness.

With four siblings, she should never have lacked for company. But before her eleventh birthday Edward was called away to a war from which he was never to return. Tom, removed from her by thirteen years' seniority and the age's unquestioned segregation of boys from girls, shrank, after his fiancee Sophie's death, into the desiccated, rigid shell of bachelordom, efficient at the routine of his deskwork but closed to imagination, a dried husk inside. As for Flo, Margery longed to worship her favourite sister, further off in years but somehow more dignified than Georgina, yet for some reason never clear, some blacked-out shock muffled under the crinolines of family secrecy, a hostility and suspicion grew up between them which no overtures of friendship could disperse.

At the heart of the family's stiffness, Margery realised, stood her mother. Nancy dominated not only her husband but the whole household with her lofty puritanical ways, lurking inescapably in the background to all that was said or done, enforcing by looks of shock, disgust or disapproval rules of conduct which could never have survived had they once been stated. Hers was a threat from which her youngest daughter could only escape by entering an inner world where imagination could roam free, paroled from the dark rambling house and the prison-like atmosphere of those few meals the family ate together. For Margery that world was reading.

'Oh, all right. Alone and palely loitering,' she once told a visitor who enquired how she was faring. Georgina began to laugh and so did Arthur, but within seconds Nancy's frown froze mirth to an icy silence.

'You should be grateful for all you have.'

Margery reached out to pass the visitor some cranberry sauce. 'Man doth not live by bread alone,' she volunteered by way of revenge. This time her quotation brought only faint giggles, from Caroline and Hazel. Hatred seized her. If this was how one was supposed to behave here, she wanted out.

And, weirdly, it was what she achieved. The fact broke on her with disbelief. All she'd observed of the working lives of old schoolfriends showed that anyone who had unhappy relations with their seniors was blocked from moving away because of the suspicion they aroused of being a troublemaker. In references and reputations signs of rebellion were always recounted. Yet in her case the escapism of the mind which drove parents and teachers to distraction brought real escape, too.

Margery shows originality in her work but is too inclined to ignore the rules of grammar and spelling, the English mistress at St Teresa's had written in one termly report. Delighted, Margery shrugged. The shaking and loosening of school blouse and tie suggested a desire to rid herself of clothes. 'So long as people know what I mean, what does it matter? Spelling can be original as well.'

Nancy merely glowered. It was not her way to debate or discuss. Not that topic, not anything. As if activated by some sixth sense she swung her scowl towards Arthur, extinguishing the hastily-suppressed vestiges of a smile.

Yet, apart from a term in which a newly-acquired enthusiasm for Baudelaire saw her emerge against all expectations as winner of the Sixth Form's Prize for French, it was in English that she excelled.

'I think we might consider putting her in for one or other of the Cambridge colleges,' 'Eggy' Eggleston, the English mistress, suggested.

'Hm.' The Headmistress was less sure. 'I applaud your wish to do well for the girl.' Like a Siberian sunrise, an icy smile edged over the horizon of cracked, hairy lips. 'But Cambridge...hm. That might, I think, be a trifle ambitious.'

'Not really. St Margaret's got two acceptances last year. And other schools in Liverpool. The number of grants has been increased.'

Miss Meade emitted a single cough, staccato and prohibitory. This was coming close to revolt. 'Perhaps we should wait a year or two and see...how far democratisation is to go.' She spoke the long word with wryness. All her life she'd defended standards, the standards she herself had once satisfied, the standards she hated to see devalued or – still worse – attained by others.

Eggy Eggleston changed gear, adopting a worried expression. 'It's the danger of being left behind. Of the school not maintaining its high reputation. Compared with others.'

The message met instant decoding. Verity Ward-Price, the headmistress at Colindale, the direct grant school down the road, had long been a threat to Miss Meade. Ever since their rivalry at Cheltenham Ladies' College. Ever since they were respectively nicknamed – humiliating though it was to recall – 'Priceless' and 'Mediocre'.

The Headmistress stiffened, her voice an icicle. 'As you wish. I won't stand in your way if you undertake all the necessary applications. Of course, mistakes and misjudgments do occur. And it does seem that nowadays the 'varsities may be less demanding, less discriminating. But I am still inclined to think you are embarking on a fruitless, and misguided, escapade.'

And so escape came. A still stranger result of Eggy's and Margery's efforts was the schizophrenia it induced in the Headmistress. When announcing her pupil's success at assembly one morning in the following term Miss Meade mumbled in such low tones that whispers of explanation were heard to spread from the front row of girls to those unable to hear the announcement at the back and the voltage of turmoil had to be reined in by a call for silence. Only at the school Prize-giving, attended by the Chairman of the Board of Governors, the Mayor, and successful local industrialist Lord Wells, as well as by a reporter from the *Globe*, did Miss Meade seem to lose her gloom and resentment, blossoming into details of the school's achievement and stating Margery's name with comparative audibility. Subsequent rumour among the girls had it that old Mediocre was in love.

Margery received the news with a theatrical waving of arms and ballerina steps. 'I'm in! They've let me in!,' she told Georgina waving the College's telegram. 'It's like when I read my *curriculum vitae*. I can't recognise myself.'

But in a moment doubt alighted, snagging her clothing and freezing her in the posture of Peter Pan in flight. 'Georgina,' she said, 'you don't think they got the papers mixed up, do you?'

Chapter 6
1948

'You can't, Margery. It'd be so rude!'

'I can. I will.'

'But it's such an insult. To the King! Come on, you'll only be shaking his hand.'

'No. I'm a republican. I don't think we ought to have a king at all. So how can I go up there and act all lovey-dovey with him?'

'It's not acting lovey-dovey. He gives Patricia the shield and she holds it up for the crowd to see. Then we file by and shake his hand.'

'Don't argue! We're in public.' Patricia, the team captain, edged as unobtrusively as possible into the line of girls queuing for the presentation. Higher up the steps that led into the VIP stand the defeated Irish Under-21 team were receiving royal commiserations. 'What's all this about, anyway?'

But Dorothy was reluctant to tell tales. All eyes turned to Margery.

'I'm not going up to shake hands with the King. I don't believe in kings.'

'How rude can you get? That's awful. Come on, don't give the whole team a bad name. You'll disgrace us.'

'No. It's simply wrong, him having all those privileges.'

The line had become an arc, the girls leaning forward to watch. There seemed nothing to be done.

But Patricia hadn't been made captain for nothing. She moved close to Margery's face, speaking in a hissed whisper.

'You do realise he didn't want that job, don't you?'

Margery stared. 'I don't get it.'

'He didn't choose to be King. He only took it on, and very unwillingly, when his brother abdicated. You know...'

'That woman?'

'The American, yes.'

'Really?'

There seemed nothing to say. The armbanded official gestured and the team tramped to the stairs. Margery followed, on her face a distant gaze that looked out over the applauding crowd, defiant.

Chapter 7
1954

Margery wasn't sure why she was in Dar at all. It wasn't the sort of place a year of postgraduate travel seemed to demand.

Perhaps it was the name: Dar es Salaam, haven of peace, the guidebook. said. After the perpetual roar and the pall of exhaust over Mexico City, the racket and shindig of the markets and the guttered side-alleys of Santiago and Bahia, the Tanganyikan port had sounded like a balm devoutly to be wished. And still less resistibly, there'd been the offer of a free flight to Nairobi.

Free? Well, there were different ways of paying.

During her student days she'd been through an anti-American phase. There were US air bases in East Anglia still, relics from the war converted to ice-buttresses of the new, chilly peace; and on free days transatlantic airmen, white and black and mulatto, came into Cambridge to saunter round, see the colleges and whistle at the girls. 'How vulgar,' Margery had thought. When others giggled or responded eagerly to the calls and palatal clicks from jeeps she turned away, disdainful.

But now things were different. Time, she felt, had eroded the prejudices of immaturity. The young officer she'd met in the Rio bookstore, tall and handsome in a sky-blue uniform of finer material than she'd ever seen on a British serviceman, wasn't the sort who wolf-whistled. In fact the first words between them had come from herself.

'Excuse me. I've been trying to reach that book. Up there.' She pointed to a high shelf.

'Why sure, ma'am. Allow me.'

It had been no problem for his six-foot reach. He scanned the book's cover.

'You like poetry? American at that.'

She'd clutched Whitman to her bosom, taking care not to conceal the latter completely and after a while realising she could raise its profile by increasing Whitman's pressure on its lower reaches. She'd raised her eyes to heaven. 'Especially American.'

After that, she remembered, they'd gone off to have drinks at a pavement café. And at his suggestion! Well no, not exactly. She herself had said, 'Isn't it hot, here? Makes you crave for a long, cold drink, doesn't it?' and had cast her best, most longing and little-girlish look at him (but not overdoing it because he was so polite and proper and called her *ma'am*) and he'd taken the cue superbly and there they'd sat deep in the deepest conversation about T.S.Eliot and F.R.Leavis (of whom he hadn't heard so she went great guns on him) and the objective correlative and whether grief plucks no laurels and all the time, the *whole* time, an hour and a quarter of it, he hadn't once looked away from her or eyed any of the Brazilian girls going by along the pavement, not even the one with a high-slit skirt and no knickers worth speaking of.

Not that he would have spoken of them. Not even if they'd been worth it. Much too gentlemanly. Even the following week in that hired room at the hotel opposite the church with statues of the tormented prophets he hadn't actually *spoken* much. Yes, he'd been very gentle and tender in spite of the continual loud shush of the air conditioning and the gekko taking an upside-down stroll across the ceiling and the snarl of traffic below, which she'd kept thinking must be coming from the tormented prophets, but he hadn't got much nearer to actually *speaking* than those fascinating low groans and gorgeous gasps at crucial moments. He was obviously the strong, silent type.

She'd extended her stay in Rio by two weeks after that. Well, she'd had to, so as to catch the flight with him to Nairobi on a US Air Force jet. He was on a special Anglo-American military mission to East Africa. The Cold War and things.

Oh, he'd looked so handsome sitting in the cockpit – what a funny word that was, when you came to think of it, calling something thirty thousand feet up a *pit* – acting as co-pilot, all swimming-pool blue in his neatly-pressed uniform. He'd been something really high up, she was sure she remembered, a field marshal or something – must have been, to have his uniform so neatly pressed. When he put it on the next morning, item by item, its light blue the colour of sky at dawn on a day that was going to be a real sizzler, it was like a transfiguration. Almost like a prophet coming down from Mount Sinai wearing a heavenly halo, only this one covered all of him. All of him when he'd finished dressing, anyway.

When he had to go back to HQ in Brazil she'd saved keepsakes of their Great Love. A beer mat she'd snaffled from the pavement café where they'd tied up T.S.Eliot and got Leavis taped. A Gideon bible from the bedside drawer in the Estado De Rio Hotel, to remind her of the tormented prophets and of all the sound effects that went with them.

But now that they'd parted - after exchanging *poste restante* addresses, of course, but before she'd received any actual letter from

Lincoln (funny him being called that, when the tapes on his airforce underclothes had a quite different name on them: Hank J.Roover) – she'd gone on to Dar and at that distance, after crossing the White Highlands and descending to this tropical coast, the whole whirlwind romance seemed to belong to another world. Like that giddy feeling when you come back from holiday and can hardly stand up straight as you wait for the bus into town or join the queue at the grocer's. Like coming out of a swaggering, romantic, pirate movie when you're a kid. Like after your first double whisky at Graduation Ball. Like that, yes, like that.

Often, strolling past the vast bulk of the old German buildings along the waterfront or looking out across the still, deserted harbour , its image of perfect tranquillity opening on to the vastness of the Indian Ocean, there came into her mind some lines from – Tennyson, weren't they?

And in the afternoon they came to a land
Where it was always afternoon.

How exactly the poets knew things.

Her thoughts dwelt, too, on her keepsakes: the beermat and the Gideon bible and the name-tape she'd secretly cut off Lincoln's underpants with her nail scissors while he was in the bathroom. Not that they were all she'd kept. Lately, in moments of weakness, she'd begun to – well, to worry in case the encounter with Lincoln (or Hank) had left behind another, less intended memento. At the time, or times, she'd wanted to speak out, to ask or explain or make sure, but at moments like that it seemed, well, base and physical. If the worst came to the worst...but she wasn't even sure how she should see it, whether as worst or best. Of course, in a way it was worrying but if you looked on the bright side, also in a way liberating. Well, whatever. Perhaps she should see it as just another scene from life's rich pageantry.

There was one other keepsake she treasured: the volume of Whitman that Lincoln, or Hank, had bought her. Continually, she took it out and looked at its gold-lettered title and strong binding. What a lovely present, a token of love. Often she stroked and caressed its leather cover. She didn't go so far as to open it. She'd never had any time for Whitman anyway.

Chapter 8
1955

'Hello. Is that Dad?'

'Arthur Munnerly, yes. Hold on, is that -?'

'Yes, it's me, Margery. In Dar es Salaam, Tanganyika. I'm phoning from the British Embassy. They've let me phone free if I don't go on long.'

'Well, lovely to hear you, darling. What a surprise! I never–'

'Listen, Dad. Is Mother out?'

'Yes. You know Nancy on Wednesday afternoons.'

'Yes, she's at Dorothy's? Dorothy from church?'

'Of course. Without fail.'

'Good, I thought she would be. Look, Dad. I'm coming home next week. Flying to Heathrow and then train to Lime Street.'

'Oh lovely. What wonderful news. We've all been wondering where you've been this long time.'

'You got my postcards?'

'Well, yes. Not that Nancy thought them all very suitable.'

'The girls on Copacabana beach? I thought that would shock her. Gave me quite a laugh. But that's not why I'm ringing. Dad, when I arrive, I'm bringing someone else.'

'You're not -? You don't mean you've got enga-?'

'No, not that and not likely to be. Dad, I've become a mother. Of a son. He's very healthy – good lungs and a kick to play for Everton. Not so good at controlling his other physical motions. I'll explain when I see you. I just wanted you to know so that at least one person won't be shocked and treat me like a pariah. You still there?'

'Yes. Yes.'

'I can't go on. You all right?'

'Yes.'

'See you, then. I should get home on Friday. It'd be nice if my room was ready for me.'

'I'll see to it. Margery, you are all right, are you?'

'Yes, Dad. Never better. Lots of love to you. Don't tell anyone I rang, will you? It'd only give them time to stoke up their prejudices.'

'Oh, Margery, that's unkind.'

'Must go. Lots of love. See you next week.'

'Yes, dear. And love from us.'

29487396. Margery perused the number, printed on its cloth tag, a fourth or fifth time.

There were numbers like it, she remembered, on the puzzles page of magazines and comic papers she'd read as a kid. Like *The Children's Newspaper* by Sir Arthur Mee (funny how she always remembered the Editor's name), an improving juvenile paper that Mother and Dad – no, it was just Dad, Mother never read much – had ordered for them - Margery and Flo and Georgina and the boys. Dad used to read it as well, so much so that at times she'd wondered whether he got it for his own benefit rather than theirs. She hadn't heard of it for years. It must have gone the way of all flesh, she supposed, like *Comic Cuts* and the Billy Bunter stories and now, just lately, *Picture Post*. Funny how those ephemeral, trivial prints carried such a deep aroma of their age.

The scent of a time, a place. She remembered the dizzy scent of cloves carried across the Indian Ocean from Zanzibar to the African coast. How mysterious the sense of smell was, moving in, invisible yet all-enveloping, moulding one's mood without one knowing, no word or thought involved.

She'd read you could smell a slave-ship in mid-Atlantic even three miles down-wind. Not so sweet and euphoric, that.

But – she returned to the cloth in her hand - this official-looking number on the tag she'd cut from Lincoln's General Issue air force underpants wasn't a puzzle – that is, it wasn't *meant* to be a puzzle – and it definitely didn't date from Sir Arthur Mee's prime before the war. What on earth was it? Magic, maybe. A secret code or key. What fun! And it brought back Rio. Yes, even a number could carry a trace, an ambience of the wonder of romance and love.

Hold on, though! Love? It couldn't be a tally of -? No, surely not even a man of Lincoln's magnetism… And no, not that, either. Probably. It was a fixed, printed number. There was no mechanism for increasing it day by day. Or night by night. And she'd noticed it on their very first day at the Estado de Rio Hotel and didn't think it had been changed upward since then. How could it? Though with a big number like that you could never be sure.

Oh dear, that was Peter yowling again. If only he wouldn't yowl so much, or at least do it more in tune. Not that he was bad when you thought of friends who'd had babies and never got an unbroken night's sleep for months. *Years.*

There, that's quietened him down. Voracious, that's the word. Utterly, suckingly voracious. Thank heavens he didn't turn out to be twins. Tweedledum and Tweedledee. He might be the monstrous crow, of course, the way he needs feeding. What would it be like to have lots of babies, like the wife of the Scottish Wee Free minister who once came to Havana House? Fourteen, did they have? Imagine it.

Or was it more? Sixteen? Not sure. Not 29487396 anyway.

That *would* stop you sleeping.

*

Uncanny how being abroad shifted your whole scale of values. A mental and moral landslip.

Having a baby out here didn't seem so bad. The man at the Embassy – he seemed to be a Consul rather than a full Ambassador but he was very nice and cheery and dealt with the problem of an unforeseen baby as if it was in the ordinary run of business like someone turning up with excess baggage – hold on, though, what was I thinking? Yes, the Consul, if that's what he was, changed my passport in no time to show there were two of us travelling on it, and booked me a BOAC flight – I've forgotten what that stands for but it must stand for something important, Bring Over All Your Clobber, maybe – to Heathrow – that's the new big airport they've built in London, well, near London, I'm never sure if it's a new name for Blackbushe or not, it doesn't sound half so spooky and exciting: *She was seduced in the Black Bush.* No. Anyway, what I was going to say – what *was* I going to say when I interrupted myself? – oh yes, having a baby outside marriage doesn't seem serious here but when I get back and the dark shadows of Havana House close in, and what the neighbours will think or, worse, say, oh dear, what then?

I'm not looking forward to that, not one tiny bit. I shall just have to be insouciant. Debonair as well, perhaps. Or with plenty of *sangfroid?* No, I'll stick with insouciance.

Trouble is, insouciance by itself, though a fine standby, may not be enough. To descend to things of low degree, who's going to pay to feed and clothe this little brute? Not the money from my poetry readings or the improving out-of-town classes on Eng. Lit, that's for sure. A good thing the family's rich and prosperous.

Or was. Until the shipbuilding collapsed and Edward's ship was sunk and Georgina got bombed out and the whole thing started to crumble. Tom doesn't show much interest in the business even though he's supposed to be the chairman and a non-executive director. More preoccupied with his architect job, and when he goes there'll be no one at all to manage things at Atlantic Finance.

Except... No, naughty! Don't do that! Oh God, he doesn't look like a tycoon in the making, does he?

Hey, stop poking your finger in my eye. Stop it!

I can see nothing but trouble coming from this one in the future.

*

Normally she'd have made a scene of it: the Return of the Native. Scenes were her thing. But to knock on the door of Havana House, baby in arms, and have to explain everything seemed too demeaning, too Orphan Annie. They could find out gradually. Still by some miracle in possession of her key to the front door, Margery slid it into the lock and inched in.

No one. Nancy and Arthur would be at church this time on a Sunday morning. Flo and Georgina as well, possibly. Or Georgina might be gardening at the back of the house. Good. Then they could discover her, not she make herself known to them. On tiptoe like a pizzicato in one of that funny man's cartoons, she stole down the hall to her room.

Or what should be her room. What would still be if they hadn't got up to any funny business, like turning it into a junk room or handing it over to squatters like an ex-army billet or renting it out to refugees from East Germany or letting Hazel and Caroline run riot in it. For a moment she paused to survey the Great Hall. Nothing had changed. The gloomy pictures of long-dead ancestors still lined the stairs, the lighter-coloured patch remained where the portrait of disgraced Caspar had once hung. Overbearing like the rest of this family mausoleum, it must – God knows - have distorted her psyche or ego or id to be brought up in a dark cavern of a place like this. She sighed, then turned the big black knob and crept in.

Unused to the austerity ration of light let in through a window shadowed by cypresses outside and by long skirts of ultramarine velvet curtains inside, she switched on the light. So this was home. Well, sort of.

With a squelch she set the baby down on the floor. Peter, she'd decided to call him, she wasn't sure why. Perhaps because it was on a rock halfway up the Sugar Loaf Mountain in Rio that he'd founded his church, well, at any rate left his visiting card. She breathed satisfaction at not waking him. Sleepy little thing, wasn't he? More a Munnerly than a Wild West boy. Maybe.

She looked round for something to wipe wet hands on: nappies had been scarce on the journey back. Ah, this would do - an old sun-dress of the sort Florence used to wear on the beach at

28

Thurstaston. She wouldn't be doing that any more, not an old thing like Florence. It would make a good towel. She picked it up, scattering a diaspora of sand on to the fluff-coated carpet that Peter was now starting to taste, and reduced her hands to a faint, keen ammonia smell by vigorous rubbing. She walked to the window and seized the curtain. At a second tug one of the hooks gave way and the velvet sagged, adopting a pose of obesity or possibly pregnancy at one end. Ho ho, here we go. Back to nothing working. Just like Paraguay.

But her suitcase! It must still be standing unguarded at the front door, stuffed with priceless mementoes of travel and tropical heat and romance, all nestling among the dirty underclothes and the undiscarded swabs enfolding sundry of Peter's bodily effusions. She started towards the landing.

But the door was already opening. Slowly, a figure appeared.

'Margery!'

'Good God! Flo!'

For a second they stood open-armed, on the brink of joining but held back by an unseen membrane of change: the older sister shrunken and pale after years of internment in the gloomy house, the younger with face creased to beaten copper by baking tropical sun. Then recognition snapped and with the strangeness of new lovers they embraced.

'You didn't write. We thought you might have had an accident. Even - dead.'

'Me? No, I'm not dead. Not a little bit.' Margery held up arms and hands in proof. 'Hey, I just remembered. My case is still outside.'

'No, I brought it in. I recognised it as one of ours - one of Mother's, I thought. Here.' She walked back to the passageway and with the labour of a navvy lifting some heavy gear lugged the case into the room.

'Heavens! It's full of iron ore!'

But as her load thumped the floor another intrusion caught her eye. She stopped short, incredulous, then with funereal step approached the weird bundle lying at mid-floor.

'What is it?' Gingerly, with a toe, she prodded the grubby shawl. 'What – on earth – is it?'

'Ah!' Margery sprang to life. In a moment she stood beside Flo, inserting a foot between her sister's shoe and the baby. 'He's all right. He's mine. Peter. I've called him Peter.'

'You've – called – him -?'

'Yes. It's his name.' Margery stooped and picked the bundle up. 'Well, he has to be called something. I suppose.'

'But... But where did you...get him?'

'Well, where else but..?' Margery patted her stomach. 'The usual way.' She waved a hand. It was all rather absurd, explaining the obvious.

'But...his father? Who's...his father?'

'Ah. Yes.' The question came unforeseen. It required consideration. What could she say? *Well, I'm not sure, actually. According to some accounts, he's called Lincoln, but according to others Hank J.Roover?* No, it wouldn't do. Too longwinded and unfinal. And anyway, she wasn't sure she liked either name. In bed she'd stuck to 'darling' and, once only before rejecting it, 'sweetiepie'. 'Cuddles' was too fulsome. She could invent a name, of course. Hank was a good one: mentally she resolved to think of him as Hank. But not to Flo.

'He was a gift from the gods.' She raised her palms and face heavenward. 'Like Pallas Athene rising from the sea off Cyprus. Or did she spring from Zeus's head? I'm not sure. Probably authorities differ.'

But Flo was serious. 'Margery, don't joke. He is your baby?'She moved aside a curtain of shawl to study the baby's head, crowned by a carrot-top of sandy hair but otherwise spherical as a grapefruit. It looked just like any other baby – a cross between a Michaelangelo cherub and Mussolini. Her face broke, close to tears.

'Of course. I don't pick up strays.'

'There's a need for that, too.'

For once a glimpse of her sister's feelings impinged on Margery: as if, for Flo, a foundling would have been a godsend. 'Sorry, yes. No. He's mine. All of him.'

'And you're not going to say how...or who?'

It was a perfect let-out. Margery performed three small dance-steps 'No,' she said, 'I'm not.'

Chapter 9
1957

'...and you, little mole,
abseil me down to your den
who once crept out of mine.
There I'll make you my home.'

Margery's poem was followed by prolonged clapping. Unsure how to respond, she made a mock-curtsey, then waved her papers in a vaguely conductor-like manner until the chairperson, Miss Welbeck, completed her complimentary remarks.

'There's a little time for questions. But not much.' Margery's reputation for voluble answers was well-known. She'd already exceeded her time limit for the talk.

A female voice – most of the Literary Society's members were ladies – piped up from the back of the hall. Unfortunately her words were mangled by the whirring, and then the prolonged four o'clock striking, of the grandfather clock which graced the stage. Something like the words *boring* and *fancyman* caught Margery's ear.

'I'm sorry, I didn't quite...the clock. Would you please repeat..?' Margery performed a characteristic twirl, making the pleats of her rose-patterned summer dress flair out attractively. She often didn't hear things but was never sure whether it was her hearing or whether it was the way her mind leaped from one titbit to another, like a leveret in spring. Leveret. What a lovely word. Some kind of rabbit, wasn't it? Did she want to be like a rabbit? Not really. At least, she supposed not.

'Would you call it a fantasy poem?'

'Ah. I see.' The question took Margery aback. She was on the point of answering *No, it's addressed to my little boy, my son. He's two, you know,* when she realised and stopped short. My God! she was spilling the beans. They wouldn't know about Peter. She'd been billed as *Miss* Margery Munnerly and with Rock Park miles away from this back-of-beyond Cheshire village they wouldn't have heard of the latest addition to Havana House. Or even of Havana House. If they did they'd be shocked. She mustn't cause a furore.

'Well I suppose so, in a way.'

Hold on, though. Mightn't the role of unmarried mother enhance her image as a poet? She halted, standing on one leg, right hand held down her side, the left raised to her lips as if requesting silence. No, best not to risk shocking them. In a place like this, preserved in amber since the nineteen thirties, there could be walkouts, even denunciations.

'That's to say, no, it's not fantasy. Not entirely, that is. One of my sisters has two little girls.'

A buzz of motherly warmth spread round the hall. Miss Welbeck picked out a few more questions – did Margery find that life in the Wirral inspired her in a way consistent with the postmodernist ethos? was the elfin spirit in one of her poems a symbol of female emancipation through libido? – and then brought the meeting to a close. Over tea and cakes she spoke to Margery briefly, before hurrying away to discuss some Literary Society business with a Mrs Stockwell.

Left with the feeling that she must somehow have been an embarrassment to her hostess, Margery was preparing to leave when she was approached by a man with a goatee beard. Cup in hand, he gave her a twinkling grin.

'My name's John Holderness. I'd just like to say how much I admired your readings.'

'Oh, thank you.' He wore an expensive, possibly angora, suit, nattily cut at collar and lapel. The epaulettes seemed exactly designed to complement the aroma of pipesmoke. Margery expanded. Pipe smokers were one of her turn-ons. 'It's just...what I do. My hobby.' She hadn't meant to say that. Writing wasn't a hobby at all, it was a lifelong vocation. But one had to say something.

'I came especially to hear you. I'm not a member here.'

'Oh, I see. So what made you -? I mean, how did you hear..?' Another mistake. Never assume people haven't heard of you. Assume the opposite, it boosts your reputation. Then most of them will pretend they know your work. Those that don't will feel inferior and have to start reading you. They could even buy your slim volume.

'Someone at another poetry meeting, one in Barnston, mentioned you. She gave me one of your poems and I loved it.'

A recommendation. That was nice. But Barnston! It was getting dreadfully close to Rock Park...and Peter.

'She didn't, this lady, say anything else about me, I suppose.'

He seemed surprised. 'No, just that she liked your poetry.' He hung back, a shy man it seemed, as if waiting for her to explain what else the lady might have divulged. When Margery merely smiled he went on. 'I live only just down the road from here. You wouldn't care to come in for a cup of tea or something, would you? I hope you don't mind me asking on such short acquaintance.'

There was nervousness in his voice. Margery hesitated. It seemed a strange invitation. But he had the appearance of respectability. A Conservative, she decided, but still nice. And she liked his diffidence, his real interest in her. No man had paid her that compliment since that night... Hm, but that hadn't turned out too well.

'Oh, that needs thinking about.' She flounced round on him, smiling. 'First, tell me which poem you liked best.'

'The one addressed to your sister's baby.'

'Oh no.That's to say, yes – ' She checked herself, again on the point of divulging information best concealed. But the other members of the meeting were busily chatting amongst themselves; no one was listening; he'd said he was a newcomer, not someone who frequented the Literary Society or knew the people who did. There seemed no harm in sharing a secret.

'No, he's not my sister's, actually. He's mine.'

'Oh.' Did she detect a note of disconcertment in his voice. 'I thought you said...'

'I only said I had a sister who'd two daughters. The poem's addressed to a son.'

'Ah, I've misunderstood. You were billed as Miss Munnerly.'

'That's right. I am.' Margery enjoyed his puzzlement. The role of bohemian rather suited her.

'Do excuse me. I was confused.'

'Not at all.'

All the same, he didn't repeat the invitation to go for tea at his house but after a few more minutes of conversation on indifferent public subjects began to make his excuses. Disappointment laid a chill hand on her arm.

'Oh good heavens, Mr Holderness, I must go.' An impulse not to be the one who was turned down stirred a flurry of fiction. 'I have to rush. For a driving lesson. A man-friend is giving me lessons. So nice to meet you.'

She hurried from the stage, relieved to have saved her status. How political human relations were. *Men should be what they seem.* Othello. But they never were.

On the bus journey up the Wirral relief took on a sour aftertaste of the kind that comes after drinking too much fizzy lemonade. She wondered why the man who she'd at first thought rather dishy had switched off so suddenly. Perhaps he'd decided she was too busy for him to take up her time. Or felt she'd deceived him by not telling the truth about Peter from the start. All the way home she pondered the question. But she could think of no answer conformable with what she was willing to believe.

*

In fact there was plenty of time before the driving lesson. The man-friend who'd agreed to give it, Arthur, wouldn't have far to come for their six o'clock arrangement. Perched on a front seat of the top deck as the homeward-bound Crosville bus wound its way through the lanes of Cheshire and Wirral, Margery felt the superiority of her high viewpoint augmented by the knowledge that she would soon be no longer in need of buses. So long as Arthur would lend her his car, that is. So long as Nancy would let him.

In one way she admired her mother for ruling the roost like that. In another it didn't seem so nice, a bit *eminence grise* and domineering. She'd heard of dominatrixes. Dominatrices, she supposed, speculating on the basis of fourth form Latin with Miss Baker. Baker*loo* they'd called her on account of her frequent self-excusals from the middle of lessons. Margery wondered if she would like to be that sort of person - like Nancy, that is, not Bakerloo. How, for example, would that pipe-smoking Barnston man have got on if she, Margery, had been heavy and overbearing like Nancy. Perhaps he'd have turned tail and run from the heavy conventionality, just as he had from herself? Perhaps run even faster? She should have introduced him to her life more gently.

She regretted, too, that she hadn't given him much chance to reveal himself. Oh, well there were other fish in the sea. Even for a woman edging towards thirty. Another unacceptable thought.

She'd entered the hall of Havana House when a wailing sound signalled more immediate emergencies. Oh drat it! Peter! With reluctant strides she mounted the stairs and pushed into the room, a disused linen store, that she'd commandeered as his nursery.

'You've had a mighty long poetry meeting.' Flo looked up from a kneeling posture beside the cradle, caught in the act of dandling a rag doll over Peter's riotous form.

'Yes. My poems excited huge interest. In a packed hall.'

'Well, thank heaven you've come. Now I can get some peace.'

'He's been good, I expect?'

Flo's look swept the idea to oblivion.

Margery was undeterred. 'Flo, I hate to ask this after you've been so kind and I'll definitely do something similar for you when I can – well, not necessarily all *that* similar but something helpful – only the thing is: could you please carry on looking after him for another hour while I have the driving lesson Father has promised me. it's *so* important.'

'No.' Flo put on her most Nancy-like look. Almost the dominatrix. How fascinating. 'Four and half hours is quite enough. Not another minute.'

'Oh Flo, and usually you're so kind. Such a good sister.'

'Not one more second.'

'But why? I suspect you secretly *love* being with Peter and you know what a wonderful, quiet, loving little soul he is. It's only for an hour.'

'Since when did any of your driving lessons finish on time?'

They were discussing details now. It was progress. Margery put on her most winning way. 'Flo, please. Just this once. I promise I'll never ask you to do it again.'

But Flo was on her feet. Fresh wails from the cot commemorated the event. 'You can ask someone else. Georgina. Mother. Someone. Not me.'

Margery accompanied her through the nursery door and along the landing. Still pleading, but to no avail. They stopped at the end of the landing where Flo and Georgina had their apartments.

'Try there.' Flo flung a pointing arm towards Georgina's door. 'She can afford an hour or two.'

Margery hesitated, for once aware of the burden she would be thrusting on someone already burdened with two daughters. Aware, too, for the first time, of a streak of resentment in her sister's tone.

'Okay,' she said. A certain pride in the *American* expression dispelled doubt. 'I'll get Georgina to stand in.'

Only as she rapped on the door did she wonder whether she should perhaps have paused in the nursery to kiss Peter. Or at least let him know she'd come back.

*

'Gently now. NO, GENTLY!'

It wasn't often that Arthur shouted. Grunted, yes. Spoke in a low, monosyllabic voice from under his greying bristle of moustache, yes. Shouted, no. Margery jammed a foot down, by good fortune hitting the brake. More slowly than before, but still

35

unsteadily, she released the gear pedal. The car juddered out of the garden into the road. This time it missed the gateposts. There was no traffic coming.

'Now don't get too happy. Calm down. No – NO, we turn right here. That's it. And then left into the main road.'

He sounded relieved that it was a left turn. As if a right might be too dangerous with her at the wheel. Margery wasn't happy about that.

'Are you criticising me?'

'No, dear. Only thanking heaven that I'm still alive.'

'The impudence.'

'Just watch the road, not me.'

'I am. I wish you wouldn't wear that tweedy jacket.'

'Please. The road, not my jacket.'

'All right. But only for now.'

On the main road Margery stepped on the gas. Another American expression. Funny how Americanisms got into your blood and stayed there, even years after the post brought nothing from Iowa or Arkansas or whereve US air vice-marshals lived. But it was great to be zooming along like this. Poop-poop! Silly, canary-coloured caravans!

'I should slow down a bit, dear, if I were you. Someone might step off the pavement.'

'No need to worry. I'm in control.'

'Do take care.'

'They'll know I'm a learner from the plates. What an experience this is, how exhilar-'

But they were nearing Birkenhead in the grey of descending twilight. With a stench of burning rubber from the brakes, the car screeched to a halt. Margery and Arthur stared through the windscreen. Pinpointed by light from the door of The King's Arms on their left, a man in a trilby was on his knees, crawling across the road. Untroubled by the stalled, steaming bonnet only a foot from his shoulder, he continued sloth-like towards the opposite pavement, oblivious. A dark trail on the tarmac extended like a ship's wake from the darkened crotch of his trousers

'My God!' Margery steamed with indignation. 'It's the bloody Irish.'

'Margery.' Arthur spoke with gentle rebuke.

'What do you mean, Margery?'

'Your language. And the racial slur. Quite unjustified.'

'Sorry.'

She didn't sound sorry. The man reached the far pavement and vanished between parked cars. The uprearing vehicles on both sides reminded Margery of the Israelites crossing the Red Sea. From a brightly-lit door – there was a pub on that side as well - two men staggered out, saw the crawler and with difficulty dragged him to his feet.

'Ah, come on, Paddy. Come in and have another drink.'

Margery turned and stared at her father, triumphant. But Arthur's mind was focussed only on how he should explain the decision to which he was moving, the determination hammered into his brain by what he'd just witnessed. The conviction that an old man wasn't strong enough to take any more of this, that this tour of duty as Margery's driving instructor would irrevocably be his last.

Chapter 10
1971

'His sixteenth birthday, Mother. Come on. It's a special day.' Margery gave a small vocal performance, her notes a fluid, musical alto.

'He was sweet sixteen
Little Peterkin,
Always dancing on the village green...'

Nancy allowed herself a smile. It was the sort of smile that left Margery wondering if her attempts at liveliness simply made her look immature and foolish. Nancy's smiles were more chilling than most people's brush-offs.

'Why won't you, Mother? Why won't you come to Peter's party?'

'It will be too rowdy for my tastes.'

'It won't. It's not the main party. He's going off down town with Red Thomas and his other pals for that, later in the evening. It's just a preliminary one – a sedate family tea party here at Havana House. Do come. Show him you care.'

Nancy narrowed her lips to greater than usual tightness, her way of saying no. Margery surveyed her mother with pity and gloom: the finely crinkled skin at temples and cheeks, the expressionless abyss of the eyes, the spidery hair circling the walled-up cave of her mouth.

What did Nancy think about all day? What had she thought about as she played lady of the manor all these years? Before the war she must have thought what instructions she should give the servants, what was to be cooked for dinner, what groceries must be bought at Dindale's. But for decades now all that had been left to Georgina and Flo. *Something* must have filled the gap.

Sometimes she seemed not to have understood that pre-war days were over. *The Telegraph* flopped through the letterbox each day but beyond scanning the headlines she never seemed to read it before Arthur at mid-morning ferreted it away to his room. Now and then she expressed views on the state of the country and the world. 'There are too many blacks flooding into this country,' or, after a Labour election victory, 'No good will come of this.' The comments followed those of *The Telegraph* but somehow, Margery felt, she seemed to express views that she thought would mirror Arthur's. Yet Arthur's had changed over the years, becoming more liberal, adapting to a gentler view of homosexual people (a class whose very

38

existence Nancy denied), a greater generosity towards the peoples of Asia and Africa. The two of them never discussed the wider world.

Nor would such matters have figured at all in Nancy's short years of schooling. Of that nothing remained.

No, not nothing. Once in two years perhaps, at one of the few domestic
tasks she still undertook – the handwashing of some delicate silken garment or the polishing with Silvo of some particular piece of sterling silver received and cherished as a wedding present – Margery's mother would utter, startlingly as if a bird were speaking, lines of schoolroom poetry she still remembered, dimly linked with what her hands were doing.

> *Out spake the hardy Highland wight.*
> *'I'll go, my Chief. I'm ready.*
> *It is not for your silver bright*
> *But for your winsome lady.'*

A winsome lady. With silver bright. Was that how Nancy saw herself, still, to this day?

As if in reply a line from Margery's own schooling surfaced.

> *Oh would some power the giftie gi'e us*
> *To see ourselves as ithers see us.*

But Nancy would never have stooped to Scottish verse.

'Mother, why did you marry Father?'

Shock. Wide eyes. Then a faint smile.

'I loved him. He was a young man with prospects. A young lady was expected to marry.'

'The earlier the better?'

'One didn't miss chances.'

'Do you still feel – close to him?'

'Close? Dear girl, closeness didn't come into it. A man had his work to do. A lady saw to the house and servants. And her children.'

It figured. Through the pre-war years Arthur went off to his work at whatever the family firm was called before it became Atlantic Finance and Shipping, leaving Nancy to run the house. And after, when Arthur retired, it was not so different. Arthur retired to his room and read while Nancy held sway in the drawing room.

What did Arthur read? How weird that no one, not even his daughters, knew. Only that Nancy disapproved of an activity that was neither business nor a domestic task. Twice Annie Smith, the woman who came in to clean, had come to Margery holding out one or two dusty books.

'I found them under the hallstand, Miss Munnerly. Hidden, it seemed like. They've got the prices in the front. I think they may be your father's.'

And Margery took them, for later, secret delivery. That Arthur should spend much-needed shillings on dusty old tomes was more than Nancy could bear.

With the invitation to Peter's party refused, Margery sat forward in her chair, a prelude to leaving. But something rare held her. Something precious in her thoughts. An openness. An intimacy.

'At least you must be pleased with your children, Mother? I mean, apart from the tragedy of Edward, all still with us and all healthy. A big family.'

It was then that Margery's ears tricked her.

'Yes, four out of five. And one more.'

'Sorry? One more?'

'Yes. A boy. He would have been your age by now.'

'I didn't know. No one ever said.'

'What was the point in speaking? We didn't talk about – bodily matters – matters of birth and death.'

'When - when did he die?'

'If you only remembered, you would know that better than I. You were with him when he died. I only found out later.'

'I don't understand. How could I -?'

'I only found out when you were born.'

'You mean...there was another...? A twin?'

And to her mother's slow, grave nod it seemed as if the watery cave of pre-birth came back, the dim prodding form with its tuberous fingers and thumbs, the floating, nudging, slow-colliding, twilight figure in the warmth of darkness; above all, the closeness never to be regained, the theft of all purpose, all love when there came sudden stillness, a dearth of response, a void which nothing and nobody could ever refill.

Chapter 11
1978

Another ripple of laughter ran through the audience, stronger this time. Better than any talk of hers that she could remember. Margery flung back a straying lock excitedly. This was going down well. She returned to her quotation:

With silent, unerring skill Burlington slid down the drain-pipe.His feet touched the third-floor balcony soundlessly, hushed by the cushion of SAS rubber boots. There remained the challenge of reaching the floor below, where the hostages lay bound and gagged. There must be no delay, no mistake.The slightest warning meant death for the captives. He crouched low, ducking below window-ledge height against the danger that one of the terrorists might stray up the stairs and see the shadowy black figure in balaclava and skin-tight forage gear, a knobbly belt of stun-bombs and smoke canisters clustered like barnacles at his waist.

Margery broke off. This time the laughter became a roar. Mirth at the yarn was augmented by the longing of a literary audience to feel superior to a best-selling popular writer.
'Well, quite! I won't go on.'
Someone at the back called out, 'Oh, do!'
'No, enough is enough. I'll have mercy on you.'
'Please don't!'
More laughter.
'I'll give you this as a donation'- she held up the Burlington paperback – 'this tawdry *Comic Cuts* afterwards if you like. Free of charge!'
When the laughter subsided she continued. 'From what I've said you can see what I mean about the banality and vulgarity of popular taste. I ask myself how long the British can go on lapping up this sort of trash. Meanwhile, the great wealth of contemporary writing is ignored. It wilts for lack of finance and recognition. Our task is to promote it as it deserves...'
As the talk's climax approached, her own eloquence and a half-masochistic pleasure in scorning the writing of her own son bore her on. Pride and satisfaction expanded like a balloon, tightening her chest. Partly, she realised, they arose from the fact that today, for the first time, she was reaching beyond the limited

field of Merseyside rising on to the regional stage. True, she hadn't been asked to read out her work, only to present a paper. Still, even to do that for the North-West Literary Association was a distinct accolade. *Accolade.* There was a good word. French, she supposed. Or was it Latin? What a gorgeous junk room of treasures languages were.

There was – and merely admitting the fact to herself brought a trembling around the heart – there was another reason why being here gave her such pleasure. She'd glimpsed him at the back of the hall the man with the pipe – was he called Holloway or something similar - who'd waylaid her after her reading to that other Lit Soc in Cheshire somewhere. Waylaid. How brigand-like and romantic! And she'd messed it up, sent him away with nothing after he'd invited her round to his place for tea. How could she do it? How *could* she?

A sudden chill entered her blood. It occurred to her, out of nowhere, that all her opportunities had been missed. There'd been Hank in Rio and then Nairobi. It might – must – have been a small incident in his life, one of many such, but to her, with the glow of remembrance, it had grown over time into a towering peak of her life. There'd been no one since then. Imprisoned in Havana House, not by unkindness or even the strict puritanism of Nancy and heaven knows, not by any great amount of care or time given to Peter or Joni, but imprisoned all the same. A mental prison more barred and chain-bound because its assumptions were unspoken – respectability and conformity and worry about one's standing in the Rock Park community in the days when there'd been one. If you spoke something, said it out loud, it could be questioned. It was the unspoken assumptions and values that crippled you. Yes, even a bohemian such as they all took her to be. *It ain't the things you don't know that do the harm*, Mark Twain had said. *It's the things you know that ain't so.* So it was with values.

And yet somehow the fault, the weakness, didn't lie in Rock Park or Nancy or the church or the neighbours or other people generally. It lay in herself. Suppose Hank had proposed, suppose the pipe-smoking man hadn't unaccountably taken flight, wouldn't some objection within herself have raised a fist and cried Veto?

The image of the ideal stood in her path. She tried to duck beneath its arm, to dodge its obstruction, but always it moved too quickly, barring passage. Another world surrounded her, a watery world in which she swam and moved and had her being, holding a promise of closeness, warmth, safety which the world could never give. She felt the probing of thumbs and stubby fingers, the joy of liquid collision in twilight, the water's transmission of gurgling, gentle sound. A second identity, different from herself yet equally loved, enfolded her within the dark submarine sac of perfect union. Nothing a born life could bring could equal it.

She felt it again, but this time in a way far more banal and humdrum, when the meeting closed and, as some sliver of her had half expected, through the corner of an eye she saw a figure she knew, approaching. The Barnston man! He was still tweed-suited, still smart; she realised she'd never really looked at him before; a country gentleman. The aroma of pipe smoke seemed to come ahead; she could smell it before the brogue shoes padded up the aisle and shook her hand. Pull yourself together, Margery. Accept him for what he is, don't compare him unfavourably with some dream, some Apollo of your fantasy. Be realistic. Learn, even now, to make allowances.

'Congratulations! A fascinating talk.'

'Thank you, kind sir.' She bobbed a curtsey, her arms sweating. She wondered, is curtseying an affectation? Or are my affectations what he likes about me? Heaven knows, there's little enough else to like.

She forced a smile. Self-deprecation wasn't her style. It had to stop. 'Last time,' she heard herself say, 'at the Literary Society, I'm sorry I wasn't able to have tea with you.'

'That's all right. I sympathise. You're a busy lady and I was taking up too much of your time.'

'Yes - no. No, it was a pleasure to meet you.' She waited. She must say the right thing, accept any invitation this time, at any cost, she mustn't be the sort of woman who rebuffed, a cold bluestocking unapproachable to men. He had a nice voice, with a burr of West Country about it. Oh God, if only she could think of his name. She must find out – and *remember* – it. If only she could manage things better. If only –

'I just wanted to ask one small query about something you said. The question of how far Orwell's *Shooting an Elephant* is fact and how far fiction. The view I've read....'

As she listened some other Margery, a sister at her side, answered and made points and added quotations while her own thoughts floundered in a pond of hopelessness. Ought she to suggest they go somewhere, to some tearoom, to discuss Orwell more deeply? *Was* there a tearoom near here? If there was, would it still be open? She daren't look at her watch to see. On no account must she seem impatient, as if she wanted to rush away, to get rid of him.

The man – what *was* his name, why hadn't she *asked* so as to avoid this dreadful appearance of indifference – was clearly deep into poetry, a man in love with words. The thought occurred: perhaps this isn't a personal approach at all, perhaps he just wants to sort out his ideas on Orwell? It's *Politics and the English Language* he's absorbed in, not *Homage to Margery*. But there was still a chance…if he would hang on… Agitation seized her. A hotel, a pub would do, anywhere. She raised a wrist, looked at the watch. But her jarring halt in mid-action only emphasised the error.

'Why don't we find somewhere nice to discuss this more?'

He seemed surprised. 'That's a lovely idea. I wasn't expecting it. I know how busy –'

'No, not at all. Well yes, but not today, specially.'

'Let's see.' It was his turn to study his wristwatch. 'I'd certainly like to. But, oh my goodness, what a shame. I've an absolute obligation to be at the Board of Governors – the local school, you know – at seven and before then I must eat and tidy myself up. What a shame.'

As he made his excuses and left she was left hollow and trembling. She searched her feelings. Regret, yes. She'd wanted, she'd been determined to get to know him. But relief, too. Not just that the ordeal was averted, not mainly that. In the few seconds when he'd seemed to be on the brink of saying yes, of showing interest in *her* and not just Orwell, the acrid censor in her brain – oh, who put him there, was it you, Nancy, was it some dim forebear, George Munnerly or Amos or some other ice-hearted slavetrader – that bleak back-of-the-mind idealist had studied her companion and felt alienation. The alienation of someone for whom only the perfect will do. The aloneness of the incomplete person, a woman whose only fulfilment lay in finding the lost companion of those years before the years were numbered and counted, before the calendar of life shed its torn leaves.

Chapter 12
1986

Margery picked the morning mail off the mat and padded back to her bedroom.

She settled at the dressing table - the right place for a poet in her negligee to open correspondence. Antique in shiny, polished walnut, it had been in the room when it was allocated to her as a girl and now, sisters and parents having fortunately forgotten the allocation, it had become her property. An inheritance from great uncle Caspar, so she'd been told, the black sheep of the family in late Victorian times. Hadn't he gone off and lived a life of enthralling dissipation and debauchery somewhere exotic after almost bankrupting the family business so that even the house was in jeopardy? Something like that. What a romantic figure! Margery had always had a soft spot for Caspar.

She viewed herself in the mirror of the dressing table. Not bad for fifty-eight. Hair still long and luxuriant, playing a sort of peekaboo in the foothills of her bosom. All filaments of grey had been painted out, the way a faded fresco was sometimes discovered underneath some later picture – a Giotto, say, or a Leonardo. Margery wondered if she could be a kind of living Leonardo and if so whether anyone would discover her. Only if she was mummified, she supposed. Hm. That wasn't so attractive.

Ah yes, the mail. She mustn't forget that. She took it up. It consisted of only one letter but quite a big one. Addressed by herself. Ah yes, she knew what this was. Taking up and brandishing her mother-of-pearl paper-knife – another heirloom from great uncle Caspar – she slit the envelope and took out, together with the poems the editor had returned, the letter that would say which ones he'd accepted.

> *Thank you for sending your poems to 'Rooster' Magazine but on this occasion we regret that owing to lack of space we cannot include them. Good luck with your submissions elsewhere.*
>
> *Mairhi Carstairs, Editor*

Hm again. So they weren't accepting any of them. Oh well. Margery crumpled the rejection slip in her hand and looked round for the wastepaper basket. Missing, as usual. There'd been a time when she'd thought of papering the walls with slips like this as a proof of the distinction of her writing (all the best writers were rejected a million times) but since having the décor of her room re-done in Louis Quinze style the rejection theme might strike a wrong note. She dropped the ball of paper on the floor. Annie would know where to put it.

Unexpectedly, she collapsed over the dressing table. Big drops fell on the torn, cheap manilla of the envelope. She found herself sobbing. Why?

It wasn't the rejection of her poems. That had happened scores of times, hundreds, without evoking tears. Something she'd eaten or drunk last night? No. There'd been the usual stabs of indigestion after supper but they'd been successfully numbed by a couple of tots from the whisky bottle she kept, unknown to other members of the family, on the bottom shelf of her best bookcase behind Bernard Shaw's *Complete Works.* One solution to the world's woes cloaking another. Why, then?

She stood up, alarmed. A shadow had fallen, not across the room, which was still bathed in bright sunlight, but along the marrow of her bones and channels of her blood, as if emptying them, hollowing them out. Her body shook. Loneliness entered the room and stood gazing with sad eyes, shaking his head down the retrospect of her life, all she'd done in fifty-eight long years, all she'd missed or abandoned, all she would never do.

'Peter!' The name came out unwilled. As if in echo she thought, *Joni.* I'm a mother, a grandmother. I brought up a son and now the line, my blood, is going on. What am I doing here alone, writing poems that no one will publish, skimming the surface of arty gatherings like a water boatman, held in place only by conventions and fashions as strained as the surface tension under the daddy-longlegs of the millpond? Why aren't I the head of a family, a revered figure with a life of love and company and merriment to look back on and treasure? Oh, Peter, Peter, why did I never realise? My best poetry is *you*!

The sobbing took a minute to subside. She dashed a handkerchief to her cheeks. She must do something. Get in touch with Peter, apologise, grovel if necessary, make it up, ask him round.

But she'd tried it so often. Recently, even last night. Before that there'd been individual visits and family gatherings but last night had been a wider range of people. Peter had come, he'd seemed to enjoy it, they'd talked. And yet she couldn't feel sure. Each time she'd meant to make real contact, to corner her son and talk, get to know him, show interest in his life. Each time, somehow, for reasons she couldn't grasp, the attempt had failed. Why? Why?

Was it what people had sometimes called her 'butterfly mind'? 'You are an old scatterbrain,' Doris Edwards used to say at school. 'A real dotty one.'

At Cambridge, too. 'Don't forget to answer one question at a time,' Yvonne Parker had called out as they went into the exam hall for Finals. And it was true: her mind did skip about, linking up things that to most people didn't seem connected. But surely it wasn't important. Didn't Aristotle say somewhere that seeing similarities was a sign of intelligence? Wasn't it what poetry was about? There must be more to her failure with Peter than that.

An inability to concentrate on others – that might be it. Because they bored her. Only her inner thoughts were interesting enough to hold her attention for long. It wasn't her fault. It was other people's, the world's. Or was she rationalising, whitewashing a dreadful, egotistic weakness?

> *...bearing, I say, the stamp of one defect*
> *shall in the general censure take corruption*
> *from that particular fault.*

Shakespeare had it just right on this, on everything.

Well, the defect had to go. She would invite Peter round again, even so close to last night's party with him and her writer-friends, and this time on his own. No writers, no Annie smith for him to stick to like a clam, nobody. Come to think, there was an even better idea. Invite not just Peter but Penny as well. Hadn't her relationship with that other man, the shifty-looking one, broken down? So wasn't this just the time to re-unite the once-loving couple? Yes! If she, Margery, could bring that about, the family could re-form, it could be a big, happy clan again, she could become the *alma mater*, the matriarch, the loved and respected head of a prosperous, thriving hive of love and joy!

Margery rushed to the bureau and flung open the stationery drawer. Today she would turn a new leaf.

*

It would take place in two weeks' time. There wasn't a day to lose. She'd spend the whole of Saturday preparing: a buffet tea with cream buns, cheesecake, fruit loaf, ham sandwiches, prawn cocktail, an expensive Portuguese white wine and Russian salad. She'd choose a time when Nancy and Arthur were away on one of their rare sorties to visit friends and an afternoon when her sisters would be out of the house. If it was fine outdoors, she and Peter and Penny could even go down and sit in the arboretum, ironing out old differences, restoring a family unit too long neglected. This was to be a meeting of minds, a feast of reason and a flow of soul.

'Hello. Come in,' she would say. Even in an empty apartment she found herself whispering the words. Angry at her own hesitancy, she raised her voice. ~~It was all so vivid~~. 'You're first arriving. Penny's not here yet.'

~~They climbed~~ the stairs, Margery not so much breathless as slowed by a hugging in her chest.

'Oh, I should have rung and told you. Penny can't come.'

Margery stopped. 'Oh dear. And I've gone to such trouble. When I rang she didn't reply – I left a message on her ansaphone both times – but I thought that was just Penny. Damn. And I could have picked another time.'

Peter shook his head. 'I don't think so. Not with me coming.'

'But you've obviously been talking to her. She can't mind meeting you so much.'

And in imagination he shrugged. 'We don't push our luck.'

Loneliness returned. The flat would be empty without the third person she'd imagined, the other half of a love rekindled. But Peter at least would be here. She must make something of that. Vaguely, in her few and scattered moments of introspection, she'd wondered if his approaches to her over the years with poems or, once, a painting had been his own attempt to bridge the gap. And she hadn't caught on, too busy with her writing and her lectures and talks. She must not make the same mistake again. She must learn by experience. She was going to win him back.

In a dither, she decided to serve Portuguese wine. That would lubricate things. As complements she would hand out the crab sandwiches and salad.

'Now. What a long time. Tell me what you've been doing. I'm dying to hear.'

'Nothing much. Grooving.'

Grooving. What a funny word. But up-to-date and with it. State of the art. Margery gave a delighted giggle in prospect.

'Have you got a job?' Best not to mention his unfortunate experiences in past jobs.

'Not...really.'

48

'What do you live on, then?' Was he still writing those penny dreadfuls, the ones about that man, what was his name, Horrabin or Westmacott or something? They'd brought in a tidy income once.

'Sometimes Red gets me a job with the council. Just temporary. Traffic surveys, that sort of thing.'

'Like Red sometimes did? You stand at a street corner and press a button on a handset whenever a car goes by?'

'Something like that. I did it for the county council at the top of Kelsall Hill. You know – where you get the view of Chester and the Cheshire plain. How's life with you?'

'Oh, splendid, simply splendid. Now, I've cream buns. You must have some.'

But though in her head she chattered as gaily as she could and handed out the expensive fare she couldn't really afford, a veil had descended on her mind. She was aware of it but only as she might be aware of an extra rattle in the car when she was driving, not really becoming *conscious* of it until the engine finally broke down. She was a dentist, talking by rote while concentrating on filling your molars.

Yet the words *Kelsall Hill* stuck in her mind. The seed of a poem germinated. She'd only been to the Hill twice, driving over it one day to give a talk at Sandiway and the other time when she'd been receiving advances, ultimately unfruitful, from a man called Hector in Winsford. But the memory of it stayed. Kelsall Hill meant love.

She put down the list of foods she would buy or prepare and looked round.

What was wrong? Had she lost something?'

But no answer came. Immediate action was the vital thing, to take a note of her thoughts. Curses, despite all resolutions she hadn't paper and pencil; she'd set them aside when putting on her best party dress. Where were they? She flapped her hands, frantic.

A scrap caught her eye, a rectangular bluish chit. She seized it and, grabbing a pencil, scribbled.

Kelsall Hill – beyond that last blue mountain barred with snow – from whose bourne no traveller returns - Hector – love fading.

It would do. The scattered phrases would be enough to awaken emotion. Then she could write them out - in a sonnet or villanelle - at a time of tranquillity. Emotion recollected in, etc. She waved her arms again, this time in jubilation. Or a pantoum. Now *there* was an idea: a pantoum! She couldn't remember exactly what a pantoum was, certainly nothing to do with a lean and slippered pantaloon, not at all, but it would be one up if she could manage that. Lovely.

Good heavens, yes. Mustn't lose *this* piece of paper with its notes. Look at it more closely and you find it's a cheque. The cheque for fifty pounds that Dad, Arthur, gave me the week before he died. I wonder why. He couldn't have foreseen death, could he? Surely not. But you never know. Hold on: must put it away in a safe place. Then take it to a bank and if it's still valid cash it. Phew.

She ran to the bureau and after opening several drawers selected the one that seemed best: most likely to be opened soon, least likely to be emptied into the waste paper basket. She shut the drawer with a slam. There! Now to prepare for Peter. No, not prepare. He was already here, she'd just been talking to him.

But the business of writing her poem-notes had taken time. How long? Five, ten minutes. No, probably more. Time with its awkward gait always went faster when you were doing things that mattered, and meanwhile...

'Peter!'

She ran to the door and opened it.

'Peter!'

She ran down the landing, peered over the banister rail. But the hall below was empty. She wondered if she'd heard the reverberation of the heavy front door being closed, slammed. But she couldn't be sure. She went to the window but there was no car outside, not that she would have recognised Peter's car anyway, not after all this time apart.

The walk back to her room took time, the tick of lonely seconds, minutes. Slowed by the return of her indigestion, tight and fierce, she sat down, head in hands, among the virtual, uneaten cakes and the Russian salad and fruits and the silver teapot slowly losing warmth. And all that answered her slow whisper of 'Peter' was a seepage of hot tears.

*

The old clock which, like the walnut dressing table and the bureau and so much else, she'd inherited without a word being spoken or written by parents or grandparents, said seven before she got up. It wouldn't do to give way. After all, she had lots to live for. What was all this silly fuss about loneliness? What nonsense!

I know. She headed for the corner of the room where a small coffee table piled high with books concealed the telephone. Within minutes the notebook she kept for addresses and phone numbers struggled free. Her way of thumbing through it had the intense, nervous deftness of a rabbit nibbling. She picked up and dialled.

'Hello. Could I speak to the proprietor, please? To Hector? Hector Entwistle?'

But she knew at once he'd moved. Years ago. Time didn't stop just because you committed someone you loved to the pages of a notebook. Nothing was stable any more, not nowadays.

The tight pain came back. Indigestion again. No, it couldn't be that, it was in her chest, not her tummy. Margery staggered to the sofa and half-fell on to it. The tightness was getting worse. A dreadful word came to her. Angina. The doctor had once said something about it when she'd mentioned her pains while at the surgery for a check up on something quite different, probably her bunions.

It had sounded serious. People died of angina, didn't they — to do with the heart. Which was where the pain was, as she understood its position. What had Dr Miles said?

The phone lay on the floor next to her sofa. She must ring now, ask Dr Miles to come round at once. If only the pain would let up, if someone would unscrew the tight and now stabbing knife driving into her. Damn, she couldn't quite reach the cradle. Lean forward, Margery, don't be so useless. A bit further. Now...

But the last mite of effort failed to bring the receiver to her grasp and when Flo, hearing the heavy thud on the floor above, came round to enquire, she found in her sister's sprawled body neither pulse nor breath.

PETER

Chapter 13
1962

'Mummy says we've not to listen,' Hazel said. 'We'll know all about it later, when we're grown up.'

Peter pulled a face. It was always the same when he played with Aunt Georgina's twins. Caroline was all right, she'd go along with a good idea, like climbing on piles of chairs you could stack up here in the nursery or racing slugs down the window panes of the old house. She was a sport.

But Hazel always made trouble. 'Then you go away and forget them,' she'd whined after the last slug race. 'One got into the butter dish.'

Caroline joined in. 'There was one in the bath.' She burst out giggling and Peter joined in. Only Hazel stayed solemn, stiff with concern about what her mother would say. Hazel cheesed him off.

'Why wait till you grow up? Why shouldn't I tell you now?'

'I don't believe what you said.' Hazel's face was a lacquer of disapproval. 'It's not nice.'

He hesitated, unsure what her objection was - untruth or not-niceness. Vaguely, he'd felt from the start that playing doctors and nurses would start a quarrel. First, there'd been Hazel's grumpiness when he'd strung the usual cotton reel on a piece of string looped round his neck and used his new-made stethoscope to prod her chest and tummy. Now there was all this trouble about where babies came from. He wished he could just play with Caroline. Why did Hazel always have to play as well?

'I bet my Mum wouldn't mind.' He turned to Caroline. 'Do you think Auntie Flo would?'

Caroline spilled fresh giggles. Peter beamed. He liked her. He felt the old alliance against grown-ups re-form. It was more fun holding your nose at teachers and stuff if there were two of you. Mrs Parker's nose, the wart on Mr Daly's neck, the way Auntie Flo, usually so mardy towards the three kids, sometimes dropped in at the nursery when Auntie Georgina was out, as if she secretly needed them.

This time, though, the alliance seemed to be more against Hazel. That was great, too.

'If you're really poorly they cut you up.' He picked up a handbrush someone had left next to a dustpan on the nursery floor. 'We could do that.'

'You should leave that alone. It's Mrs Smith's.'

'If it's Annie's why's she leave it lying about?'

'P'raps she forgot. It won't be your Mum's. She never dusts.'

He and Caroline laughed again. He wondered whether to go ahead with an operation. The brush wasn't much like a knife but he could use it as a pretend knife and then brush up afterwards. He put on a professional look. He moved towards Hazel,

'Yours seems a serious case. I think we have to cut you up.'

But Hazel dissolved in tears. 'You leave me alone. You're not nice. And you,' she turned to her twin, 'you go along with him, you encourage him. I don't want you for my sister at all.'

Peter sensed big trouble. Left another instant, his cousin would call in her mother. There'd be a trial and he'd be found guilty – he wasn't sure of what. It was always the same. The need for action was urgent.

'Here,' he tugged at his pocket and, together with a filthy handkerchief and two conkers, pulled out a crumpled sheet of paper. 'Have you seen this? It's one of Mum's poems.'

In a second the tears stopped. Three minuscule critics clustered round the poem, heads down, a miniature rugby scrum.

'Read it out.'

'Where d'you find it?'

'In her stockings drawer.'

'She still wear stockings? No one wears stockings now.'

'Some women do. I've seen.'

There was a moment's silence. He decided not to explain. He drew himself up like Margery did when she read stuff at meetings, a different, professional look.

> *Loved shrimp, I pick your name*
> *not from black family Bible*
> *incensed with dust nor from*
> *octopus grapple of blood*
> *or cascade of generations*
> *but from a rock pool of love,*
> *you whom, with your fringe of feet*
> *and concertina shell*
> *only love forbids me eat.*

Another pause. Caroline wrinkled a nose. 'What's it mean?'

'Dunno. It's poetry.'

'Poetry still has to mean something.' Hazel seemed sure.

'Not if it's, like, posh.'

Caroline summoned courage. 'It's about a shrimp. It's caught it in a rock pool.'

'What's that about a Bible, then?' Peter wasn't convinced.

Explanation fell to Hazel. The other two listened in awe.

'She's christening her baby.'

'I never got christened.'

'Doesn't matter. It's poetry.'

'Is she wanting to eat him?'

'Prob-ab-ly. They do that in some places. It says it in that Arthur Mee book. They're called cannibals and –'

'What?'

'I don't know. And he's like a shrimp.'

Peter puffed his cheeks. He stuffed the poem back among the conkers.

'I'm not like that.'

No one argued. How could you deny truth?

Chapter 14
1968

When the girl reached the end of the bicycle sheds Peter stepped out. For a moment they stood breathless, sizing each other up.

'You're Peter Munnerly, aren't you? My Mum knows yours.'

He decided to play it cool. 'I know. You're Penny Green' He twiddled his school pen as if it were a cigarette.

'Your Mum's called Margery. They met once at a parent-teacher evening.'

The subject seemed exhausted. He jammed his pen back into his breast pocket and pointed to his school bag.

'Do you read *Eagle*? If you do I've got some.'

'Old ones?'

'Not that old.' He fished one out. 'What's today's date?'

'Don't know. What's it say?'

'Fifteenth of March.' It didn't seem to help. 'They're sixpence.'

'Where do you get 'em from?'

He raised his head, narrowed his eyes: *Don't get too snoopy.* 'Want to buy one?'

Penny Green wrinkled her nose. Even in a show of disgust there was something fascinating about it, pert and upturned. Peter felt his breath quicken.

'I can get girls' stuff as well.'

'What like?'

'*Girls' Crystal. Miranda.* They're a bit old but you could have them cheap. Five for two bob.'

'Do you make pots of money that way?'

'More'n you think.' Giving nothing away.

He wondered how much she would think. Girls didn't think about money, only what they could spend it on – clothes and make-up and things like that. They didn't read good stories where you could *become* Dan Dare or Dr Who. He bet she didn't even know what it was like, living Dan Dare's life half the time. And the other half Superman. Girls were silly. All the same, when you looked at her...

She gathered herself as if to go and in haste he put a hand on her forearm. Sleeve rolled up for deskwork on a summer day, her flesh was fresh and delicate, starkly contrasting with the orange nicotine stain, the dark hairs of incipient adolescence on his own.

'You ever been in Wardle's shed?'

'Wardle?'

'Our groundsman. He used to play goalie for Rovers.'

'He's to do with your school. Just because ours is next door doesn't mean -'

'You want to see it. It's great. Just down the path there, the cinder one.'

She seemed reluctant. He sensed the need for charm and smiled, at the same time tightening his grip on her arm. 'It's easy to get in. The lock's broke.'

'Why do you want me to go in there?'

But even while asking she half-understood. She stood expressionless, staring at him. Shock? he wondered. Or the bubble of excitement?

'Come on./ No one'll know.' He reached in his pocket and took out a handful of sales money. 'Here, you can have a shilling.'

Her eyes gleamed. He felt the thrill of discovering a like mind. He'd waylaid her for her looks, the long dark locks curtaining her eyes, the enticing way she walked. And the stories about what she'd let you do. But this was something more. The romance of shared capitalism.

She pawed the ground. with her foot, undecided. When she spoke her answer was a challenge. 'Half a crown.'

She didn't even check the coin as their feet crunched down the cinder path.

Chapter 15
1969

All through his childhood years he tried to win her.

After his fifth birthday there came a day when she walked with him to the local school and waited in the yard alongside other mums and a few dads until a teacher lined up the new children and led them in croc into the single-storey, ranch-like building. At the door he looked back and saw his mother waving but the reassurance was only momentary. A sense of aloneness such as would never come again engulfed him, the feeling of a lone swimmer being swept out to sea by irresistible currents.

During the days that followed he forgot her, carried away by playground games and activities with the other children. He became popular for suggesting new exploits for himself and his classmates but at the same time resented for the trouble he so often brought down on them, a boy whose status hovered between leader and subversive. But when he drew pictures in class it was Margery who emerged most often on the crayoned sheets and when the bell rang at half past three, always taking him by surprise, it was the high point of his day to pelt into the yard and down to the gate, socks round ankles, hair askew, satchel flapping, to find her waiting there.

'And what have you been doing today?' she would ask; and he would show with unsure pride the picture he'd drawn of the big house hedgehogged with far more chimneys than it could truly boast or the view across the Mersey to the big city, its cathedral tower owing more to what he'd been told than to any real observation.

'Lovely,' Margery said the first time he offered one of his masterpieces. 'May I keep it for ever?'

The surge of joy at having bestowed an eternal gift was inexpressible. After that, whenever she asked, 'May I keep it?' he would wait and if she said no more would ask, 'For ever, Mummy?' And Margery would reply, 'For ever.'

He showered other gifts on her: a strip of frilly crimson crepe-paper left over from the Christmas decorations; a piece of shiny agate one of the other children gave him ('It's very precious'); a mouse he found, sleek and peaceful in death, in the cellar of Havana House. But though she always responded with a jump of enthusiasm it died away too quickly for his true longing. Within a minute she would turn her attention to other things - the tinge of evening blue on the slate roofs of surrounding houses or the height of the tide that by now, she said, would have cut off Hilbre Island from the mainland against which it once nestled. 'Mummy,' he would say to entice her back, 'Mummy.' But though she took the outstretched tiny hand, within seconds it would be lowered again, unheld, forgotten by the dancing butterfly of her mind.

It was the same when teenage years took him to grammar school. As always, his career sprang differing, sometimes violent reactions. Within a week he decided which masters he respected, which not. And within a further week the teachers had responded in kind: their opinions of him were of his choosing. Some masters detested him for his awkward questions, questions bringing out the shortcomings in their knowledge, questions unmotivated by any desire for knowledge, only by mischief. Others saw the maverick as possibly clever, capable of reform. But except in History, and then only in the chronicling of wars and revolutions, his schooldays trudged by like war-prisoners, rigid with a boredom only the pleasures of sedition could relieve.

'How are you getting on at school?' Margery would sometimes ask. And because he'd heard her enthuse about education, because she herself had been to Cambridge, a place he viewed with a mixture of awe and suspicion, he tried to hold out hope, an offering of some token success.

'I got top mark in History.'

'Oh very good. Alfred and the cakes.'

Her attention vanished like a passing swallow and he was left relieved and yet let down. He hated to disappoint her and yet would have preferred anger at his general mediocrity to the sparsity of her interest when he excelled.

Two or three times over the years he gained a good mark for an English essay, one on Shakespeare's portrayal of the King in *Henry the Fifth*, another on Dickens' treatment of the French Revolution. Then he would leave the essay lying about in Margery's writing room, longing for her to see it. But her comments showed no sign that she noticed the alpha mark, but flew immediately to the issues the essays discussed. It was as if, with her, only ideas and words counted; he, her son, was, except in brief moments of affection, a stranger. The gulf between them widened. Every approach became a rebuff, a plea for love rejected.

The incident that hurt most arose in his final year. The school's chief game, occupying two terms of the year, was football and at that Peter had shown energy and skill. But his inability to restrain a ferocious keenness in pursuit of the ball had had him sent off the field so often that he was now banned. Nobody imagined he intended harm. In conversation, other boys focussed more on the day when, asked by the refereeing master whether he played as striker or defender, he had to admit that he didn't know. 'He's just mad,' was the common opinion. 'A screwloose.'

And so for Peter sport came to mean cricket. Out on an elm-surrounded field, clad in white flannels, he seemed to imbibe the gentlemanly pedigree of the game. He batted fiercely and raced to great effect in the deep field. Away matches, where no master would be present to watch, were a special joy. The team prospered. Before long he was made captain of the second eleven.

'You'll be leading the team and representing the school,' the sports master, 'Porky' Price, told him. 'It's an honour.' The teacher had no idea how to interpret the low mumble with which Munnerly received the news, the head-down shambling way he walked from the changing room.

Peter had no idea, either. He'd taken responsibility before. He'd booked halls for Margery's literary evenings, managed the monies collected at the door. He enjoyed doing a Saturday delivery round with the electric dray, especially when the milkman, Fred Dooley, was off ill and Peter was in sole charge.

One customer, a well-heeled lady from a near-mansion on the waterfront was unsure if she'd paid her bill for the previous month and Peter, without checking, assured her she hadn't. When the accounts proved otherwise he kept the money, a boost to his cigarette fund. 'What a charming young man,' he heard the lady comment to a neighbour. The clash between reputation and reality, already a seed in his consciousness, took root and deepened. As with all things that grow big in the mind, wherever he looked he saw it.

It made the offer of the cricket captaincy a Greek gift, a move that might bring enjoyment but which dragged him on to the side he opposed, the platform of faces he watched on prize-giving days, the rows of bloated officials bestowing rewards on those who would one day become like them. The conflict burned irresolubly. If Porky Price wanted him to be captain there must be something wrong with the position, something somehow underhand. Wasn't cricket a game the rich and privileged played, the ones who hadn't made money for themselves but inherited it from their fathers? Yes, he would get rich, but not by any means they would approve of. At any price not that way.

And yet he accepted. Unwillingly, with constant grumbles and professions of dislike, he found himself enjoying the role, a secret unadmitted vice. At the end of term, when the school's final and most important game against their local rivals approached, he voiced his thoughts at the breakfast table.

'We're playing Holton High on Saturday. Do you want to come and watch?'

Margery roused herself from abstraction and beamed on him, a genuinely pleased, loving smile. 'Of course. I'd love to.'

He told her the time of the match, the place, how to get there. He assured her there'd be plenty of seats; there might well be people she knew from parent-teacher evenings or just from ordinary social life. She beamed throughout; and yet mistrust nestled, a hidden traitor in his heart. When he spoke he was never sure if she was really listening.

When the day came he reminded her again over breakfast, re-told her the way to the ground. He watched, smiling because her smile lit him up, yet uncertain that she took in anything he was saying.

On the field he arranged his field thinking not only of the game but still more of his visitor. For himself he chose unusual positions, at gully when the batsman at one end faced the bowling, at mid-on for the other. That way, he had constant view of the entrance to the ground. He could watch his mother come in and take her seat to watch her son command his players, lead his team to victory.

But the match began, and went on, without her. By the end of an hour Peter knew she wouldn't come. She'd meant to, he never doubted that. The smiles and assurances were genuine. But what chance did good intentions and resolutions have against a fanciful mind, a straying attention, an absorption with a world inside herself that alighted on him only as a humming bee hovers over a passing flower? The betrayal was total, the worst he'd ever known. The incurable nature of human weakness assailed and stayed, a lasting wound and a never-forgotten lesson.

One other matter stayed as a scar on his body. For thirteen years it never arose. Then, soon after his fourteenth birthday some talk among the other boys in his class struck a pang of loneliness. Moved to voice it, he followed her to the kitchen one evening.

'Margery' - his mother insisted sporadically on his using the personal name - 'why don't I have a father?'

She raised her eyes out of contact with his, as if at some unspoken joke. 'Everyone has a father.'

'Who is he? Why don't we live with him?'

But the answer breathed unreality, a text from melodrama. 'He's Heathcliffe. He came in the night and now is gone.' She hurried through to the hallway, more intent on her moment of theatre than on answering. Peter sat in gloom, feeling lonely and cheated.

But in the way the mind has of rallying to support its needs, a half-substitute appeared. One afternoon in the summer holidays of his tenth year Margery went out for some unexplained purpose, leaving Peter in the care of Annie Smith. With Peter's imagined help Annie was moulding pastry for an apple and bramble tart when there was a knock on the apartment's door and the forbidding figure of Aunt Flo appeared. It wasn't the first time she'd dropped in over the months. Always in Margery's absence. She glanced round the kitchen as if making sure the coast was clear.

'I just called in in case Margery might like a chat.'

'Peter saw Annie suppress a guffaw. 'She's at a meeting. Poetry.' Annie said it as a Presbyterian might say *nudism* or *wife-swapping.*

'Ah. And how's Peter today?'

'I'm okay.'

'What are you doing, then?'

Though it was obvious enough, unease with Flo stopped him admitting his role as assistant baker. But when you were making conversation you had, he supposed, to say *something.*

'Waiting for Annie's tart to be ready.'

'I see.' She wasn't finding it easy going. Was it loneliness that drove her here? Peter wasn't sure. Whatever, something prompted her to mention Edward.

'Your Uncle Edward was a great one for tarts. And pies.' She added the last words hurriedly - to avoid ambiguity, Peter decided. 'It was what he missed most at sea.'

'Was he the sailor one?'

'Yes. Sailed everywhere. A great tar.'

'Where d'he go?'

'Everywhere. The North Sea, the Irish Sea' – Aunt Flo faltered, handicapped by the limits of her Geography – 'wherever there were enemy to fight.'

'What did he do when he fought them?'

'He attacked them. Hoisted the flag and attacked.'

'What like with?'

'Oh, guns and things. Then there were submarines. U-boats.'

'How did he attack U-boats? They're under water.'

He listened with rising elation as Aunt Flo floundered from invention to invention. A surge of joy at having her on the run, lost in unknown territory, arose as he fired question after question, merciless. But it wasn't just that. There was pleasure in the figure she painted of Uncle Edward as well. A man murky and undelineated but for that reason all the more heroic, someone who'd really gone to sea and fought, someone he himself was going to be like. In a while he let his questions flag and, sure enough, Aunt Flo's initial gusto began to revive. Confidence returned; the tales of derring-do expanded. He thought of one of the few films Margery had taken him to see, one in which the hero - a man called Finn or Flynn – led a cavalry charge of six hundred men on horses carrying lances and beat the enemy almost singlehanded. That was what a man should be like. That was the sort of man he would be.

When Aunt Flo left he went to his bedroom and, taking paper and pencil, sat at the dresser. He sucked the pencil, searching for a name. Like the man in that film, James Bond, named after a posh street called Bond Street. Those three days when Margery had taken him to London, had they seen any posh streets? Yes! They had. Enthralled, intoxicated with the character of another person as an actor might be on stage, he moved his pen over the paper.

Across the icy plain of Balaclava the enemy outnumbered the British by twenty to one. But nothing could daunt Horatio Burlington or damp his indomitable valour. For him the day would bring either victory or death.

Chapter 16
1971

They, too, met in Wardle's shed.

Where Wardle vanished to in the afternoons wasn't clear. 'Rip' Kirton, the school football captain, said he needed two hours' rest each day because of a cracked skull he'd sustained colliding with the goalpost when he once dived to prevent Wensham Nomads scoring in a local derby. In contrast, Bob Tommelty, the fat boy of the class, insisted that Wardle had a mistress down at Claythorpe. Pressed to give details, including a blow-by-blow account of Wardle's more adventurous trysts with her, Tommelty merely ducked his head into his shoulders in fits of uncontrollable splutters. Scattering saliva, he pressed a finger to his lips to indicate that the subject was too delicate for public discussion. Only his hands, gesturing as if to caress a gigantic egg-timer, left no doubt about the mistress's main attributes.

Whatever the explanation, after three each afternoon the shed stood empty, its lock still unmended. Peter and Red Thomas hung some old sacks, used for drying the cricket rollers in wet weather, over the shed's window and lit up.

'Well. Did you do it?' Red Thomas's attention was barely impaired by the need to flick ants out of the hole in his ankle-socks.

'Yeh. I've got it here.' Peter unfolded a typed sheet from the inside pocket of his blazer. 'All it needs is signing.'

'Let's see.'

'No. Your hands, you'll muck it up. I'll hold, you read.'

Red Thomas peered at the letter. It took a while to digest.

'From Purlock to them – the Army?'

'Dead right. I want out of here.'

'An' the beak's supposed to be recommending you. Saying you're what they need?'

''Course. That's what you say in testimonials.'

Red Thomas searched his mate's face. Slowly they exchanged grins. Red began to laugh but broke off when Peter snatched back the letter, scowling. Derision went too far.

'So you're going to sign it? Write Purlock's signature?'

Peter shook his head. 'Needs a real good fake. I'd be no good at it.'

'Who, then?' At the last syllable Red's voice faltered.

Peter raised his head, blew smoke rings into the shed's grass-smelling atmosphere. 'Who's best at writing sick notes? Who's the expert?'

Red sat up, alerted. 'Oh no, that was different. That was signatures from mums and dads. No one knows how they write.'

'With Purlock, you'd have something you could copy. See here.' From another pocket emerged Peter's last-term report. At the bottom, as usual, the Headmaster had scrawled his name. 'You're good at that.'

Red backed away. An exploratory ant halfway up his trouser leg demanded prolonged attention. 'Nah, it's too risky.'

Another high-blown ring of smoke. 'Do you enjoy it when I fix up for you to come here after school?'

'For me to -? Yes. What do you mean? Not -?'

'Or are you happy to stay on your own, like? Not share the good things in life?'

'Hey no. You don't mean – Carol Jones?'

''Course, if you don't want to take it in turns, if you prefer to find a bird for yourself...'

Red swallowed, his face colouring to match his nickname. Beads of distress bubbled to his forehead. He lurched again towards the letter in Peter's hand.

'*A fine young man...worthy of the best traditions of the Army... from a long-established Liverpool family.* Grief. We'd be in deep trouble if Purlock found out.'

'You would. But he won't. It'll just go into a Ministry of Defence file. I may not see it again – ''least, not till I'm a field marshal.'

The enormity of the plan sank home. 'You mean it? Con your way into the Army? You're really going to do it?'

'Yeh. We are.'

*

It seemed not to be a recruiting office at all. The name, *Advice Centre*, stood out over the doorway, painted in striking black letters. Window displays flaunted outsize pictures in colour: soldiers driving an armoured car over desert; men in white uniforms skiing over dazzling snow-slopes; a squaddy hunkering down to give sweets to Arab children. Peter raised a celebratory fist and marched in.

The room contained two advisers. One, with no stripes on his arm, sat at a large desk behind a tabloid newspaper. As he lowered it to take in the unusual sight of a customer, the scantily-clad girl on the front page subsided to table level and a middle-page spread of several totally unclad came into view. The other soldier, a sergeant, stood at the window, his forehead plastered in a black slick which concealed yet drew attention to the ebb-tide of hair. The style gave him a faintly Hitlerian appearance.

He swung round and marched without obvious purpose to the centre of the room. 'Good morning, sir. And what can we do for you?'

'I want to join up.'

The statement seemed definite enough but it loosed a flow of sales talk. 'Ah yes, well just let me tell you. If you want to learn a trade, see the world, get ahead in later life, then it's just the place for you. You won't regret it. There's a wide choice of skills you can learn – gunner, electronics specialist, driver, signals operative, mechanic – there's tanks as well as light vehicles – engineer, bridge-builder, you name it. And there's practically unlimited scope for advancement. The pay's good. People don't realise that. They think it's like in the past...'

While the torrent flowed Peter released a half-smile. Images of a holiday brochure flitted to mind. *Come to sunny Korea. Enjoy hide-and-seek in the forests of Mount Kenya.*

'Yes, I've already decided. I just want to sign on.'

'Ah.' The sergeant seemed taken aback. Recruitment wasn't usually so simple. 'So what, er, regiment were you wanting to apply for?'

'The SAS.'

Again a pause. 'It's not easy to pass the selection procedures for that.' He surveyed Peter with doubt. 'You reckon you're tough enough?'

'I played rugby at school. I went on mountain outings.'

'Well, you can try. If you don't pass there's lots of not-so-demanding regiments you can transfer to.'

'I want the SAS.'

'Discipline's strict, you know. Instant obedience to orders.'

But Peter shook his head. 'I'll give the orders. I'm going for a commission.'

The sergeant cleared his throat and walked to the desk. Its expanse stood as empty as the desert in the recruitment poster. He sat down and from a drawer pulled out a pile of forms.

'Right, then. We just have to fill this in. I'll do the first bit, then the rest's up to you.' Again the note of doubt. 'That all right?'

It took a moment to interpret the question. *Can you write?*

'Yeh, that's fine.'

There was silence as each of them took his turn with the form. Address, telephone number, nationality. When Peter came to *date of birth* the other man craned forward.

'1953?'

'Yeh. I'm eighteen.' He stared at the sergeant's eyes. If you lied confidently enough you could get away with it. With anything.

'Okay. Now if you'd just sign here.'

The signature, written with a flourish, spread far beyond the allocated line. The sergeant viewed it with a mixture of doubt and disapproval. He took back the pen.

'Right, that's it, then. You'll be called for a medical in a week or two. Subject to that, you'll get your call-up papers in a few weeks.'

Peter raised clasped hands like a boxing champion. But the sergeant contributed only a laugh. As Peter walked to the door the sales talk fell away under the crossfire of cynicism.

'You poor, bloody sod.'

*

On Wednesdays Margery went out to one of her English classes. It was as good a time as any to pad along the west wing and call on Flo. Peter was about to tap on the door when it swung wide open. He gave a start, alarmed to have been observed.

'And to what do I owe this mouselike approach, young man? On what new felony are you bent?'

Peter looked both ways along the hall. He raised a finger to his lips. 'Can I come in?'

Victorian pelmets and velvet curtains made the big room pleasantly dark. They settled opposite each other, she in a high armchair with wings, he perching at the end of a chaise longue. Facing yet distant, they brought to mind the stork and the fox in Aesop's fable.

'So? What have you got to confess?'

'Er, nothing. Well' – a prickle of truth made him falter – 'actually, I came to ask a favour.'

'Oh yes? Well let me make this clear. I will not underwrite your bouncy cheques, if that's what you're asking. Or stand bail for you at the local cop shop.' She enunciated the last words with precision, proud of her technical vocabulary. 'Or turn out at night to recover you from drunken collapse in a local gutter. Or adopt your illegitimate children. So, what else? It leaves plenty of scope.'

Peter's chuckled uncertainly. 'It's not as bad as that. Nothing like.'

'Go on.'

'You see, the thing is, I'm joining the army.'

'You – are – *what?*'

'Joining the SAS and –'

'*Joining the SAS?* You do realise, I hope, that, first of all, your mother wishes you to stay at school and take you're O levels, followed in due course by your A's?'

'I know. But I've decided not to.'

'Oh have you? Don't you realise that the army will object to boys of – what is it? – fifteen trying to sign on in their ranks, however big and tall you may have grown recently?'

'But I pass for eighteen. People often mistake me for that.'

'Dear boy, there are forms to be signed, legally binding commitments and contracts. How can you plan to lie to your sovereign in writing?'

'In the First World War lots of people did it. It doesn't do any harm, it helps the country. Remedies the recruitment shortage.'

Aunt Flo took a deep breath. Her voice sank in pitch. 'Deranged nephew, what do you know about the SAS?'

'I read a book about it. It'd be great. I –'

'They swim as frogmen to plant limpet bombs on the bottom of battleships. They crawl through swamps to blow up enemy ammunition dumps. They break into houses where gunmen are holding people hostage. They carry grenades in their belts which could go off and blow them to smithereens. They –'

But words failed. Aunt Flo subsided into silence and disbelief.

The time seemed ripe for renewing the attack. 'I wouldn't ask you to recommend me for any of that. I mean, not blowing myself up –'

'I have to admit that breaking in does sound more like your line of expertise.'

'The thing is, when I signed on they wanted an address and the name of a responsible person. Someone to refer to.'

'I see. To verify your age. Your eighteen years, your sobriety of character, your immaculate record at school and elsewhere. Quite. And so you want me to perjure myself as no one else possibly could?'

'It's just a general character reference.'

'Hm.'

'It's only – you know. General.' He paused, waiting.

His aunt's head nodded slowly. 'Yes, I know.' A moment of silence passed. Flo drew breath. 'As it happens, they rang me yesterday, the HQ of the SAS. They wanted to confirm certain statements you'd made in your form of application. As they burbled on it took me several seconds to sort out what this fantasy, this charivari of untruth was all about. But then I remembered you and the pieces fell into place.'

'What – what did you say?'

'I certified, I endorsed, I confirmed all your long novel of falsehoods. I perjured myself. I even accepted the false name you gave me.'

Peter's voice was barely audible. 'Steve's.'

'Yes. My fiance.'

His aunt gave a long sigh. 'Why do I do it? Why do I let myself become accomplice to a future Crippen, a Houdini of misdeeds, a Savonarola of heresy? I don't know. Envy, perhaps? A little. A feeling of *there but for the grace*? Perhaps. But, dear boy, I suspect at bottom the truth is more simple. For some reason unfathomable to man and inexcusable before God, I have a fondness for you. And there you have it.'

He felt it as a relief for her as well as him when he made his excuses and left. In the silence of the hall he wondered why it should distress her to admit affection or how she could be surprised at loving someone as decent and admirable as himself.

Chapter 17
1971

'Down off Market Street,' Artie Wellings explained. 'Second house on the left. There's some real crackers.'

They came to the fence skirting the camp. The palisade of vertical metal spikes gave off occasional glints as the moon battled its way between dark clouds.

'You go there often?' Artie's nocturnal absences without leave from the billet had excited speculation. The town's red light area was most people's bet.

'Once a week. You wanna try it.'

'Get caught out of barracks, you're on a charge.'

'It's only the same as now. You was just drinking, I had nookie as well.'

'Yeh, s'pose so.' Artie had come late to the Farmer's Arms, delayed by greater attractions.

'Worth the risk. You should see 'em. Nadia. Ooarh.'

They halted. Peter stared at the fence, eight feet high and without footholds. His mind flickered between doubt about surmounting it and the charms of Nadia off Market Street. 'How do you reckon -?'

'Easy.' Like a storeman checking supplies, Artie counted the staves leftward from one of the fence's periodic concrete posts. At the seventh he grasped the metal stem and twisted. The stave turned and slipped from its attachments at top and bottom. Ducking heads, they slipped into the camp. Artie replaced the stave.

'Look out!'

Again they ducked, this time behind a three-ton lorry parked, by good luck, at the roadside. It hid them until the officer had passed. Then, with gently lowered feet reminiscent of ice-skaters, they slipped over the road and towards the billet.

B Squad occupied part of the old barracks, the third floor. 'Built for the Crimean War, this place was,' company sergeant-major Turgreeve had announced when they first clattered in. 'Been condemned five times but the nation's taxpayers can't afford a replacement, so we're waiting till it collapses and smashes some of you rookies' heads. That'll be no great loss.'

The pessimism was justified. On the day of their arrival Peter had commented on the green-edged patches suggestive of lichen that stained the wooden timbers overhead.

'Won't hurt you, mate,' Artie Wellings had muttered back. 'You could do with a shower.'

'I shan't feel it. I'll be safe in the arms of Morpheus.' The smattering from 'Beanie' Minning's classics lessons helped to maintain Peter's status.

'Well, chuck him out. We don't want any dodgies round here.'

The exchange created comradeship, the warmth of mutual insult.

They avoided the door at the front. Just inside it, the partitioned space allotted to Ramm, the Squad's stubby Welsh corporal, presented too great a chance of trouble. Ramm's loyalties weren't to be trusted. The chance was especially great when, as tonight, the house's lights were, unusually, still on. Artie led the way to the fire escape at the back.

They climbed with stealth. At one point they heard footsteps on the tarmac not far away and froze till the steps passed. Another pause gave Artie time to re-tie his bootlace, fastened too hastily when parting from Nadia. At last they reached the back window, its panel painted with the words *Fire Exit*. Artie grasped the steel door and pushed.

The door didn't move. He heaved again, applying his shoulder. He cursed under his breath. 'I left it on the latch. Some bugger's gone and –'

But suddenly the door swung open. Artie drew back, then tiptoed forward again. But before he could enter the lit-up billet a bristly face appeared in the doorway: Company Sergeant-Major Turgreeve's.

'What the hell d'you think you're doing, eh? Why are you out at this hour? And what's wrong with the proper door? All right, get in. You're in real trouble, I can tell you. Real bloody trouble.'

They stood in silence while the tirade boiled. The rest of B Squad craned their necks from beds and viewpoints down the billet. Peter wrestled with perplexity. Beyond doubt it was Turgreeve's appearance that accounted for all the lights being on. Turgreeve, and Ramm standing beside him, a look of suppressed laughter on his face. But what had brought Turgreeve round to the billet at this hour for what seemed like a snap inspection? Ramm? Had Ramm, always given to sudden and unpredictable treachery, got Turgreeve to come round for an unscheduled snoop?

'So, where've you been?'

Artie answered. 'Just a walk round the camp, sarnt-major.'

Turgreeve pulled down the ends of his mouth. 'Don't come that one. A walk round the camp that lasted half an hour? That's how long I've been here. Haven't I?' He turned to Ramm, who nodded vigorously. A crawler's assent. So this *was* all Ramm's doing. Ramm must have noticed Artie's absences but didn't want the odium of turning him in for them. So, never liking Artie much and wanting the joy of exercising malicious petty power, he'd called in the CSM. But why, exactly?

'Corporal Ramm here believes you've been absent from the camp without leave before. Says he saw you in town once. In other words this isn't the first time. Is that right?'

Unsure what story would stand up to questioning, Artie hesitated; but in the gap memory came to Peter's aid. There'd been the night Ramm and Artie woke the billet with the racket of boots and raucous voices as they piled in from town in the early hours. By all accounts, from Market Street. That night Ramm hadn't felt able to catch Artie for going AWOL without incriminating himself. So this time he'd engineered Turgreeve's appearance so that the CSM found out for himself. Either that or Turgreeve had pressured him into sneaking on his one-time fellow-in-crime.

'Excuse me, sarnt-major. I think there's a mistake somewhere. I'm sure it can't have been either of us that Corporal Ramm saw down town. We've never been to the Market Street area. We wouldn't know this girl, Nadia, that the Corporal's talked about even if we met her. I mean, I don't know how familiar Corporal Ramm is with –'

But the last words were drowned by Ramm's coughing. The fit lasted a full half-minute, leaving him red-faced and discomfited.

'Sorry, sarnt-major. A cold coming on.'

'So what do you say to this?' He turned to the Welshman.

'Well, yes. Yes, he could be right. I take it back. When you called in unexpected-like, I didn't have time to think. They could have, like they say, just been for a walk round the camp.'

As the sergeant-major, glowering, stumped from the billet, Corporal Ramm seemed in haste to return to his cubicle, away from the squaddies.

*

It made Peter grin. Every morning at seven the intake paraded on the square in squads and companies. The ranks were inspected, colours presented; the regimental sergeant major bawled insults and orders which could be heard a mile away on a quiet day. The sight of RSM Brant bellowing to the whole universe, the sheer

71

enormity of the way he gave commands obeyed by five hundred men, brought a huge, vicarious thrill.

'Terrific. Just the power, the dominance,' Peter confided to Artie after one parade. 'I'd love that.'

'Takes years to be an RSM. You'd spend your life getting there.'

'Don't bet on it, mate. Don't you bet on it.'

*

'Then there could be times when you have to use an old World War Two weapon. You never know. Could happen, the MOD being strapped for cash, or thinking they are. Like this sten.'

The weapons instructor paused. A razor moustache and sharp nose chimed exactly with the ham-dramatic manner of his talk. He fondled the sten gun like a lapdog.

'This isn't like your telescopic-site rifles and it's a lot smaller and lighter than your mortar or your modern machine gun. Nor, for that matter, your hand-held rocket-launcher. But that makes it easier to carry. And it's a fearsome weapon, fired from the hip. You spray it on 'em. No need to be that accurate, there's enough bullets to wipe out a company in the dark.'

He held the sten up, exhibiting. 'See here, this is the bolt-hole. The bolt rackets backwards and forwards two thousand times a minute. Got it – two thousand times a minute? So keep your fingers out, as the lady said. Got it? Don't stick your hand in, not in any shape or form. Two or three intakes ago, someone did that and lost two fingers, sliced right off. Any questions?

A voice from the front row piped up. 'Yes, sarge. Did he get discharged?'

'That's enough of your lip, Munnerly. Self-mutilation's an offence under Queen's Regs. Right. Get into rank, now! I said *move!*
*

It was chiefly the put-downs, people trying to come the boss over him, that cemented determination. The day after CO's parade the Company's team played D Company at rugger. Twice Peter was close to scoring a try but twice the same opponent, a man called Colby whose neck was wider than his head, brought him down within feet of the line. Mildly frustrated and with the match clearly lost, Peter started to kick in the opposite direction. The new tactic brought a surge of morale, the satisfaction of individuality.

The referee, a young lieutenant, blew the whistle.

'Hey, you. Which way are you kicking?'

72

Peter rubbed his chin. 'That way.' His arm wavered vaguely down the sideline.

'You're in a red shirt. You kick that way.'

'Oh no, I wouldn't want that.'

'It's not a matter of what you want. You're a red, you kick over there. Don't forget it.'

The next time the ball came his way he kicked it sideways. The ball soared out of the field, thrilling as a meteor in space. The lieutenant blew his whistle, waved a card in Peter's face. But even in walking off the field there was satisfaction. The kick had been a way of making his mark, of being himself. At the sideline he stopped to join in the general belly laugh at his behaviour before breaking into a trot towards the changing room and the exhilaration of the showers.

Somehow, he was dimly aware, it was that incident that led to the next. They were in the billet shortly after breakfast a few days later when Tubby, a former Billingsgate porter, broke into song.

'There was a bloke, he was no good.
He took this girl into a wood.
Bye bye, blackbird.'

'Aw, shut it, Tubby,' someone at the far end of the billet objected. 'We've heard that one scores of times.'

'He took her to a place no one could find her.
He tied her to a tree with her hands behind her.'

The objector reached over to his locker. Within seconds the sound of a transistor radio played at full volume drowned Tubby's serenade. 'Today,' intoned the plummy voice of a BBC newsreader, 'is the birthday of Her Majesty the Queen.' A drum roll rattled in huge crescendo. Then the band's brass came in with the stentorian chords of *God Save The Queen.*

People turned in protest, their hands held to their ears. Pulling a grotesque face, Tubby stopped singing. But the music went on.

Peter couldn't have said why he did it. Some combination of the stirring harmonies, the lingering love affair with power he'd contracted on the drill square and sworn to make his own drove him to action. He sprang to his feet and stood stiff beside his bed, his arms straight, pressing down his sides.

'On your feet! Get up, you idle men! ATTEN-TION!'

For a second the squaddies were stunned. Burgess, a slightly-built and sickly-looking youth, made as if to obey the order but when no one else moved shuffled to a standstill. 'Creep!' someone hissed at him. Then the spell broke.

73

'For Chrissake Munnerly, sit down and shut up. Who d'you think you are?'

'Heading for stripes, he thinks he is.'

'He'll get stripes across his face if he goes on.'

'Get back on your bunk, idiot. It's not passing out parade.'

The music ended, followed by six pips, five short and one long. The plummy voice, its volume turned down now, began reading the news. In a moment there was a click and the transistor fell silent. Peter climbed back on to his bunk.

A grin rose to his lips. It was a new experience, being unpopular for doing the patriotic thing. He'd rather enjoyed it – the odd-man-out role, but this time with the establishment presumably on his side. There was an originality about it, something that picked him out. Yeh, great.

Burgess had almost obeyed. Maybe if he had, the others would have followed suit. Peter mulled over the thought. He did seem to have some magnetic quality, something that made others take orders. A leader. A chuckle vibrated his chest. It'd be worth trying again.

*

They were polishing boots and brasses when the door burst open and the lieutenant commanding the Squad marched in. He halted in mid-floor next to the coal-burning stove.

'Which one of you's Munnerly?'

For a second no one answered. An instinct not to sneak held them immobile. Then, as if realising that no sneaking was involved, the squaddies' eyes moved towards Peter.

'I am.'

The officer waved a sheet of paper in his hand. 'What's your date of birth?'

Peter coughed. 'Er, 1952.' The document could be his application form. He wished he could remember what he'd written.

'What month?' A pause. 'Come on, you must know. How old are you?'

'Eighteen, sir.'

There was a moment of scrutiny. 'Mm, you don't look eighteen. And you're not, are you?'

'Yessir.'

'No you're not, don't lie. Regimental office rang up your old school and asked. They said you were fifteen. Or' – he peered at a second paper under the first – 'just turned sixteen. Anyway, you lied about your age. Didn't you?'

Peter swallowed. The game was up: a fighting withdrawal was called for. He raised his eyebrows in hurt innocence. 'Me, sir?'

'Yes, you. It's no good-'

'Excuse me, sir. Who did you speak to at my school?'

'I don't know, it wasn't me. Your headmaster, I suppose.' He shuffled the papers. 'Porlock? Here it is. Purlock. Purlock.'

Peter's face broke into an understanding smile. 'Oh, old Purlock. Ah, I see now.'

'What's so funny about that?'

'Well, sir. Ha! I don't suppose you know old Purlock. If you did... Ha!'

The lieutenant sensed he was losing control. 'Look,' he broke in, 'the fact is they've rumbled you. You'd better come with me to the office. And don't lie to them. It won't do you any good.'

'Me, lie, sir? It must be some clerical error. We'll have it sorted out in no time.'

But this time the officer had a retort. 'No doubt. And in no time we'll have you chucked out. Come on. Quick march!'

Chapter 18
1972

'Midge' Sprewls, a form master antagonistic towards Peter long before his pupil's inglorious discharge from the army and return to school, walked down the aisles collecting the answer-scripts. At Peter's desk he halted, picked up the boy's script and studied it. Returning to the previous desk, he took up Boothroyd's. There was jubilation on his face.

'How do you explain this, Munnerly? Your answer to Question One contains, the same sentence as Boothroyd's. A strange coincidence.'

Peter swallowed. The Scouse accent he'd mutinously adopted was for once silent.

'How do you explain it, eh?'

'I don't know, sir.' He stared down at the desk. The lie was safest. Best not to divulge his own and Boothroyd's pre-exam system, the prediction of questions, the memorisation of paragraphs from books.

'If you're not going to answer, it'll be clear to me what's happened, Munnerly. You've been cheating, haven't you?'

'No sir.'

Sprewls returned to the script. 'These answers are exceptionally long, not like you at all, Munnerly. Whence this superior knowledge?'

'Good memory, sir. Keen interest in the subject.'

An undercurrent of laughter shook the classroom. Sprewls glowed with pleasure, a perceived popularity compensating for his five foot three stature.

'A likely story.'

'It's true.'

Midge Sprewls rolled the exam script into a scroll and brought it down smartly on Peter's head. Peter winced. What was all this about? He'd done nothing wrong. Or was it body language? He bet that was it. Body language always brought him trouble.

'Open your desk, Munnerly.'

'Why? It's not relevant.'

'*Do as you're told, boy.*'

Reluctantly, Peter raised the lid. Midge Sprewls leaned forward and rummaged. A kind of fascination held him like unset gelatine as his fingers turned over the books, loose papers, an old sock, three conkers from two seasons before last, an old football lace. Peter sat upright, staring into space. There'd be trouble now. Sprewls might notice the strands of tobacco from old fags. He couldn't fail to see the bookie's ticket, the glossy mag under the junk.

Yet oddly, after prolonged searching, it was a sheaf of loose papers that Sprewls took out. From its unmanageable foliage he extracted a handwritten sheet.

'What's this, Munnerly?'

'Don't know, sir.'

'Then I'll tell you. It's someone else's answers to a class exam. And you have it hidden in your desk. It's a crib, Munnerly.'

Peter remembered. Schofield's paper, left over from last term's test had lain among the melee for months.

'It's an old one. It's not to do with today's exam.'

'You'd better come with me to the Head, Munnerly. *Now! Come on! Look sharp!*'

As they entered the Head's room Mr Purlock slammed shut one of the drawers in his desk, removing from sight a book he'd been studying. Peter's mouth curled in a cynical grin: it was well known that Purlock was working for a Master's Degree in Education. With exuberance Midge Sprewls levelled his charge.

'Well, Munnerly, what have you got to say for yourself?'

'I didn't cheat. Really. I've never broken any rules.' At the final falsehood his voice quivered on the brink of mirth.

'It won't do any good playing the innocent, Munnerly. Mr Sprewls has told me your answer was identical with Boothroyd's.'

'Only a sentence or two.'

'You don't convince me, Munnerly. Two sentences is a lot.'

'Mightn't it be Boothroyd who cheated?'

The Headmaster glanced towards Midge Sprewls but the Geography master's face derided the idea.

'Mr Sprewls clearly doesn't believe a word of that. Well, Munnerly, are you going to admit what you did? We haven't all day.'

'It's not true.'

'And what about the other evidence? Mr Sprewls tells me you had a crib stowed away in your desk.'

'It was Schofield's answers from last term. I picked it off the floor when he dropped it.'

Again, a glance towards the Geography master; again a scornful shake of the head. Where their two stories conflicted Mr Purlock had no choice: he had to believe the teacher.

'Right, Munnerly. I'm going to let you off lightly this time. Detention on Thursday next week and you're grounded, not to leave the school premises or visit the tuck shop at all this term. That's all. You can go.'

Grounded. Tuck shop. Purlock's attempts to make this place sound like a public school would have been funny if they hadn't been so sad. As the door closed behind him Peter felt his will harden. He was seventeen. He didn't have to stay in this racket a day longer. Margery wouldn't care, wouldn't even notice. She'd hushed up his links with Penny Green. Nancy, of course, was different. God knows what would happen if she found out. An enforced wedding at the least, a lifetime of penurious drudgery. The prospect debilitated his mind, its ramifications huge and unknown. No, not that. But not this, either.

He'd get a job. If the Munnerlys wanted him to be so respectable they could fix him one – a decent one, one he could bear. Meanwhile, he was quitting. They could stuff their A levels.

In a moment he smiled: the sweet scent of irony expanded his lungs. He'd been punished for an act of cheating he hadn't committed. And yet Sprewls hadn't noticed the tobacco shreds, the half-smoked reefer. All he'd confiscated, with Schofield's script, had been the copy of *Penthouse* with its array of naked women. Wrapped inside the sheaf of loose school notes, he could peruse it at his leisure. Private study. Peter could see him absorbed in its pages, glued to it, until there fell out of its folds another unforeseen treasure.

The image was side-splitting. Peter threw back his head and filled the school yard with laughter: Sprewls flushing scarlet at sight of the condom packet's gleaming square. Sprewls outraged, shocked beyond speech. Yet too mortified to report to Purlock or anyone else that evidence of Munnerly's further depravity.

Chapter 19
1973

Havana House,
Rock Ferry.
3 March 1973

Dear Peter,

I write to you on a matter of some seriousness.

As you will be aware, I have, in accordance with what I take to be your mother's wishes, been in touch with former colleagues in the business world for the purposeof enquiring whether suitable employment can be found for you. I have done this with coniderable misgivings after hearing of your early departure from school withno attempt to take the leaving examination and I hope that nothing I am doing now will be taken as a mark of approval of your behaviour in that respect or, indeed,many others. The business world has no place for thefrivolous or flighty. It requires assiduity, hard work and a sense of commitment over many a long and arduous travail. To secure for you admittance to one of our city's oldest and most well-established companies is to put at hazard the trust which our family has always inspired in Liverpool's trading community. I hope you will never forget this. However I propose to take that risk and have secured for you a post with the family company, Atlantic Finance and Shipping, a leading firm in both fields. Though the family's direct link with the company is limited to the part-time directorship held by your uncle Ted, the family's reputation is nonetheless closely bound up with the firm's fortunes. Your position will be one which many a young man would be deeply grateful to obtain. I can only hope that you will take it up with gratitude and a deep sense of responsibility. It will, I understand, from an early stage involve dealingwith sizeable trans-actions on behalf of the Company. Such a post is not to be treated lightly. I shall, so far as my health permits, follow your progress with close interest and can only trust that you will not betray the trust I am placing in you. As a token of my intentions and good wishes I am also enclosing the certificate for a substantial block of shares in the Company which I have transferred into your name in the hope that this will cement a sense of loyalty in you. I desire no thanks, only a commitment to further the good name of our family, for which I have worked all my life.

You are to report to the Company's offices on the waterfront at 9a.m. next Monday and to request to see the Chairman, Mr Charles Scrimgeour.
He will acquaint you with yourcolleagues and duties.
I can only add my best wishes for your future career.
Your caring and concerned grandfather,
Arthur Munnerly
*

'Yeh. Ten thousand. Yeh, that's what we want. Excuse me, don't I have to sign something? Really? Okay. Okay, I'll expect that. Ciao.'

The telephone, one of three gracing an otherwise empty desk, clanked on its cradle. Peter slumped back in his chair, breathing deep. He turned to his room-mate. It had come as a surprise to find that he shared an office with an old pal from school, Bob Tommelty.

'That's it, then. Ten thousand dollars sold.'

'That's small stuff. You'll get more than that. Much more.' Tommelty refused to be impressed.

'What gets me is, it's all by word of mouth.'

'Has to be. Paper'd take too long. There's an invoice on clearing day.'

Through the third floor window Peter scanned the waterfront. The bronze birds that gave the Liver Building its name and the neighbouring Cunard Buildings stood immutable in their apparent solidity, the latter's concrete stilts and flood-prone basement concealed from view.'The thing is, I never see all this money I buy and sell. I might not even have it. In a way I don't. It's all abstract.'

Tommelty's rotund form bounced with giggles. 'That's nothing. Wait till they get you on to derivatives.'

'Derivatives? What's that?'

'Things like options to buy in the future, sold at a price fixed now. Then there's futures – you fix the price now but by the time you have to pay it the market price'll have changed.'

'So it's guesswork?'

'Part of the job. Paddy down the corridor buys dollars in London at one price, then sells them on the phone to New York for a cent or two more.'

'Is it worth it?'

'If you get a better price.'

'A cent or two better?'

'A tiny fraction of a cent, if you buy and sell enough.'

The information took time to digest. 'You really can buy and sell money just like that?'

'Not just money. There's blokes sell iron, lead, coffee, sugar, wheat. Anything.'

'Where do they store the stuff?'

'They don't. It's notional. The right to it.'

Peter's stare pierced the dirty pane. The Liver birds with their raised wings shone golden in the spring sunlight. He bit his pencil. 'Hold on, can I just be clear? You buy some huge amount of dollars now at one price and by the time you sell them the market price has risen. So you make a packet?'

Tommelty nodded. 'Or, if it's fallen, a loss.'

A pause. 'Yeh, I see. So you have to guess right.'

'You're catching on.'

*

'He said it word for word.' Peter lolled back, balancing on the back legs of his chair. 'Word for word, exactly.'

Bob eyed him, waiting for more. 'So?'

'*With the help of appropriate hedging the risk factor was minimised and a turbulent market turned to our advantage.* It's what he said. Scrimgeour read it out at the conference.'

'So? What's so surprising about that? You wrote the speech for him.'

'No, it doesn't surprise me, you twit. And I don't give a damn who wrote it. The point is, he didn't know if it was true. He was just parroting.'

'Wasn't it, then?'

'Wasn't it what?'

'Wasn't what you wrote true?'

Peter gazed at him, wide-eyed. 'How the hell should I know? I don't do the hedging.'

'Why did you write it, then?'

'Because' – Peter broke off under the impact of another convulsion of mirth – 'he told me to. Then at the meeting someone asked him…whether   he favoured…a high gearing for the Company…or a low one.'

'And what did he say?'

'He said – he said - he left that side - to the engineers.'

They looked at each one moment, then broke into fits of laughter. Bob Tommelty wobbled with mirth, a jelly in a suit.

'He…didn't…know what the question meant. He didn't… know if what he said…was true. It could have been…a complete fraud.'

A full minute passed before sobriety began to steal back. Peter was first to regain equilibrium. A sly smile creased his face.

'You know what, I'm looking for another job.'

'Honestly? Where?'

Peter reached in his pocket. The paper was neatly folded, typed on the electric typewriter he'd bought for his room at home. 'See this. I thought it worth photocopying.'

Bob Tommelty pored over the neat words. With the curious habit of half-literacy his lips moved as he read to himself.

The Prince regrets that since accommodation is provided free of charge at the grace and favour residence in Great Windsor Park, and in view of the generous living-in allowance,no bonus will normally be envisaged further than the basic£40,000 salary. The appointee's duties in the FinanceDepartment will normally occupy at least two and at peaktimes as much as three days a week and, where stock market turbulence requires, the usual three months' leave may bereduced at the Prince's discretion to two. Applicationsshould be submitted by the 1ˢᵗ June…

Tommelty searched Peter's face but there was no sign of a spoof.

'You applying?' he said at length.

'Already have.'

'God! You never said.'

'They interviewed me at the weekend.'

'Crikey. What happened?'

Peter hadn't considered how the story would evolve. While giving the question thought he pursed his lips and narrowed his eyes.

'Promise you'll keep it secret. Just between us, nobody else.'

''Course.'

'Right, then. I got the job.'

'You got it?'

'Still unofficial. They're going to confirm it in writing.'

'When?'

'Later. The job doesn't start till – quite a while. A few months, they said.'

'Grief!'

'There'll be no grief on pay like that.'

*

Lunchtime seemed a good time to sit alone and savour the practical joke. And to think seriously about the urgent need to get out of office work, a real change of jobs. His reflections might have born fruit had they not been blotted out by the arrival of four secretaries and a receptionist who, unprecedentedly, sat down at Peter's table, laughing flirtatiously. They asked continual questions about his own life, as if all suddenly struck by his charm and eligibility.

*

High finance alternated with office-boy duties: Between his dealings on the money market Peter laboured over the chores of checking the monthly stationery order and settling payments for washroom laundry. Contact with the firm's directors was minimal – a glimpse across the cafeteria to their more expensive, screened-off area, a nod of greeting when they passed in the corridor. Summer had sidled away unnoticed and Birkenhead Park was awash with red and brown leaves before Peter was summoned one afternoon to Charles Scrimgeour's office.

Entering the Chairman's carpeted office for their first meeting since he joined the Company, Peter wondered whether he ought to be feeling nervous and overawed. A glance dispelled the idea. The Chairman stayed for several moments poring over a typed sheet which, curiously, lay upside down to his field of vision. The title, easily legible to Peter above a column of small monetary sums, read: *Cost of repairs to plumbing at Company Head Office, 12 September 1973.* After a sufficient pause Scrimgeour looked up, his movement accidentally revealing a cutting of *The Daily Telegraph*

83

crossword previously hidden by his forearm. With haste he shoved it beneath the repairs account.

'Ah, Munnerly.'

Peter waited while his employer tightened his tie and coughed. 'Do sit down. It shouldn't take long.'

'Now,' Charles Scrimgeour searched his desktop in a fruitless, faintly manic manner. 'I don't seem to have the exact figures to hand but they're not really important. The important thing is to congratulate you on your recent, very considerable success in the money markets. We've never had success on this scale before. I can see I made a good choice when I took you on at your grandfather's request.'

'Thank you very much.'

'Well no, thank *you*.'

There was another pause. Peter surveyed his boss with dispassion. Something about him – the fustiness of his tweed suit, a suggestion of weakness at the chin, the continual, rabbit-like nibbling movements of his nose - suggested that, contrary to expectation, the Chairman was himself nervous at meeting an employee forty-five years his junior. The ends of his sideburns danced in time with his heavy breathing.

'Er yes, a happy choice for our team.'

Then it was as if the strain became too much. Scrimgeour, with an unconvincing show of sudden remembering, reached to his tray and took out a wad of neatly-typed papers held together by staples. 'It was just - do you think you could kindly take this down to the printer's. Sally will tell you the exact address, it's off Bold Street, I believe. Keep close guard on the papers, won't you. They're my Report to the shareholders and won't become public until they're sent out in a fortnight. I hope you won't mind. It's actually quite an important errand – job, that is.'

Smothering a smile, Peter reached out for the Report. 'Is that all – just to take it to the printer's?'

'To the Head Printer, that is. Personally. Mr – er, Mr – I forget his name. Sally will tell you. It's vital it reaches him without intermediary, you see.'

On belated impulse, Scrimgeour slammed open one of his desk drawers and, tugging out a large manilla envelope, proceeded to ram the Report into it. 'Can't be too careful, can we?'

Peter took the package. The interview seemed to be at an end and he stood up to go. But Charles Scrimgeour stayed his movement with a gesture.

'Oh, while you're here, just one other thing I thought of mentioning. Only as background, of course. Can you spare a moment?'

'Yes. Of course.' Peter sat again. The boss's change of manner was puzzling, yet something about it betrayed that this was the real point of the interview. Why was Scrimgeour so desperate to conceal the fact? Dim memory of some Victorian novel in which a boy and his father change places filtered into his consciousness. *Vice Versa* - that was it. He waited, his calm oddly growing in line with the fuddy-duddy Chairman's agitation.

'It's a long time since I was down at the coal face, so to speak, ha! Up here we deal with the broader outlines of policy. No, I just wondered if you could remind me of, well, how exactly you manage to swell our profits so satisfactorily. Not the technical details, of course. Just the general gist.'

A bead of sweat trickled down the genteel face to his neat, trimmed moustache. A smile creased the furrows of forehead and cheek with an air of enforced avuncularity. But under it, too strong to be concealed, Peter perceived distress. The old man hated asking his questions, admitting ignorance. Every minute humiliated him.

Peter began slowly, cautiously. 'It's just normal market ops. Sometimes we sell foreign specie forward, other times spot.' He paused. Charles Scrimgeour was nodding, too vigorously to have understood. Peter went on a little faster. 'There's times when a contango's in order, of course.'

'Yes, yes, of course.' The last words were half-choked into a cough. Scrimgeous took out a handkerchief and blew his noise.

'Depends how market conditions are responding, whether traders are unwinding or looking for better collateral...'

'Quite. I mean, just the broad gist -'

'...or dealing at arm's length. Or if leverage is increasing...'

'Quite, quite. I see. Now if you'll excuse me -'

But triumph surged inside Peter, a general whose enemy was on the run. Words he'd heard, words he'd vaguely hoped one day to learn the meaning of, flooded out in a tidal wave of confidence. So it was true. You could get away with anything at all if you blarnied enough. 'Then there's times when the reverse discount ratio -'

There was a click behind Peter's chair. The door opened and with belated recall Peter realised that his boss had pressed the summoning button on his desk. He swivelled to see Maurice Libsey, the senior Finance Director, approaching across the pile carpet.

'Maurice, I've just been congratulating Peter here on his marvellous success in the money markets. But unhappily I have to rush away - an appointment with my stockbroker down town. I wonder, would you be so good as to take over and let him explain the exact methods he's using so successfully. Then, if you would, perhaps you would drop me a memo passing the secrets of his magnificent success on to me? I'd be so grateful. Just for the record.'

Before he finished Scrimgeour had moved to a coat-stand near the door. With a smile of anguished joy he pulled it open and, giving a further glance at his watch, vanished down the corridor. Peter waited for Maurice Libsey to follow.

But Libsey had seen the envelope in Peter's hand.

'The boss been giving you some important papers?'

'Dunno. That's to say, yes - his Chairman's Report. I've to take it to the printer.'

'He's hauled you out of the office just for that?'

'Said it was important. Secret till it's published next week.'

Libsey eyed the envelope. 'Is it sealed?'

'Actually, no, he's forgotten. I'll get some sticky tape and see to it. More secure than just licking the flap.'

'And now he's off to see his stockbroker.'

'Yes. What are you suggesting?'

But Maurice Libsey didn't answer. His eyes stayed fixed on the envelope. For a moment it seemed as if he might stretch out and grab it. In a moment he made as if to end the conversation. 'Perhaps I should see my stockbroker, too.' Absently he added, 'It won't affect you, I suppose - how the firm fares.'

But Arthur's recent gift came to mind. 'It might. I've got shares as well.'

Libsey raised an eyebrow. His thick lips bulbed into an anemone smile. 'Better be careful. Risky times, these.' He plodded away down the corridor.

*

'Aren't you going, then?' Bob Tommelty lounged back in his swivel chair, grinning. 'An hour or two out of the office.'

But Peter still hesitated, the bulk of the envelope heavy in his grasp. 'It seemed as if they were both going to sell their shares. Both Scrimgeour and Libsey.'

'Which shares?'

'In the Company. As if things weren't going well.'

'What's gone wrong, then?'

'I don't know.' The envelope sagged in his hands. The unsealed flap buckled under its unbalanced weight. 'I've got some as well.'

'Many?'

'Dunno.' A five-digit number flickered in memory. 'A lot, I think.'

'So you gonna sell?'

'Dunno.'

'I didn't know you were a filthy capitalist. Have you got others, too?'

Peter sighed. Normally, Tommelty's nosiness, as bouncy and irrepressible as his girth, would have annoyed him. But the sense of an important decision bypassed annoyance. He leaned forward. 'Can you keep your mouth shut?'

'Yeh. Gonna open the envelope?'

'It's open already.'

'Gonna take the Chairman's Report out?'

'Remember, you said you'd keep your mouth shut.'

''Course. What d'you think I am – a bleedin' bletherer?'

Peter reached his hand under the flap. The sheaf of papers was heavy. It formed a neat, uniform block, newly printed, aromatic from the photocopier. He sat to read. Bob Tommelty levered himself to his feet and stood behind him but the phalanx of small print demanded concentration and he sat down again, waiting.

> *Much may depend on the outcome of the forthcoming*
> *OPEC meeting, which will effectively settle the price of*
> *crude oil for the coming year. Any substantial rise would*
> *be deeply damaging to the Company's shipping operations*
> *while a sudden shift in payments from the industrialised*
> *countries to those of the Gulf would hit any British*
> *financial institution engaged in foreign...*

Peter rose to his feet, thrust the Report back in its envelope and sealed it. He picked up the telephone directory and searched. Ah yes, here it was, the firm Arthur had once mentioned as his stockbrokers. They would do.

He would have dialled at once but in the event he waited for a little silence, a silence delayed by splutterings from across the office as Bob Tommelty chortled to a pal, describing how Peter had sneaked a preview of the Chairman's Report.

*

He'd hoped the storm of publicity would only affect the directors. But two afternoons later, leaving work at the main door of Atlantic House, he saw his mistake. Men in leather jackets and car coats interspersed with a few hard-looking young women, all with pencils and notepads at the ready, swarmed round him like bluebottles.

'Excuse me, you work for Atlantic Shipping and Finance?'

'Only at a low level. I'm not a director.'

'Are you a shareholder?'

'Well, I was.'

'You sold your shares?'

'Yes but... What is this?'

'How do you answer the charge of insider dealing people are raising?'

'Insider dealing..?'

'Using inside knowledge to sell early before the share price fell.'

'I haven't any inside -' He halted. Memory plucked his sleeve. 'Has the price fallen? I didn't know...'

The man's grin flaunted disbelief. *We've heard that one before.* 'There's moves to make dealing like that illegal.'

'But has anyone done it?'

The grin of complicity widened, flaunting its slyness. Peter's eye fell on a newspaper that stuck like a folded truncheon from the man's coat pocket. 'I haven't seen today's news.'

Whether at last believing him innocent or with an impulse to expose his guilt, the reporter tugged the paper from his pocket and like a bridge player setting out a grand slam unfolded it for viewing.

Dramatic oil price rise. Billions knocked off shares, the headline read. But the reporter's finger traced a line under a lower report, laughing as he prodded its message home to Peter, a sharper breaking the bank in some card game. *Big preemptive share sales. Was best practice ignored?*

'No, I don't know anything about that side of it.'

Peter turned away, hacking a way through the thickets of pressmen. But a quavering in his voice had confirmed their suspicions, the evidence gleeful on a score of cynical faces. Those who salivated for guilt always found it. To them he was proved guilty. As guilty as if he'd known what the Arab oil cartel might do or what best practice was.

As he hurried away, the month's lessons drummed in memory. The inured, regular fiddler knew the ropes; he always escaped unscathed. Not so the tyro. The arch-crime was innocence.

Chapter 20
1974

'Mum.'

'Oh, hello. I didn't hear you.'

'I did knock. Are you busy?'

'I'm always busy. You know that.'

'With your poetry?'

'I had a poem accepted for *Spangles.* It's a highly regarded publication.'

'Well done.'

'And I won the Mayor's Literary Competition. The award was presented by Lord Moreton. There were sixty-two people present at the ceremony including the Sheriff and Mayor. We had champagne and strawberries.'

'Well done.'

'Picked on the Wirral. The strawberries.'

Peter hugged the sheet of paper he was holding. 'I just wondered if you'd like to hear a poem I've written.'

'I'm always eager to hear your outpourings. What sort is it? The Movement, modernist, postmodern, structuralist, post-structuralist, epiphenomenal...what sort?'

'I don't know. It's just a poem.'

'How does it deal with the problems of rhyme, metre, rhythm, internal assonance, masculine and feminine endings, the status of women, writing in the post-Marxist environment? And so on.'

'I don't know. Can I read it out?'

'Not just at the moment, dear. I've got a class to go to at the college. It's important that I do all I can to encourage young writers.'

*

The rejection came back to him two decades later, recalled by another quite different experience.

They were lying on a beach in Spain one evening. A scatter of fishing smacks at anchor dotted the bay and dwindling sunlight freckled the low Catalan hills to westward, as if borne in on the offshore breeze that had sprung up at day's end. Yet the midday scent of pinetrees lingered. He couldn't remember the girl's name. Only the pink billow of her bikini top and the small burn mark on her left thigh. Was it Angela?

The sleep of paella and red wine and lovemaking had almost overtaken him when she released his hand and rolled over on to her side, tilting a trickle of sand on to his chest and arm. She kissed his flank, then, straining upward, his mouth.

'Tell me you love me,' she said and with words that lingered added, 'even if it's not true.'

'How can you say that? *Of course I love you..*'

It came to him that his false assurance then was as genuine as any Margery ever gave.

Chapter 21
1974

'Your Grandad wants to see you.' In a characteristic way of hers, Margery turned away as she made the announcement. Usually she would have had a laugh or smile on her lips; today she seemed serious.

'What about?'

'He'll tell you that.'

Peter searched his mind for things he might have done wrong. Especially at work. Ever since Arthur had got him the job he'd had two bosses to keep sweet: Scrimgeour and his Grandad. But, perplexingly, there seemed no reason for trouble to have arisen.

'Can't you give me a clue?'

Margery hesitated. Through the unspoken telegraph linking mother and son he felt it wasn't to do with work. What then? *Sex?* Oh God. How could that come into it this time? He couldn't imagine. But that would account for the look of indecision on her face: the wanting to reprimand him but not feeling well placed to do it; the hint of a laugh scowled to silence by the Munnerlys' sense of propriety. No one at Havana House ever mentioned sex.

'He'll tell you. You'd better have a good story ready. Go on. He's waiting.'

A daunting sense of heaviness clodhopped with him along the landing. There came to mind the walk to Purlock's study at school, the interview with Scrimgeour at Atlantic Finance, the summons to appear before the major at Training Camp. They did it to elevate themselves; they summoned you to make themselves feel important. That was what they wanted most of all, more than money, more than power or sex, these people who never told you anything, never talked about the things that mattered or that motivated them most. If they'd been his sole source of information he'd never have found out how the Munnerlys made their money on the shipfuls of fetid human flesh plying between the Gold Coast and Barbados; he'd never have found out how babies were born. No, it had been up to Red Thomas and the other lads – the very people the Munnerlys despised - 'gutter urchins' he'd heard Nancy call them - to tell him anything like that, anything that mattered in life. Hypocrisy like the sugar coating on crystallised fruit encased the family he was supposed to be so proud of.

Never trust anyone. What else could you conclude?

He knocked and waited. In the house that was your own home you had to knock, then wait. Always you waited. And why? Not because they were busy: Arthur and Nancy, especially Nancy, were never busy. Because it made you feel small. You waited on them because that was what menials did.

In a minute the door opened and Arthur stood there.

'You wanted to see me.'

'Yes.' He gestured Peter in. To invite him by speaking would have been an indignity.

Another gesture of the head directed him to a chair. Peter stood waiting, pretending not to see, looking round the room.

'You'd better sit down.'

It came to him that his grandfather wasn't acting freely. Nancy wasn't there (Why not? If this was about trouble at work she would be. She liked nothing better than to play the police inspector, to interrogate, to play at exerting power). But Arthur was obeying her orders. A feeling of pity grazed Peter's cheek. This old, grey man had made the money that kept Nancy silken-dressed in her drawing room. He'd exempted her from employment and housework alike, lifelong. Yet he'd spent a life as her slave. Poor fool.

Arthur took an armchair, half-facing him but at an angle. How they feared eye-contact. As the guilty always did. He was fingering a paper.

'I've received this letter.'

Peter reached out and took it. It was written on green, lined paper, in a rounded, female-looking hand.

Dear Mr Munnerly,

    I am writing as my daughter Penny's mother to tell you something you may not know and unless I tell you may not find out. Penny has been a close friend of your grandson Peter for a long time now, they were at school together and I am sorry to say that she is now pregnant. There is no doubt who the father is. It is your grandson Peter and I think we ought to make arrangements for them to get married as soon as possible.

    Please would you get in touch with me at the above address to arrange this?

                      Yours faithfully,

                           Emily Green

'Well. What have you got to say?'

There was no point in denial. 'Do we have to get married? Doesn't seem a good idea to me.'

'Your Gran insists on it.'

So. His guess was right. 'That settles it, does it?'

He sensed aggression now. 'Yes, it does.' How afraid the man must be, of his own wife.

'What sort of wedding does she want?'

'A proper one, of course.'

He was trembling. Beads of sweat stood out above his moustache. He was terrified, utterly terrified. Any question, however harmless or factual, sent the old man close to rage.

'You mean white?'

'If it can be made to seem appropriate.'

Peter had heard it all: Nancy as analytic as a bridge fiend, discussing other girls' weddings, noting every detail, checking every convention: where the bridegroom stayed the night before the wedding, who were chosen as bridesmaids, if there was to be any promise to obey; whether the bride wore white. For Nancy every symbol had a meaning. Truth came a poor second.

He expelled breath and gave in. He wondered to whom his yielding brought more relief, himself or his grandfather. 'Okay, I'll go and see her. Mrs Green. Only' – he couldn't let it pass – 'why couldn't Penny tell me herself?'

'I put that question to the girl who delivered the letter. She said Mrs Green didn't want you and Penny to be alone together.'

*

'Hello. I'm Peter Munnerly. Can I come in?'

With reluctant hostility the woman - it must be Mrs Green – let him in. The end-terrace at Canal Street contrasted starkly with Havana House. Its front door opened direct on to the street, its frontage barely four yards wide. In the parlour where he was ushered lace curtains shut out the prying eyes of passers-by. Even on a sunny day they cast shadow over the worn, heavy sofa and armchairs, the empty, black-polished grate and, at its side, the potted cheese plant standing sentinel, as an aspidistra might once have done. An upright piano, also polished but devoid of music under an overload of ornaments and photographs, gave the impression of never being played. Too cramped for any social activity, too dark for sewing or reading, the room stood museum-like, eloquent of the mismatch between standards aggressively preserved and a sense of lost hope or purpose.

'Well, it's you that did it. What are you going to do?'

For once he stood wordless. At Havana House it had never seemed that there was any choice what he should do. His Grandma, Nancy, both directly and indirectly through Arthur, had decreed marriage. But here he felt there might be alternatives, room for negotiation.

'You ought to make it right by her. By Penny.'

It was not in Peter's nature to take orders. He took a breath, preparing to argue. But something about the little woman's sad pride held him in check. A woman struggling to keep her house decent against all odds, gloomy and cramped as it was in its wasteland across the street from the canal's rubbish-tipped water. Fighting a losing war. Was that why Penny had never asked him round or introduced him, ashamed of her home and sole surviving parent? Or was there some deeper, bitterer hostility between them?

'I ought to talk to her about it.'

'She's out.' The words were half-swallowed. 'You ought to do the right thing. It's yours. The baby.'

'I know.'

'You're wayward.'

Pity at the scene swamped the reproach in Mrs Green's voice. Against a fiercer accuser he would have fought back, defended himself. But this lonely, sad figure with her low, grief-stricken voice, her half-crouching posture and the waves of grey yet still comely hair – she'd been pretty once - brought him shame for adding to her troubles. They cast Penny in a new light, too. The girl's perky manner and jokiness, seen from this house, took on feverishness, a desperate attempt to escape the awfulness of life in Canal Street, the covering-up of a home which, once exposed, might destroy her one means of escape.

'What does Penny want? Does she want us to get married?' The weirdness of it surged up, overwhelming: he hadn't once seen Penny since the pregnancy was known.

'Yes. She does. Soon.'

It was out in the open. He faced the decision like the prospect of a new and unknown job, his body empty, uncertain. 'A quiet one?'

She nodded. 'A quiet wedding.'

There seemed little else to say. As he edged past the hallstand to the cheap coloured-glass mosaic of the front door his eyes noted, without taking in, the black leather of the studded jacket suspended there. Only the polished hemisphere hinged on the door's streetward side, the half-globe with which he'd rapped for entrance, spotlighted the sudden, freezing reversal in his feelings about Penny. Cold brass. Knockers.

At another, less stunned moment he would have looked up more quickly to the flurry of a lace curtain in the bedroom window overhead, the instant disappearance of one – no, two – faces. But a glimpse was enough. One of the faces was male and unknown; in the other he recognised his future wife.

*

'There will be a proper wedding. But the bride cannot wear white.'

Nancy looked away at the last words, mortified by the reason for her latest prohibition.

'But Penny doesn't want that. Nor does her mother. They want a quiet wedding.'

'I understand that we – that is to say, your Grandfather and I – are paying for this wedding. In the absence of any father on the bride's side.'

'Look Gran, we can't force a wedding on them that they don't want.'

At the familiar mode of address Nancy blenched. 'I would like my friends and social acquaintances to be present.'

Peter gazed. Early in life, before her marriage to Arthur, Nancy had moved for one brief season among the Aichison-Booths, the family of the Hon. Wilfred le Marchand, that of Lady Victoria Drage and the sons of Colonel Hunt-Browne. Unseen and unheard-from for sixty years, they haunted her still. From their ghosts arose the ambiance of gentility in which she lived and had her being. Almost all would be dead now. But in her assumption of social superiority and her blindness to change they lived on. *For a thousand years in Thy sight are but as yesterday, seeing that is gone like a watch in the night.*

Extraordinarily, the unaccustomed recollection from his early years sparked an idea in Peter's mind.

'I know. Why not a quiet legal ceremony and then a service in church when it's not news any more, when the spotlight's off us and people take the marriage for granted? And its consequences?'

Nancy pondered. The strings of her neck alone carried the rigidity of someone shocked by some improper suggestion. 'To which my friends could be invited?'

For a second he wanted to shout, *It's our wedding, you meddling old snob, not yours. Choosing the guests is our business.* But to what purpose? The world of reality and Nancy's had no point of tangency. The dead had no visiting cards.

But this time, to his amazement, Nancy relented. Weariness had won the day where reason failed. She raised a languid handkerchief like smelling salts to her face.

'Very well,' she said. 'Yes. If that's what you prefer.'

*

The queue stretched along the registry office's corridor and round the front and side of the building. The couple had to retreat fifty yards down a sidestreet to find the end.

Peter's first thought was to expect youth; but the motley trail was hard to interpret. Slicked-back male hair, oiled against the run of fashion, betrayed streaks of darkened grey; the mushy slouch of beer bellies gave deceptive suggestions of age. The brides wore skirts that flared like parasols to reveal podgy thighs; stiletto heels prattled on the pavement, or off it when the effects of alcohol made balance unmaintainable. Most striking of all was the timbre of the hubbub they emitted, a tangle of high shrieks from the women and, beneath them, a low choppiness with the nasality of Scouser twang mixed with ever-spreading Estuary-speak.

As they took their place a woman some yards ahead lost balance and fell in the gutter, tearing her white stocking at the knee. Her bridegroom, beercan in hand, staggered to help her up. An uproar of laughter turned to sympathy, then again to mirth. The couple, tottering upright again, embraced, his hand groping her bottom as his lips emitted slobber down the plunging arc of her cleavage. There were more cheers.

Peter turned towards Penny. With relief he saw she was laughing. After at first wanting to marry here he'd later grown lukewarm towards the idea but she had insisted. Yet only he felt guilt at sight of the grotesquerie ahead. He'd seen the imbalance of remorse before a dozen times: those most guilty of error or deceit untouched by shame, the crook proud of his crimes. Who it was that felt himself open to blame lay beyond rationality.

The queue moved uncertainly forward. He wished they'd decided otherwise. This was *Carry On Getting Married*. Even a church wedding would have been better. But Penny's latterly swollen condition, once revealed, would in any case have made Nancy rule that out. He thought, too, of the jibes there would have been: about Penny, her other men, her continuing history – well-known locally, as he now learnt – of youths taking what they could get with her. He remembered Mrs Green's bar on their meeting while the marriage was arranged; the black leather jacket on the hallstand at Canal Street; the man at the upstairs window.

Even so, when he looked ahead to the planned service at St Giles's, doubt reared as to whether it would really be better.

*

It was strange that someone like himself, with his Merseyside accent and friends who did manual and transient jobs along the quays and round the office-blocks of the waterfront, should feel more at ease in a church. Strange, even with Nancy silenced by shock at the visibility of Penny's condition.

Silenced yet still all-powerful: the combination seemed fitting for a service of divine worship. There'd been strict orders: the organist must play traditional music – Handel's *Water Music* while the guests gathered, the Mendelssohn *Wedding March* as the bride entered, Widor's *Toccata* when the service ended. The bridesmaids – two of Penny's cousins - would carry bouquets of whatever flowers were seasonable – at this spring season, friesia and monbretia. The ushers – a role into which Red Thomas and Bob Tommelty had been pressganged – must wear morning dress, even if Peter had to bear the cost. Necessity was bowed to with dignity. This wedding was of the Munnerly heir. It must be an act of high commitment.

Most important of all, the two families were to be segregated on opposite sides of the church. This stipulation proved the hardest to carry out. Apart from her mother and the bridesmaid-cousins Penny had no family to muster. The cousins' parents lived down south and were unwilling to make the journey. Her grandparents were dead. All contact with aunts and uncles had long ago died. Facing the problem over the telephone on which Penny made contact from her nextdoor neighbour's house, Peter saw the church as it promised to be: on one side, Arthur and Nancy, together with Margery and her sisters, hemming in Hazel and Caroline and Peter's own friends headed by Red Thomas and Bob Tommelty; on the other side, the bride's mother and the two cousins.

'I'll see to it,' he told Penny. 'Don't mention it to anyone. I'll sort it out.'

Which, on the day, he did. The three figures perched on the front lefthand pew were not alone. Behind them, ranked in dark suits and white shirts and with unaccustomedly brushed and slicked-back hair, the school's recent first and second elevens – batsmen, bowlers, fielders in all positions – formed a solid phalanx of supporters, croaking an undertow of miscellaneous notes during the hymn-singing, whispering muffled wisecracks under the cover of prayers, exchanging sly sidewards smiles as the couple made their promises. Nancy, he reflected, must have wondered how the bride came to have so uniformly young and male a circle of friends and family; but the propriety of the occasion kept the thin lips clamped. Peter avoided eye contact, gratified but taking no risks. Even the cricket teams with their records of dodgy conduct kept to the rules. It amazed him how much loyalty was evoked by the assurance of unlimited free beer at the reception in Havana House afterwards.

'Dearly beloved, we are gathered together...'

He hadn't expected to be moved by the intoned words or the hymns, had even felt small flames of rebellion stirring. But the actuality quelled revolt. Throughout the chants and psalms, the lessons and solemnisation, he rejoiced to be free from the depression that had come over him on the rare occasions when Margery had cajoled him into church: annoyance that the service had been turned into a family entertainment. On those occasions small children squawled and ran up and down the aisles. Adults whispered among themselves with no break or pause. Smiles were exchanged, jokes passed, people waved to friends across the nave. How good to be clear of that.

'...which is an honourable estate ordained of God...'

Yet that wasn't how it felt. He glanced down at Penny, standing at his side, her form swelling against the white frothy fabric of her dress. She was smiling broadly, the prettiness of her schooldays returning.

'...nor taken in hand unadvisedly, lightly or wantonly...'

The minister bent over his book with over-earnest concentration, struggling not to notice the bride's giggles and restless jollity.

'I will.'

'Those whom God hath joined no man put asunder.'

And suddenly the vows were all over, the plunge taken. He became aware of the singing. The choir, specially paid by Arthur for their services, struck up the anthem.

Rejoice in the Lord always
and again I say rejoice.
Let your moderation be known unto all men.
The Lord is at hand.

But while the notes soared to the barrel vaulting the sense of uplift died. At last the congregation stirred. There was an upsurge of whispering and shuffling of feet pierced by the cries of infants who sensed a familiar level of disorder returning.

Anger flared in Peter's stomach. At the call for anyone to speak now or else forever hold his peace he'd felt alarm: there were goons here who might feel this a time for practical joking. There'd been embarrassment, too, fear of the sudden meaningful silence or audible guffaw that could punctuate the prayer book's words on avoiding fornication. But those had passed without humiliation. What stayed now was the sense of being robbed. Nancy, though he hated to admit it, was right. Marriage should be a high endeavour. Even an enforced duty could be undertaken in earnestness. And at the end this gathering, the kids and the genteel along with the rough and boorish, the snobs along with the yobs, even the bride herself, had robbed him of that.

Taking Penny's mirth-shaken arm, he clamped a smile on his face, a death mask of resolution. As Widor's *Toccata* shook the slender columns and tracery the couple processed down the aisle, their emotions solar systems apart. He wondered how much better this had been than the grotesquerie they'd witnessed at Wormley Row registry office.

Chapter 22
1974

The morning haze promised equatorial heat. After calling a taxi at sunrise and helping Penny up the hospital steps Peter was directed to a small cell-like room to wait until summoned.

Another young man sat opposite, not speaking, pulling at cigarette after cigarette like a piglet voracious at its mother's teats. When the placebo of nicotine failed he stood and stamped up and down, whey-faced, until the upheaval inside him became too much and he rushed into the small adjacent lavatory to vomit. Peter checked himself for qualms. No, nothing noticeable. What was the fuss all about?

'Mr Munnerly?'

A diminutive nurse showed him into the maternity ward. Under a single sheet Penny lay sweating, attached in some imperceptible way to a machine whose dial displayed the flickerings of a hyperactive needle. For a moment she smiled, then resumed her frown of concentration, preoccupied with the eruption to come.

The knoll of her belly summoned phantasmagoric images: bottom-heavy Chinese dolls which couldn't be overturned; a Russian doll with another, identical doll inside; an igloo buried under snow. But a nurse who stood anxiously watching the machine dispelled fantasy. When a young man in white coat, presumably a doctor, came in, they conferred in agitated mumbles.

'I'm afraid you have to leave,' she said when the doctor vanished. 'There are complications.'

'Can't I stay and watch? Hold her hand?'

'I'm sorry.' She moved towards the corridor. 'The doctor...'

Restored to the waiting cell, he kept the door open. Through the gap he could see the door of Penny's room, closed but magnetic. Minutes passed; the hands of his watch crept round their track. After what might have been forty minutes – but in truth he'd little idea of the crawl of time – he got up, angry and impatient, and tiptoed to the maternity ward door. Silently, with infinite care, he eased it a fraction open.

To watch unobserved brought visceral excitement. A camera scanning Penny's body, a spy in the innermost court of life, he stood drugged, his eye drawn through the millimetre crack of the door. Images blossomed: an old-style football overinflated, the bladder forcing itself through a gap in the leather; the extrusion of a pate, its quiff of hair wet and dark as an oil-slick; an earthquake groaning, the entrails of the earth excreting.

With a frisson of the skin he found himself moved as if by profound music. Tears greased his face, a thin uncontrollable glycerine that welled up without will or spring. Bewilderment blinked his eyes. He wasn't weeping from sorrow or joy or any known emotion, as if the turbulence rose from some limb or organ he didn't possess, had never possessed. The shudder and wrench of heart were an implant, unknown and alien to a man. And yet the tears flowed.

Chapter 23
1975

Like an ancient photograph, the marriage turned brittle.

Peter wondered if it would have stood stronger if they'd had money to get a place of their own. In the two rooms allocated to them at Havana House there was always the sense of surveillance. By Georgina, by Flo, by Nancy.

Still more he wondered if they'd have been happier had the marriage been freely entered into. Nancy's words - *'You are about to become a father. You must be married as soon as possible,'* - echoed in the back of his mind during every argument at the chilly breakfast table, every exchange of fire over dinner. What might have been a mistake for which he had only himself to blame became a source of grievance, something all the more hateful for being imposed.

Just as sour was the slow realisation that he found Penny hard to bear for the very qualities that had at first attracted him. Her air of whimsiness and unreality, the faint dottiness that had made her seem in need of protection from a devious world became tiresome, a never-ending burden. Though she shared his relish for making money, their ideas on how to use the money ran along opposite shores, she wanting to spend every gain as soon as it was made, he to put it at risk in some new venture, for the kick it gave him and to try to make more profit. Dimly at the corners of his mind he dodged the thought that he'd seen in Penny some glimpse of the eccentric zaniness he loved in his mother. But instead of endearing him to his wife the idea estranged him from Margery, bringing fresh unease to their encounters.

Only Joni, when she arrived, pink and enchanting at thirteen pounds, drew the newly-weds together. Peter adored his daughter. Every step forward in her life seemed a triumph offered to him alone. 'She smiled,' he shouted, running through to the kitchen the first time a dandled finger enticed the chubby face into a tiny ecstasy of giggles. 'She smiled!' Each new advance in the baby's behaviour was the first time any baby anywhere had acted so. The joy at having her tummy tickled, the way she waved her hands upward when he wheeled her pram under the huge oaks of the park, her habit of falling asleep with her arms still held up rigidly like wires – all were as momentous as the discovery of fire or the wheel.

At times like that Penny would try to use the little girl as a catalyst to reconcile herself with Peter. But instead of bringing them together the attempts frayed and split still further the bond that joined them. Penny's entry into the nursery broke the spell of his daughter's presence. He resented her footsteps, her speech, her irruption into his magical love for Joni. Before long, tactic produced counter-tactic: he began to neglect or speak scathingly of his daughter in order to hurt Penny. When autumn gave way to winter he went back to his old way of spending the evenings in bachelor haunts – *The Fox and Goose, The White Hart* – with 'Red' Thomas and other old friends from schooldays. Penny was left under the high-ceilings of the big, neglected house to care for the baby alone.

*

Among the horse brasses and inverted wine-bottles the old camaraderie rekindled.

'You can't help but strike it rich,' Peter insisted, not for the first time. 'The bookie always wins.'

But Red was unimpressed. 'What happens if the regular bookies spot you and report you to the rozzers?'

'They won't. We'll operate outside the racecourse and then move on. Anyway there's never any rozzers around. If there are, you just grin and give 'em a wave. Friendly like. That way they think you're all square.'

Red had a way of staring into blankness when he didn't believe you. His hand strayed to push back the red hair that gave him his nickname. In a second or two, following another habit, he changed the subject - whether as a tactic or because his mind had blacked out, Peter never knew.

'Have you tried this Match Box thing down town?'

'What thing?'

'Computer dating. You fill in a form and they allocate you a girl. 'It's meant to be scientific.'

Peter shook his head. Yet the suggestion exerted a tug. A couple of years back he'd have leaped at it. But duty towards Penny, his wife for all her maddening faults, clouded enthusiasm.

'The bird who run's it's quite something.'

'I can't. I'm married.'

The injustice of having to waste an opportunity because of a dead marriage stung like a burn.

'You could do it just for a laugh. Not serious, like.'

'What's she like, then, this bird?'

'That organises it? Aw, you should just see.' Red pursed lascivious lips. His hands made convex gestures in front of his chest. 'A real gold blonde. Anita Blackett, she's called.'

'You can't date her, though?'

104

'No, she only organises it.'

'She gives you a girl's name and number?'

'Yeh. Asks you a lot of questions, then allocates you someone.'

'Then what?'

Red shrugged. 'Up to you whether you ring her up and fix a date. Your choice.'

'I couldn't ask her out. I'm married.'

'If that's how you feel.'

'I mean, I couldn't phone or anything. I'd only do it for a lark.'

'Okay. Sounds like a non-starter for you.'

Peter pondered. Frustration and anger surged. Why should it be a non-starter? When one business failed you tried another. You couldn't stay beached for ever.

He drained his glass. 'Okay, you're on. When do we go?'

*

The girl he rang was a nurse. At The Arches' bar counter over glasses of wine she was talkative, telling him about her sister and her friend, Nan. They were close she said, like their names: Nicola and Nan. She was eager to know about Peter. When he mentioned Havana House her eyes widened.

'One of those big ones on the waterfront?'

'It's gone to seed a bit. Used to be really grand but not now.'

'Even so.'

While she talked and even, he realised, while he himself was talking, he scarcely listened. Words bounced to and fro between them as devoid of interest as a game of ping pong in a nearby room while his eyes, normally as alert for scents as a hunting dog's, barely took in the crossed legs on the next stool, the shoulder peeping from the coy asymmetry of her dress. However he tried, the interview with Anita Blackett continually elbowed back into his thoughts.

'You been out with anyone else from Match Box?'

She shook her head with vigour. 'No, just you. Really.'

'You going to?'

'No. Not if we – you know. I don't want to.'

Indifferently, like well-fed mice his eyes ran over her and, as if brought on by the feeling of being inspected, a faint flush permeated her cheeks. The speading pink caught his attention. He tried a longer stare and to his satisfaction the flush deepened.

'What nights are you free?'

105

He took a notepad from his pocket and wrote down her answer. He looked at his watch. 'I've got to go. Look, I'll ring you in a day or two and we'll fix something. Okay?'

She nodded with even more vigour. 'You haven't told me what you do. Your job.'

'Oh, haven't I? I'm an executive. In a think-tank.'

'What do you do there?'

'I'm not allowed to tell. It's hush-hush.'

'Can I ring you?'

'We're not allowed private calls.'

'I mean at home.'

'Okay. Only' – he tore a sheet from the notepad and scribbled – 'you'll need my new number. The old one's out of date.'

His smile widened to a grin at the eager way she took the chit. He wondered who would answer when she rang, whether she would disturb some blameless family man or an old bachelor longing for romance. He hoped she wouldn't go back to the blonde manager of Match Box and confirm his real number. He only longed for the blonde herself to use that.

In the doorway he turned back with a smile that transmuted into a laugh. The nurse laughed and waved back. She was all right, quite nice really, but not his type: not enough frontage. A inkling of insight visited him. It wasn't just that, the flat chest and the egghead job, that had put him off. Being married had stayed his hand, too. That mustn't happen again. Ever.

It was strange how a whole hour with one bird could be dominated by other women who weren't even present: Margery, who he could imagine going all uncertain and fluttery if he ever told her of his evening; Penny in the background, censorious and deliciously hurt if she ever found out; but most of all, all the more ineradicable in his mind for having been lost through his moment of excess conscience at the interview, the blonde hair and pulse-arousing convexity of Anita Blackett.

*

The impulse was unexpected, unprecedented since the stories he'd written as a boy. It reawoke the day after he met the nurse, after the daydreams of Anita Blackett. In the first-floor room Nancy left vacant for him to occupy when he wanted solitude he found dusty paper and a still usable biro. He sat down and wrote.

A fanfare of trumpets shook the air. Two guards wearing enormous curved scimitars pulled open the mahogany gates

106

of the palace and drawing himself up to his full six- foot four Burlington walked with dignified steps into the Maharajah's court.

'What do you desire, Sir Burlington?'

'I desire a bride chosen from the chambermaids attending your royal wife, oh king.'

The Maharajah gestured to his right and there, in one heartstopping moment, Burlington beheld the royal consort in all her legendary beauty. But as she called forth a train of maidens for him to inspect it was not upon the maidens that his eyes rested. Instead he stood magnetised by the Maharajah's luscious companion herself, her capacious bosom glittering with diamonds and rubies, a braid of topazes and sapphires decking the golden blonde locks of a majestic head.

Burlington sensed destiny within his grasp.

Chapter 24
1979

In anything else, there were ways of learning, people who'd teach you. In marriage, there was no way and no one.

'Don't you even remember?' Penny had cried when he forgot their first wedding anniversary. 'Does it mean so little to you?'

Guilt-ridden yet at the same time baffled by her anger, he'd said he was sorry a dozen times. Belatedly he went out to buy her a present. But even that was ill-chosen, a milk jug ringed with blue lines, something he remembered from one of the poems Margery had enthused over and which he vaguely thought would look romantic and decorative on the kitchen shelf. But Penny already had a milk jug and the price, which she scolded him into revealing, was exorbitant.

'How can you waste money on a thing like that?' she'd screamed, hurling the jug to the tiles of the kitchen floor. Picking the pieces up had been like retrieving a dead child's body.

He longed for approval with the longing of a small boy desperate for affection. With the same hesitant earnestness with which he'd once approached Margery hugging his poems and stories he now brought home small token gifts, nothing expensive enough to excite her anger but enough, he hoped, to win back her affection. But each attempt failed. Penny received the gifts coldly, setting them aside in a manner that labelled them inept or redundant: a mirror for her dressing table, where one already stood; a bottle of scent she disapproved of as having been made from the body of a slaughtered animal; a red necklace at war with her colouring. A sense of inadequacy infiltrated him, the more demoralising for being unfamiliar. The girl he'd seen as a conquest, a helpless pretty thing, now emerged in a score of trivial but weirdly important ways as knowing more than he did, his superior. When he responded with resentment Penny let his snarls pass by, unscathed. The terrifying thought came to him that she'd written him off, determined to live her own life her own way, as if inwardly acknowledging that she'd bought a dud.

Memories that the purchase was forced, not freely chosen, made the hurt still harder to bear. For a while he tried, without conscious plan or intent, to recover her through her friends. When she invited their friends Jane and Ted round for the evening he found himself putting on an unaccustomed jocularity that stopped just short of backslapping.In retrospect it unnerved even himself.

'Good to see you. Let me get you a refill. How's things at Howard and Deague's, then?'

But Jane had no conversation of interest and Ted, who'd been a year behind Peter at school, brought no news from the council office where he'd sat bored and inactive since joining. He responded to the joviality with counter-questions.

'I hear you left the finance job. Didn't you like it, then?'

Peter's hand on the wine bottle slowed with suspicion. 'It was all right.'

'Got another job yet?'

'Not yet. I'm looking.'

'I heard Atlantic Finance's shares took a bit of a hammering.'

'Yeh, I think you're right.'

'Do you see much of Bob Tommelty these days?'

With the mention of Tommelty suspicion became certainty. There'd been tittle tattle, whispered gossip and chortling, behind Peter's back. Memories of the shared office at Atlantic Finance crossed his mind like a revenant. In any talk with Bob you could pick up at secondhand the conversations he'd had in the White Hart or the Fox and Hounds. You could tell what he'd said, what others had added. Often you knew exactly who'd spoken. Now, with Ted, it was the same.

In a while even the conversation dried up and after a few attempts entertaining at their respective homes ended. It should have been a relief when Penny took to meeting Jane unaccompanied, in Asprey's coffee room on Thursday mornings. But though the removal of a need to talk was welcome, the change came as another amputation of Peter's shared life with Penny. He fought the fear of loneliness by whistling as he peeled the potatoes or swabbed the kitchen floor – tasks undertaken in a desperate attempt to impart some life to a dead relationship. But each time he looked round during or after a task he found no one there: Penny had taken refuge in some other part of the house.

*

It was in late October, early on a morning when he and Red had taken a day off, that there came a knock on the door of his own and Penny's apartment in Havana House. He put down the paintbrush with which he was re-coating the secondhand rocking horse he'd bought for Joni and awkwardly, with the two paint-free fingers of his left hand, turned the doorknob to open.

'Oh! Hello.' He backed away to let Aunt Flo enter. But instead she stood her ground.

'I don't think you'll have heard. Gran asked me to come and tell you. Your Grandad died last night.'

'Oh!' The news took time to digest. 'I'm sorry.'

'He had a good life. Five children. Not many men can say that.'

A panorama unrolled before Peter. His own life had always been linear, a progress along passageways full of bends and offshoots but with few windows and those opening mainly on blank walls or central wells of the kind pre-war office buildings contained, or on glass panes which boarding-up had turned into mirrors. But Arthur's seemed different, a landscape spreading from east to west, from far sunrise to sunset. He'd been a patriarch, the head of a clan, the Munnerly clan of Victorian England among whom he was born, not an isolated atom thrown about without bond or support. Why had he, Peter, never felt the strength of belonging to a large, wealthy, respected family? Was it just him? Or had every family disintegrated in this century, reduced to a heap of fragments barely in touch with each other? It must be six months since he'd spoken at any length to Arthur.

'I'm sorry,' he said again when the first turmoil bubbled low. 'How sad.'

Flo looked at him as if struck belatedly by the same melancholy. 'He kept the family business going. The ship afloat. A respectable man.'

Something in the last word snagged on his mind, a tribute added in conformity with a respected recipe, yet smacking of faint praise. For some reason he thought of Caroline and a special way Flo had of looking at her. A look of loss - like today's. An idea flitted past his mind's window, too quickly to call back and question: the sense of his aunt's holding back, the deflection of her gaze from her niece as if checking some impulse of materni- No, it couldn't be. And yet...the shared tallness, the long face? It wasn't possible - was it? Not Aunt Flo?

For a second their eyes met. Between nephew and aunt unspoken thoughts passed. Between generations. Between the oceanically-divided morals of her youth and his, of *then* and *now*. He wondered, are we really allies in this war? Is Flo, after all, on our side, one of us?

110

It was Flo who broke the silence. 'Gran asked that you should go and see her, when you've got over the shock. She has something for you. Something she'd like you to do.' She turned, again as if sheering away from some upsurge of undesired emotion, and within a second had gone. For the first time he could remember, feelings and thoughts which the interview had prompted lodged in him, hanging about like guests who'd outstayed their welcome.

Then the unfailing habit of presentness took over. Nancy. What could she want? In his early years he'd been overawed by her severity, the brow clenched like those of the ancient matriarchs whose pictures darkened the walls of the staircase in the great hall. She 'had something for him'. Not a good omen. The last thing she'd lumbered him with had been marriage. There'd be no more Greek gifts.

He washed his hands at the hot tap, dislodging some paint on to the sink and wall-tiles. That would annoy Penny. Good. More paint came off on the kitchen towel but a detritus of stickiness still coated his fingers. So what? He turned the doorknob and, detaching his hand, set off along the landing.

*

'The funeral will be on Monday. You will have a seat in the fourth row of the church. Dress is formal.' Nancy's long face was inexpressive nowadays but the tone of authority remained. 'But a lounge suit, smartly presented, will be sufficient.'

He remembered the army, how he'd stood before the major to hear the news of his discharge. The same sense of disapproval, of being resigned to hopelessness. He nodded, hoping it an adequate response. When Nancy turned aside to resume her game of patience on a nearby card table's green baize he felt someone must speak.

'Aunt Flo said you had something for me. She didn't say what.'

'I was coming to that.' A tone of reproof. Oh, what a mistress of disapproval she was, always had been. And how deeply the springs of conditioned shame were planted. With stately dignity Nancy swivelled to lift a large cardbord box from its perch on top of a pouffe – the only one Peter had ever seen except for hassocks in church - and held it out, unmoving. Peter lurched forward to take it.

'These are family papers. They belong to your grandfather, Arthur, and to Edward, your late uncle. I would like you to sort them out.'

'Yes, of course.' Peter kept the box on his knee. To put it down might seem rude. As dominant as Flo, though less from force

111

of personality and more because she instilled in him a sense of inadequacy, Nancy still reminded him of his aunt. 'I'll do that.'

But it wasn't enough. Below the centre parting of hair his grandmother's stare intensified. 'Is that all you have to say? Aren't you going to ask what they are?'

'Yes, of course. What are they? And' – uneasily he tried the box for weight – 'Enough to sink the *Titanic*?'

The fecklessness was too much. Nancy snatched breath, then exhaled with superhuman restraint, mercifully averting the attack of vapours she sometimes suffered in moments of stress. Her next words were faint.

'Young man, it is time for you to take on responsibility. Your grandfather has now passed away. Unhappily, owing to Margery's absurd love of secrecy, we don't know who your father is. This means – do you realise? – that you are now the head of this family. Do you understand?'

'Oh. Yeh.'

'I take that inarticulate grunt to mean yes. Am I right?'

'Mm. Yeh. Yes.'

She turned aside with a hope-abandoning flap of the hands. 'Three small cards from the patience game fluttered to the floor. 'So how will you fulfil your responsibilities? Will you take over the business – the same business you left in disgrace?' A pause. 'No, of course you won't. Fortunately, Mr Scrimgeour and his colleagues are still, for a few years, with us to see to that. But when they retire will you be a fit person to come back and resume your broken career? I doubt it.'

She was almost talking to herself. Pity, lacrimose as ammonia, infected his eyes. She was attacking him but in reality the inadequacy she feared was her own. Brought up under one man's tutelage until her father passed her to a place of honour and uselessness in her husband's house, she'd never had to face the world, to move to a strange town, settle in hired rooms, live alone, earn a living or, even in her own home, do more than the most genteel tasks. Birth and upbringing in the social milieu of crinoline, topper and hansom carriage had raised her to a lifetime of debility in every practical thing. Arthur had made every decision, borne every stress, done everything for her. And now terror transmuted to blame.

'How is Penny?'

Subconsciously he'd seen it coming. The flanking attack. 'Fine. She's really well.'

She leaned forward. 'There's been talk of disharmony.'

'Yes. No. I mean, well, a bit now and then.'

'You married that young lady. So just let me tell you. You have a duty to care for her, to see that she's properly looked after.'

The dressing-down took minutes to subside. Peter felt embarrassed but, curiously, no longer intimidated. The fierce voice of propriety that had hustled him to the altar no longer brought fear. Had it only been the knowledge of Arthur's support that had made her so alarming? Had she, all along, been her husband's proxy?

He lifted the box a moment. 'Sorting these papers – do you want it done urgently?' Concrete tasks bred embitterment. He'd learnt that with Penny.

A faint indeterminate gesture. 'Not especially. If there's anything of interest, I'd like to know.'

''Course. I could show them to Joni, too. She's interested in the family.'

'Yes.'

He took the repeated feeble gesture – that of an ageing duchess - as a dismissal. He rose to his feet and left. The stricken whiteness and gauntness of his grandmother's face in the presence of bereavement stayed with him. He found himself asking how Penny might look if it came to a break-up in their own marriage. There'd be hardness, toughness, resentment, but also relief. Surely not this incapacitating panic. Only the same feelings he himself would have. Just as, for most people, marriage no longer had to be called in to regularise an unintended pregnancy, divorce wasn't any longer the dreadful end of a dream. Nothing was as Nancy imagined.

He wondered if the lifelong union that old people talked about with such approval was really founded on love at all. Might it not result simply from the past dependency of women?

*

'When you've finished your homework,' he told Joni, pushing the box across the floor to her with his foot. 'Just tell me if there's anything interesting.'

That got rid of that. He breathed deep with relief. 'Yes, I'm going through them with a toothcomb,' he would tell Nancy the next time their paths crossed. As he watched Joni crouched on the hearthrug, absorbed in an explosion of old letters, photographs, official-looking documents and yellow newspaper cuttings, he let the bars of a song escape his lips.

With a little bit - of luck
With a little bit – of luck
Someone else can do the blooming work.

It wasn't often a job of work was so easily disposed of.

'They're about Uncle Edward,' Joni said later that week when he enquired about progress. ''Boy, did he live!'

The phrase stuck in Peter's mind like a splinter. Uncle Edward, it seemed, had lived. Which was the aim of the game.

Peter wasn't sure if he'd lived. The word had an glorifying resonance, a sunrise glow about it that didn't often seem to come his way. Edward had fought at sea during the war. Images flocked to mind: Errol Flynn defeating the Japanese singlehanded; Charlton Heston calling down fire from heaven; John Wayne routing the bad guys with black hats and on black horses. The next time Joni was busy with homework he approached the brimming chaos of Nancy's scrap-box and peered in. He picked up a ring file, old but as neat as if still new. Its title on the stiff board cover read:

Memoirs of Navigating Officer of Submarine E
in the Eastern Mediterranean
1941-44

The file fell open in his hands. Its entries were neatly typed, and dated. A diary! Plumping down on the floor, he chose a page at random.

4 a.m. Observed Italian battleship 'Dante Alighieri' steaming due south, escorted by one destroyer. Proceeded to attack,

5 a.m. Fired port bow tube, the torpedo striking her amidships and exploding. She immediately opened a heavy but ineffectual fire on our periscope, but it was seen she was a doomed ship. Taking a heavy list to starboard she sank in four minutes from the time she was struck. The escorting destroyer, ignoring our proximity, began the work of rescuing the survivors. They had picked up all who were floating in the vicinity when a destroyer of the 'Tiberius' class appeared on the scene from nowhere and proceeded alongside her confrere *prepared to relieve her of some of her human cargo. This was too much even for our patience, as it was considered a quite unnecessary proceeding; so swinging broadside on to her we let go the starboard beam torpedo but apparently had allowed it too much depth as it*

*passed directly underneath her doing no damage. Without
waiting for the inevitable rain of shells, we dived and made
a course for a safe position. In the circumstances it was
inevitable we should see no more of the lost torpedo but that
did not worry us at this stage of our voyage. Besides which,
our minds were fully occupied calculating the probable
emoluments resulting from the destruction of such an
important and large-sized victim as the 'Dante Alighieri'
and with her complement of 800,*

officers and men

7.10 a.m. Rose to the surface. Hands to bathe.

Peter paused. There were sounds from the kitchen. He
remembered it was his turn to make the dinner. But the story he'd
just read left him excited and tingling. The story of a real hero, the
officer who'd sunk an enemy battleship. It was as good as – better
than – any story he'd read or heard, and to cap it all, it was true.

Or was it? He paused. A cynicism born of observing the
boss class at work crept in. He returned to the ring-file. This man,
the navigating officer, had been happy to sink a ship taking survivors
on board. Hm. It might be all right, an excusable tragedy. But that
wasn't clear. And when he'd fired their starboard torpedo – it
sounded like a scarce missile, something they couldn't afford to
waste – he'd missed. It didn't sound too skilful. Not like John
Wayne or Errol Flynn, who never missed. Maybe the story wasn't so
heroic after all.

He was about to put the file down when another thought
arose. Was this Uncle Edward's journal at all? True, his postings
had been kept secret not only at the time but for long afterwards, but
hadn't he been in the ordinary navy, not in submarines? And if so
what was this file doing in his papers? Had Nancy somehow got the
wrong memoir? Had Arthur even seen this one? A fascinating
possibility came to him. Had Nancy, aloof from the world and
longing to believe well of her son, imagined this log was his?

There was another doubt. If Edward had drowned how had
the author of the file survived? They must have been assigned to
different ships at a later date. The account might be relevant to
Edward's career or it might not. But Nancy - no one at Havana
House - seemed to have questioned it. They believed it because they
wanted to.

Should he voice his doubts? To ask the question was to know the answer. Doubt was unthinkable. He must keep quiet. Within the family Edward's memory was sacred.

The memory of Scrimgeour pretending to understand derivatives came to mind, and, further back, Midge Sprewls feeling smart for detecting a cheating offence that had never taken place. This wasn't another bluff, was it – yet another?

'It's ready. I shan't wait any longer. I'll let it burn.'

Penny's voice from the kitchen awoke him from a sinking reverie. God, it had been his turn to cook.

'Sorry. Coming.'

He hurried along the hall towards the smell of burning. At the entrance to the kitchen he halted. When he resumed he moved with a limp as if in pain.

'Sorry. It's this leg. I pulled a muscle coming out of the Fox and Hounds with Red last night.'

For a moment doubt flickered in her eyes. Then she pursed her lips, accepting the story.

The surge of cynicism was overpowering. How many of the successful, those the world honoured, were undeserving, at best the beneficiaries of wrongly awarded praise or mistaken identity? You can't fool all of the people all of the time. But Abraham Lincoln was wrong. You could. You really could.

Chapter 25
1980

'Look, it sold pretty well, didn't it? Six hundred copies. That's a good start.'

'You'd expect stuff about the last days of the Raj to sell. The War's different. There's lots of books on that already.'

'Not like this one.'

'Bet there are.'

'Doesn't matter. That's what the punters want - romance against the backdrop of a world war. That's what novels are about.'

'Nah.'

They met in Peter's room when Penny was out shopping. Supposedly keeping watch over Joni, in practice Peter consigned her to a playpen in the nursery across the landing, leaving the door open in case of distress. If she cried he shut it. Every so often, if he remembered, he would slip back and take a look at her. Strangely, with the incomprehension of infancy, whenever he entered the debris of building blocks and crayoning books, string and softballs and thick wooden jigsaws, she would always stop crying, welcoming with gurgles of joy the daddy who'd neglected her. Often ten minutes passed before Red Thomas could lure Peter back to the writing room.

'It's going to be scholarly, this one. See, I've got these books I can bring in. I'll work in all kinds of true-life stuff, real events and people. With footnotes and a bibliography, like what old Hartson used to talk about in history lessons. It'll be really convincing.'

But scholarship was too rarified for Red Thomas. He pointed to Peter's handwritten sheaf. 'So how are you going to get Burlington out of this fix?'

Peter frowned and took a deep breath. 'Right. So let's remember where he is. He's been parachuted into Berlin disguised as a Wehrmacht officer.'

'What if someone talks to him in German?'

'I told you, he's fluent in German.'

'Oh yeah?'

'Yeah. And in the early hours of Christmas morning, when no one's around, he breaks into Gestapo HQ.'

'HQ?'

'Headquarters. In the Prinz Albrechtstrasse. I looked it up. He breaks into the safe where they keep details of all the Fuhrer's orders, so he'll be able to find out where the Reich's store of gold is kept.'

'What's it matter? You can't win a war with gold.'

'You can buy war materials - metals and things. It's a vital mission. But then the Obergruppenfuhrer comes in and he has to hide in a cupboard.'

'What's the Oberwhatsit doing in the office at three o'clock on Christmas morning?'

'He's been celebrating. We can think of a reason. He's passing on his way home and just drops in. Or he calls for a glass of water.'

'You said Burlington had to be ready when the British planes came over, to signal where they should drop their bombs.'

'He does. That's the problem. How can he do his signalling when he's trapped in the cupboard?'

'Well?'

For a moment they stood in silence. The slow moan of a crying baby arose down the hallway. Peter moved to the door and closed it.

'I've got it.'

'Go on, then.'

Red Thomas's tone was one of challenge, almost derision. It was the 'then' that annoyed Peter most. That was Red Thomas all over: never making any suggestions of his own but always ready to pour scorn on other people's. Peter adopted his putting-down manner.

'It's obvious, if you've any idea what an Obergruppenfuhrer's like. He's been celebrating with his mistress and he's brought her back. They make love in the office and while they're busy Burlington sneaks from his cupboard and tiptoes out the door. That way he's in position – Burlington is – by the time the British planes come over.'

He stood for several seconds daring Red Thomas to object. Only when Red started to clear his throat did he make a hurried move. With crushing decisiveness he plumped down into the chair beside his writing table and seized his pen.

As the last of the drunken revellers staggered away to their orgies the Prinz Albrechtstrasse fell silent. Burlington cast a final glance along the darkened thoroughfare. Then with one superhuman effort he leaped up to the carelessly unlocked first-floor window. Within seconds his cat-like tread had brought him to the door of the Geheimnisamt where, cold in the Christmas moonlight, the crucial steel safe stood which in its gleaming depths held all the documents of the thousand-year German Reich.Here lay the key to the outcome of the world's titanic struggle, thesecret of victory to come

Chapter 26
1977

The next spring Penny moved out. She could stand no more, she said. A friend wanted someone to share her flat in Pitt Street. There'd be no problem about Joni: the neighbours were tolerant of children and in any case held their property as a second home, spending most of their time in London. The flat had plenty of room for an infant.

There was no row. It was as if embitterment flagged with proximity. Ticking off, on a list of their possessions, which were hers, which Peter's, she spoke little.

Was she feigning casualness? If so did it hide regret? Uncertainly, he decided it didn't. Accident had brought them together. It seemed right, mutually agreed, that choice should set them apart. When the taxi arrived to take her away she allowed him a final kiss on the cheek as they said goodbye on the pavement. Only by holding out an open hand could he be sure that no rain was falling to explain the moisture dampening his lips.

Drained of the woman he'd skirted and avoided for two years, the house seemed empty. The previous autumn Caroline had left home to work in Manchester, a departure he viewed with envy from his desk at Atlantic Finance, and for a while he tried to convince himself that her absence was the void in his life. But the scepticism that coloured his view of others extended to himself. A wife's presence, even bristling with hostility at breakfast, even presenting a knobbly backbone as she lay frozen in a parallel declivity of the partitioned matrimonial bed, gave a hidden substratum of something – was it security? The fact was, he missed Penny.

As compensation he wandered more often into Margery's rooms or into the shared family kitchen, hoping to find her there. But the scenario wouldn't integrate. It reminded him of some bizarre stage comedy in which a man tied to one woman vainly seeks the favours of a second. The pieces of his life's jigsaw never fitted. Co-existing in one house, the three moved in different worlds.

The failure seemed another rejection. Peter took to having breakfast early to avoid competition for space round the toaster, the sink and the big, rough-hewn kitchen table. It left him with time to kill before he set off for the office and, rather than risk frictions with Margery about where he'd put the butter or the way he'd used up all the milk, matters that seemed so trivial he couldn't believe they were the true causes of conflict, he sat in his room and calculated the odds on runners at current race meetings. Only when Margery was away at one of her literary weekends did he linger in the kitchen, hoping someone else – Flo, Georgina, Annie Smith, Hazel or, when she was visiting, Caroline - would come in and chat yet, when they did, wary lest they should be allies of Margery rather than himself. In fact, though, the sisters seemed to regard him with a mixture of amusement, disbelief and despair. Lack of shared interests cemented the estrangement.

At times sheer loneliness turned his thoughts back towards Penny. Then he would make tentative telephone calls, effectively inviting himself round to see her and, more especially, to see Joni. When he arrived in the big room they occupied he would present Penny with a bunch of flowers – showy chrysanthemums or dahlias, bought at reduced price from the local florist, a girl he'd known with some intimacy at school – and after Penny had accepted them with a sceptical smile, recognising their role as a kind of appeasement, he would produce a second present, a doll or windmill or wooden–wheeled dog, for Joni. While he settled on the floor or beside the playpen to engage the little girl in improvised games Penny would hover in the background, constantly thrusting her head into the living room from the kitchen where she cooked or washed clothes. Her hovering brought an uneasiness or perhaps a reproach for his part in their split-up, a pang he dispersed by recalling that if it came to the point she would never have dreamed of taking him back.

The doctrine of avoidance took root. 'It's best they don't see you as reliable,' he told Bob Tommelty over coffee at work, referring to their employers. 'That way you don't get bogged down with responsibilities.'

'Dead right there.' Bob nodded with vigour and resumed an account of his plans to quit Atlantic Finance. 'Independent financial adviser,' he said. 'I quite fancy that.'

Peter surveyed him with disbelief. Bob had always been close to the bottom of their class at school.

At home the split with Margery ran in parallel. Vaguely, Peter recognised his mother's detachment as a distorted mirror of his own relationship with Joni, an affection fragmented by the continual straying of attention, an inability to accept or even understand the nature of family ties and duty. Just as, once removed to Pitt Street, Joni seldom crossed his mind and then only with a sense of surprised guilt at having to catch up on her life, so Margery, in her whirlwind of engagements and public readings, classes and adjudications, seemed to forget him entirely. The image of a flywheel came to mind, forceful and capable of strong propulsion yet forever bounding between engagement with society and family and total detachment. What worried was the question: if you were made like this, what else could you do?

He asked it most when, as ever, he took his writing to her. Notebook in hand he would halt outside her door, his ear to the old oaken panelling, a private eye on the snoop for shenanigans. Sometimes he was rewarded with sounds of lieder, the chest-puffing notes of *Die Winterreise* or *Der Erlkonig* bizarrely transposed to alto range. Sometimes it would be an aria from *Carmen* or *Trovatore*: Margery favoured bohemian roles. Some days recollections of school English lessons would well up as, standing arrested at her door, he tried to recognise the poem she was reciting:

'*You blocks, you stones, you worse than senseless things!*
Oh you hard hearts, you cruel men of Rome!
Knew ye not Pompey? Many a time and oft
Have you climbed up to walls and battlements,
To towers and windows, yea to chimney tops,
Your infants in your arms...'

When the torrent at last subsided he knocked.

'*But hark, I hear the footing of a man.*'

Peter cleared his throat. 'Well not just any man, actually. It's me.'

'Oh.' The information seemed to flummox her. 'Ah. Come in. What do you want?'

He wanted to say *How can you ask what I want, how can you look at me as if I was something the cat brought in? For heaven's sake I'M YOUR SON!* But it would be another mistake, it would start another row, yet another. It was as if they'd neither of them ever learned a vital technique, didn't know how to discuss a disagreement without the reproaches and accusations rebounding to and fro. Surely two rational grown-up people could do that, surely. But no, like some nervous tic a patient can't uproot, the mechanism stayed ingrained and ineradicable. Peter stared at his shoes, disconsolate.

'I wrote this.' He raised the notepad like an oblation. After the Shakespeare it seemed pitiable, a sacrifice to an inassuagable god.

'What is it?'

'It's, well-' He hadn't thought what it was. It took time to decide. 'It's about Africa - Dar es Salaam. A prose poem.'

'Ah.' Her face lightened.

'You went there once.'

'I did. Before you saw the light. My worldly journeyings.'

For a moment the religious tone of her comments made him half-expect a scriptural text. But her rhapsody went on.

'The Mountains of the Moon.
Tanganyika, Ruwenzori,
Chimborazo, Cotopaxi
Stole my heart away.'

She stood with hands clasped, a Victorian maiden, a cameo of *Souls Awakening*. But it was her own imaginings that transported her, not his poem. He waited, tense with anxiety, till the flow ended.

'Would you like to read it?'

'Yes, of course. But' – she swung, by habit, into changed mode – 'first, I have duties to perform. They'll be expecting me at the Institute. Leave your poem here. I'll read it later.'

Already she was moving, gathering up her handbag, keen for the excitement of literature. She took her coat from a stand, pressed a kiss on his cheek.

Anger as never before broke from him. 'You say you like my writing but you never read it. You're not interested. You've no real contact with me, not with me or anyone else. You live in some artificial world that Cambridge created, an eggshell of falsity you've built round yourself. You never tell me who my father is, you won't read my writing, you never ask about my job or my plans to quit, never speak or act from the heart. It's all false, false, false.'

She stood staring at him, aghast. 'How can you say such things?'

He felt ashamed to go on. His voice was a sullen mutter. 'It's the truth. But truth's something you're past recognising. I'm leaving this house. I shan't come back.'

'No. No, you mustn't go. I'll read it.'

He shook his head. 'You said that last time, you said it all the other times. But did you ever? No.'

Under attack, hardness returned. 'I have other duties. Can't you understand that? You can't take up all my time.'

For years he'd taken up none. There was always something more pressing. But it was useless to go on. For all the protestations, he was her lowest priority.

He twisted the poem, his peace offering, the words he'd written in a longing to live up to her and be like her, and hurled the crumpled paper into a corner. As it skidded into one of her ornaments, the replica of some Aztec deity she'd brought back from South America, the hollow bronze emitted a small whimper like the cry of a baby in distress. The cry of Joni.

He turned and stormed from the room, set on his final departure from Havana House.

Chapter 27
1978

Throughout the autumn Penny allowed him visits to her new flat to see Joni.

At first the visits were, at her insistence, fortnightly and when he began to arrive at the door every Saturday there were protestations and tears. On a visit just before Christmas he asked if he could move in with her and then her resistance was total.

He took to Fabian tactics, swept her room while she was in the kitchen, brought in groceries he thought she needed, washed Joni's nappies unasked. An excursion into ironing her clothes when she'd gone out to the corner shop brought disaster when he singed one of her favourite blouses. The opening of every window to disperse the smoke and the rapid purchase of a similar replacement at Marks and Spencer neither concealed the blunder nor proved adequate compensation. The process of slow erosion he intended failed in its purpose.

'No, no. It'll be another catastrophe,' she said, almost in tears again when he repeated his request. Her small frame shuddered as if with mental and physical revulsion. He couldn't believe she really felt that. There was nothing else for it.

The following spring, one night when Penny was visiting her mother leaving Joni in the care of a babysitter, he packed an outsize suitcase and co-opted Red Thomas to drive him round to her place. Reassurances and a few pounds persuaded the babysitter to admit him and then to leave early. When Penny came home at half past eleven she drew back the blankets of her bed to find it already three-quarters occupied. The *fait accompli* was complete.

And with it the old frictions returned. Familiar though they were, they underwent subtle transmutation through the change of surroundings. The new habitat brought fresh feelings to the old question: why did he and Penny not get on? As he struggled with the conundrum an unforeseen answer formed in his mind: the trouble between himself and Penny was that they could never both be happy at once.

He remembered the wedding, that final slow procession down the aisle to the roar of the organ: how she had been aglow, he shaky with worry at the loss of freedom. When they moved into their rooms at Havana House, an apartment granted through the good grace of Arthur and the condescension of Nancy, Penny had been excited and full of ideas for decoration and furnishing. He, in contrast, had felt the presence of his mother and grandparents a threat, the failure at start-out of a marriage which should have brought release, an escape from the Munnerly family.

Yet even about that he wasn't sure. Wasn't it also that, presented with opportunities for improving things, for choosing wallpaper and paint and rearranging the old oak sideboard and the old leather armchairs she bought as if to convert the flat into a West End club, Penny became the organiser? Her suggestions became orders, her tentative thoughts dogmas. 'I know. We'll have that old rug out for a start. Now, we'll clear those old books off the shelf. Pooh! They're thick with dust. Who's supposed to keep this place clean? We'll have to see about that Annie woman. Now, we need some new lightshades. The telly can go in that corner. Next door can be for Joni, her nursery. Come on, give me a hand.'

And daunted by the core of steel he felt hardening in her, he obeyed and bit his lip.

Several months passed before he realised she was biting hers as well. Through his unmarried years he'd lived off the land, the advance party of an invading army: made his own breakfast from whatever was in the fridge, not knowing or wondering where Margery was; collected his mother's subventions and his pay and spent it as he pleased when he pleased, at the Fox and Hounds or the racecourse; picked up a tip, a drinking companion or a girl when he wanted one. The taming process didn't come easily.

'You aren't doing your share of the housework.' Penny stared in tears at the big drops forming on the ceiling, where a century of weather had forced its finger through rotting timbers. 'You don't help.' But when he'd applied himself to one household repair she would unfailingly follow it up with another until he became afraid of helpfulness. To help was taken as a sign of weakness.

The thought nestled yet never took root that he might be like Margery: full of good intentions which evaporated as soon as action was needed.

Their disagreements unveiled another impasse.

'Sorry,' he would say when Penny pointed to one of his duties done badly or not at all – a picture insecurely hung, a loose floorboard unnailed. But even while he was fetching the stepladder or the hammer the fact of his apology seemed to loose her fury, released by glimpse of a crack in the complacency she'd for years longed to smash. 'Yes, you should be sorry. You go off with your cronies and leave me here alone to look after Joni. Do you ever give her a thought? Do you take her for walks, push the pushchair up the stairs? Are you even aware she's here?'

He stood open-mouthed. 'Of course I am. I do. I think a lot of Joni. I'd give the world for her.'

'No you don't. If you did you'd give time and effort to her.'

'I do. I took her to the park only this week. I love her.'

She broke into tears. What he heard through the choke of sobs might have been, 'You don't love me.' When he protested she pushed him away, drawing strength from his defensiveness. When he thought of the quarrel afterwards he saw her as white-faced and demented, a waif of a thrown-away doll, nothing like the girl he'd married, the schoolgirl who'd shown him the treasures of Aladdin in Wardle's shed. It was right, what she said: he didn't love her. Whatever love was.

He learnt not to apologise, not to explain. Instead he stood silent, mute and obstinate at her every accusation. In turn, she hardened. If he could shut himself off, so could she. He wasn't the man she'd married.

'I sometimes wonder what I'd think of you if we weren't married,' she said; but by then he was too frozen, too fenced off from allowing himself to feel anything to see the remark as a danger signal. Within six months, after their biggest and fiercest row, he walked in stiff silence, yet with the calmness of hatred, from the room, leaving her in shaking iciness. The next day while she was out at Joni's toddler group he threw his possessions – startlingly few among the tidal flotsam of Penny's make-up bottles, her multitude of shoes and their daughter's toys and clothes – into his suitcase and left. There was no note: she would know why he'd gone.

From the urine-smelling draughtiness of a public callbox he phoned Red Thomas.

'You were talking about that old mill you thought of renting on Wensham Hill. Is it still going? Great. Listen, then. All right if I come and join you there?'

*

At once he felt happier. For Penny, he realised, Havana House had been an escape – from Canal Street, from poverty, from her mother. For him it had been a life sentence. For her it had been a climb up to higher sunlit uplands, prosperity, the middle class; for him a detested imprisonment. Most, though, it was her happiness that had come across to him as the assertiveness of a hidden, repugnant masculinity. Only when she'd wept or been sad had his heart gone out.

Never the theorist, still he wondered. Was there a given amount – a 'quantum' – of happiness between them, which, if one had it, the other lost? Some law, like Newton's vaguely-remembered laws of motion? Come to that, hadn't there been situations like this before? At school Midge Sprewls had been glutinously happy, brimming with self-satisfaction, as he inflicted – his *happiness* inflicted – pain on all around. In making him happy, Peter had taken pain upon himself.

The mill, though, was sheer delight. Perched on the highest outcrop of the Wirral coast, it stood like a lighthouse casting its view round two hundred degrees of cliff and sand and the all-encircling sea. To the north Hilbre Island at low tide cast its arm of sand back to join hands with the mainland; to the west the low girdle of the Clwyd Hills slung a dark chain along the horizon, pimpled by the Jubilee Tower, one brow answering another like mountaineers calling between belays. Beyond, when the mists cleared in the far west, Snowdon prodded a snout into the ozone.

And the interior was as good. The sandbank of last year's beech leaves at the door and inside the porch, the cradle-rock of the ladders joining the mill's three floors, the rust-engraved bath with its leaky tap and the sweet inescapable smell of creosote with which the landlord had failed to conceal the intrusion of rain and the sweat of old wood – were all causes for delight. A house like this needed no cleaning. With spindly unshielded lightbulbs dangling in the gloom it would be hard to read after dusk. Great!

'You have the top floor, I'll take this.' Red Thomas's assertion was shouted with a grin, more a challenge than a diktat. But what the hell? This was fun. 'Okay. I'm nearer the bath, so I go first.'

'Go ahead.'

It was more easily said than done. The bath, though its installation preceded by many years the age of environmental preservation, drew its water by gravity from the mill's conical roof. But the conduits for the rainwater had long since become clogged and when Peter twisted the spigot that served as a tap, gungy leaves together with small twigs and the corpses of black beetles dribbled into the tub in a speckled cascade. Heating the water posed more problems. Added amounts, heated in a smaller tin tub over gas from a cylinder, were necessary to make the temperature tolerable. The process was slow and laborious. By the time the last bucket of hot water was added the first had grown tepid. Even so, Peter luxuriated in the tub, lathering himself with the thin gruel of soapy liquid as from time to time he flicked dead beetles with no great accuracy in the direction of his housemate.

'Right. Where's the nearest pub?'

It amazed him that Red Thomas had to stop and think.

'It's the Ring o' Bells up at Bidston. Twenty minutes' walk.'

'God, what a dump.' They had overlooked the essentials. 'There's nothing here, I suppose.'

'Iolo Roberts would know.'

'Iolo Roberts?'

'The landlord. He's due to arrive in a few minutes. He wants to tell us about the place.' Red Thomas paused, mouth open: an idea had come. 'Yes, there *is* some drink here. I saw it in the cellar.'

'Cellar?'

'Ground floor. Hold on.'

When he emerged from off the shuddering ladder five minutes later he was carrying a six-pack. He paused to regain his puff.

'They've all been opened, I'm afraid. Funny, that. Still, they're full. Let's toast the mill.' He raised a metal cylinder to his lips. Peter, still naked and wobbling in all parts from cold, grabbed another and reciprocated. 'To our new home.'

'Our new home.'

A moment's glugging passed before Peter, now searching for his clothes - removed, he suspected, by Red during an inspection of the floorboards for mice-holes - raised one more point. 'How do we heat this place when it's cold? I mean, winter?'

Red grimaced. 'Dunno. Hadn't thought of that. Let's ask Iolo when he comes. Judging by the sound, that's him.'

*

The landlord was short and thickset with a dark bristly chin. He shook hands with vigour but otherwise centred on talk.

'I think you'll like it here. A home from home. See the view, all the coast of North Wales and, if you want it, to eastward, Liverpool.' His hand swept a semicircle round such tiny fragment of the horizon as was visible through the mill's slit windows. The virtual nature of the view didn't seem to bother him. 'The last tenant was very happy. He was a refugee from Syria.' He lowered his voice. 'Quite illegal, mind you. He loved the *anonymity* of the place, the way it didn't exist as an address. Do you get much mail?'

Red Thomas looked blank. 'Not a lot.'

129

'That's good. It's the people who get mail who're in trouble. The last postman didn't recognise our existence. The new one does, but not often. It's hit and miss.'

Peter recovered a little. 'What about bills? The water?'

'No, most of the water's off the roof.' He broke off. 'I say, boyo, you'd better get dressed, hadn't you?' A pointing finger targeted the pendulum of Peter's nakedness. Peter clutched his towel downwards. 'Drinking water and that' – it wasn't clear what the *that* meant – 'you get from the tap outside. Have you seen it? It's all right – a bit rusty and brown from the iron ore but good stream water. Comes down from the top of the hill. Very pure. Only look out for dead sheep.'

'And if there is one?' Peter's look expressed anxiety.

'Oh, then you're in trouble, boyo. The last-but-one man here, not the Syrian, another one, he got trichiasis, a turning-in of the eyelids. Very painful, it is. Affects one in a hundred thousand people, almost an epidemic. We don't know why but it might be the water. On the other hand, you never know.'

Iolo stood back, chin tucked in with satisfaction, a man who'd laid another problem to rest.

'So – what else can we drink?'

'That's the problem. There's bottled water from the Spar shop at West Kirby, of course, but that might be no better. You know the tests they've done: more bacteria in bottled water than you get from a tap. Except there's no tap here, not from the reservoir, that is, not filtered and chorinated. Not that chorine's that safe, a deadly killer in fact. It's a bit pot-luck, I'd say. But' – he returned to the vista behind the mill's obscuring walls – 'the view's wonderful.'

'And the heating – in winter?' Peter summoned resolution.

'Oh, that's a real problem, that is. You can get gas canisters down at Irby, it's only a few miles, well maybe ten. Or there's paraffin in Bidston if you've got the right stove. A kite mark's the thing, proves it's safe. Except it wasn't for the last-but-three tenant, a girl – well, woman – that stayed here. She let it flare up while she was adjusting it. Standing naked, she was, only it flared up and burned her hair off. It was a month before she could walk normal again. You need to be careful, boyo.'

There was more about the safety of the floorboards, the roof leaks, the tendency of the ground floor to flood. But the beds – he indicated Peter's pallet, crushed on the floor to a fraction of its height when new – the beds were comfortable: the tenant last-but-five had said so. No, they didn't last long, tenants.

130

Tended to move on. That was the way of the world nowadays.

As the landlord moved out, still in full flow, a last gem of advice came to him.

'By the way, talking of what you drink here. Well, you know the latrine's outside, don't you? Just a cabin with a hole in the ground. No need for emptying, it empties itself down the hill. Only the last occupant didn't use it much. Didn't fancy getting up in the small hours and picking his way down the stairs in darkness. So he used old cans and things as a kind of chamber pot. Sometimes forgot to empty them. Not a very sociable idea, I thought. Mind the stairs, won't you? The last occupant broke his leg.'

And without more warning the landlord was gone into the setting sun.

Chapter 28
1978

He'd thought the storm was over. 'Insider dealing,' they'd called it, his sale of Arthur's gift shares with allegedly 'inside' knowledge that the firm was in trouble gleaned from the confidential Chairman's report. With the historian's readiness to call any event inevitable once it had happened he found reasons why the matter had to be closed. How could he be penalised when the Chairman and his Deputy, no less, had committed the same offence? Not a legal offence at that, merely a departure from what was called 'best practice'? Wasn't the offence worse when committed by experienced, highly-placed men, directors, than by himself, a mere junior? Knowing of their share sales, didn't he even possess a gun to hold at their heads, a threat of exposure that must prevent them sacking him?

But he'd reckoned as an outsider unfamiliar with the British tradition. It was eight months later that a memorandum was circulated,. It drew on a report by management consultants who, Peter remembered, had paid his office a brief visit one afternoon several months before. The memo's contents were vague, heavy with high-sounding but nebulous words: 'downsizing,' 'close-focussing,' 'restructuring'.

'What's it mean, restructuring?' he asked Bob Tommelty.

'Don't you know? It's American. You come to work one morning. There's a janitor at the door and he tells you you're finished. Out on your neck.'

'You mean – they're sacking you?'

'Firing, mate. It's American, don't forget.'

So that when the expected happened there was no appeal. The sacking was carried out on the recommendation of independent consultants, an impartial judgment. It would be absurd to conjure up any connection with an employee's share dealing in the remote and forgotten past.

'What you gonna do, then?' Bob Tommelty enquired in the Fox and Hounds after Peter, arriving at work one morning, had been met at the door by a janitor, escorted to his desk and allowed to claim only his personal possessions before leaving the firm for ever.

'Dunno. They didn't let me touch the computer, you know.'

'Too worried you'd foul the whole system up in revenge.'

'Suppose so.'

'So what'll you do?'

Peter reflected. 'We could expand the racecourse business.'

'How do you mean?'

'Red Thomas and me. We earn a bit as bookies outside the course. We could build it up.'

'You allowed to do that?'

'Sort of.'

'Don't you need a licence or something?'

Peter shrugged. 'Forget the bureaucracy. No one catches you.'

Chapter 29
1979

'Well, it's your problem.' Margery treated her unexpected visitor to one of her ballerina swirls round the kitchen, one of the things that made it impossible to take her warnings seriously or not to love her. 'Don't blame me when they get on to you.'

'They won't. Red Thomas and me –'

'I.'

'Sorry?'

'Red Thomas and *I*.'

'We've been doing it over a year now, ever since Atlantic Finance chucked me out.'

'Without a licence?'

'Yeh. If you stick to small racecourses no one checks.'

'And the legal bookies?'

'They don't get to know. We make a packet.'

Margery gave an elfin shrug, her way of changing the subject. 'Do you ever see Penny now?'

'Quite a bit. And Joni. They're doing fine. We had coffee down town with Aunt Flo the other week.'

He watched her attention alight on the news. There'd been doubt, criticism, in most of her questions but an elation of movement showed underlying pleasure at his meeting with Flo - a deserter from the family and an outlying member still keeping in touch. The monstrous row when he'd walked out of Margery's house sank to oblivion.

'There is one thing, though.'

'Yes?'

'I happened to see that book you wrote. About a man supposedly called Burlington. Someone left a copy lying about in a restaurant.'

He knew at once she was lying. Margery never ate out. She'd hunted for the book. Only pride forbade her to admit it.

'Oh yes?'

'I think it's a disgrace. It's chauvinist. I don't care how well it's written' – so she'd studied it a bit – 'or how much research you did. It degrades women. There.'

It might have been a schoolgirl speaking and yet, because she was serious, he felt ashamed, a small boy in trouble. He tried to read her mind. It was as if she needed a pretext for her reprimand, wanted to indict him for all his other misdeeds, the shotgun marriage and its breakup, the failed job, the illegal bookmaking down at the racecourse. Yet she couldn't. Her own disregard of convention had ranged as wide as his. His birth was one proof of it.

'They bring in money.'

'They? Don't tell me you've written another.'

'I'm on my third. *Burlington and the Mekong River Plot.*'

'You never told me.'

For a moment there were tears in her eyes. It wasn't mainly concern for women, the way he depicted female characters in his books as sex objects, spicy dishes for Burlington to sample and discard. What hurt was his alienation from the Munnerlys, the respected, solid, ramified family that had made Merseyside its life and its prosperity. In all her independence, she drew security from it.

He stepped forward and put his arms round her shoulders. The smallness of her build, the meagreness of advancing middle age, started pity, a desire to comfort. But she shook him away, unwilling to seek warmth that might seem weak or beholden.

'They'll be on to you,' she said again as she showed him to the door. As if relenting, she bestowed a small kiss on his cheek. 'They will.'

Down at the racecourse her words came back like an echo as Red Thomas hurried up outside the gate.

'Look sharp, Pete. The cops are here. They're on to us.'

Chapter 30
1979

'So you don't think it'd wash,' Peter said, 'the story about Pike-Lees giving me permission?'

'As I've said, there's no chance. It's not a starter.'

'I've got a witness. Red Thomas'll swear to it as well.'

The solicitor's sigh reminded Peter of a deflating tyre. 'Look, you've already admitted to me that you had no licence to run a bookmaker's business. So we can't maintain that in court.'

Peter's face puckered with puzzlement. 'But if it'll get me off.'

The man from Rignold and Foley seemed to stiffen, the tyre reflating. 'You seem to have entirely the wrong idea about the legal process, Mr Munnerly. I'm not here to tell lies for you. I'm here to present your case on the basis of the facts. You admit that you ran an unlicensed business. All I can do is find extenuating circumstances – excusable ignorance or error – and present them to the judge.'

'But if you do that I could be found guilty and fined.'

'I am aware of that.'

It seemed preposterous. 'What are lawyers for if they're not there to get you off?'

Another sigh followed. 'If you are found telling untruths in court, especially after delaying and obstructing this case for so many months, you may be found guilty, additionally, of perjury and the sentence could be still more severe. Even custodial.'

'But –'

'In any case Mr Pike-Lees couldn't possibly have given you permission. Even the racecourse Chairman has no power to do that. He doesn't own the course and he doesn't make the law.'

The injustice of it was as distressing as its incomprehensibility. Peter's opinion of his legal-aid lawyer, supplied in response to a plea of poverty from which any mentions of his earnings as a writer were conveniently excluded, sank to its nadir. As always, once they had you on the run they put the boot in.

'Besides,' Edgar Rignold went on, 'if you were once to be caught out in untruth the prosecution would undoubtedly do all it could to throw doubt on your moral character. Your record at Atlantic Finance and Shipping, for example.' He gave a meaningful look.

'My record at... What do you mean?'

'The little matter of your sale of shares after unauthorised reading of the Chairman's then confidential Report?'

'The sale was perfectly legal at that stage. They only changed the law later.'

'Nonetheless, it was a departure from best practice. And you seem to have left the firm soon afterwards.'

'Not soon. It was quite separate.'

'A court wouldn't believe that.'

'And not knowing it was off-colour is no defence?'

The lawyer nodded. Some of the legal aid papers he'd spent twenty minutes filling in slid from his desk and fell in confusion to the floor. 'A basic axiom.' His satisfaction was intense.

'Pike-Lees has got it in for me, always has done. Ever since we had a fight at school, ever since I knew him before he changed his name from Pickles. Can't we tell the court about his moral character?'

Edgar Rignold shook his head, gathered up the fallen papers. He made as if to stand and end the interview. 'It will do no good to atempt to blacken the name of a leading member of the Jockey Club and a professional man.' He eyed Peter askance. The pride at his refusal to help took Peter's breath away. 'Think of some excuses, Mr Munnerly, extenuating circumstances. Then we'll try to make the best of a bad job.'

*

'Stehen Sie auf!!'

Burlington brought himself back to attention with a click of the heels so violent it drew tears to his eyes. Even in a rigged court like this, most of all in a court like this, it was vital to show respect .The Bosch were suckers for kowtowing.

'Ach, so! You have been found guilty of trying to escape from Stalag 534, an offence punishable by the severest penalties, up to and including death. Herr Kommandant here has sworn to this fact. Before I pronounce the verdict, now you may speak. Have you anything that you wish to say on own behalf?'

It was his last chance. Burlington clicked his heels again, moregently this time, and bowed to the judge. Herr Doktor Major Schinkenheimer reciprocated by creasing his face, a movement vaguely suggestive of indigestion. Furtively with his left foot Burlington shoved through a crack in the dock's wooden floor the soil that had fallen from his camp uniform,

137

telltale evidence from the tunnel in which his breakout had failed with such disastrous consequences. He cleared his throat. When the last of the soil seemed disposed of he reached in his pocket for thephotographs.

'Herr Doktor Major, this entire story is fabricated. Herr Kommandant has invented it.'

Another sour smile of cynicism.

'This is a very serious charge. Be careful how you speak. Why should the Kommandant do that?'

'He hates me because I have seen him in a guilty situation. And here I have proof of it.'

Leaning forward, Burlington handed the photographs to the military court's usher, a young officer standing below the dock. The. lieutenant passed the photographs to the judge.

Crumpled and stained though they were, the acetate sheets told their story. The Kommandant stood in the officers' bar, a venue just visible from the prisoners' quarters. He was in conversation with the Judge's wife, leaning towards her, his hand amorously lying on her arm. The other hand encircled her waist. The images told a clear story. Taken with his concealedminiature camera and skilfully blown up and doctored during a nocturnal visit to the camp warders' developing room, they carried the authenticity of first-rate forgery.

The Captain gazed, his face whitening. At last he spoke, his words bringing a surge of joy and liberation to his prisoner.

'These are most interesting. I adjourn the court. We will hear more of this.'

His eyes settled with vengeance on the Kommandant.

*

'A lower court has already found you guilty of running a betting business without a licence. In addition I now find you guilty of perjury and of obstructing the police in the execution of their duties. Is there anything you want to say to the court before I pronounce sentence?'

'Well, seems to me I was entitled to defend myself. I mean, it was a purely formal offence. The other bookies do it with licences, I did it without. It's the same activity.'

'The matter of your trading without a licence has already been decided and your fine determined. Have you anything to say relevant to the other charges?'

'Not if just standing up for rights is going to get me into worse trouble. Not if just defending yourself gets you further and further into the -'

'That will be enough. In addition to the heavy fine already determined, I sentence you to a term of six months' imprisonment. I hope you will have learned your lesson. The court is adjourned.'

*

With reduction for his time under arrest and what the prison governor with a wry twist of the lips described as good conduct, six months became ten weeks. Even so, the term split Peter's life in two like a cleaver: from then on, there were separate ages - innocence and experience, pre-Strangeways and post. *[handwritten: Walton]*

Curiously, what divided the eras most, almost more than the interminable drag of time, was not his duties cleaning the exercise yard and the cafeteria with their detritus of dumped food, fag ends and improvised betting slips. The wall between past and future was built most during his hours spent in the Education Centre where, on the prison's notepads, the exploits of Burlington, hitherto a casual hobby, grew to become an obsession, a shield against the present and a gateway to a future suddenly graspable in his mind – the career of a writer.

The elapse of months was needed after his release to digest the events of a period which at the time stretched endlessly. Because he'd never thought about it, he was surprised to realise that imprisonment punished by depriving a prisoner of his freedom of movement. The stroll from the office across to The Fox and Hounds for a pint with Bob Tommelty and the others at lunchtime, the chance to nip down town on impulse and spend some money on a free day, at first no more than a niggle, soon became a huge constriction. The loss of Saturday afternoons watching Tranmere play in company with Red Thomas, even mid-afternoon amblings down to the cafeteria to gossip about Atlantic Finance's top brass, chafed and irked like some heavy, irremovable garment.

The other prisoners' compulsive need for hierarchy also dug deep. He recognised it as part of himself, the craving to excuse his own offences by pointing to those who'd committed worse. New prisoners were routinely sent to the jail for their first few weeks and since Peter's sentence was short he was not transferred elsewhere. Graded in criminality by the courts, the inmates, once they arrived, found themselves again classified and branded according to status: the child abuser lowest, the woman-attacker less so, the crack burglar a figure for veneration. Everyone was ranked. The non-judgmental world of the social worker had no resonance here.

In other ways, though, the sheer ordinariness of his fellows at first started surprise. Some had what he took for a criminal look – the clenched eyebrows and receding forehead – but most, at first meeting, could have been anyone: street traders, office workers, even policemen. But as acquaintance deepened the impression changed. There were weird, small characteristics which, Peter realised, sprang from inadequacy. Many could neither read nor right. Most had superstitions: the day of the week or month, the number at table, rituals with salt, silver coins, the order of putting on clothes. For every misfortune luck was the unfailing explanation. In a world out of control, ju-ju stepped in with its magic.

One man, a Scot who'd worked as electrician at a local jam factory, burst into sudden, fierce hatred when a mate spoke well of another jam manufacturer's product. Someone's mention of a liking for gin brought forth a similar outburst: a man had to drink whisky. When he found a fellow-Scot, the two formed an anti-English alliance: in Peter's third week a white-collar criminal, an Englishman, was found lying unconscious in the lavatories, beaten up. No one was ever found responsible though no one had any doubt. Under the strain of imprisonment, tribal loyalties glowered and burned.

After that, the English fraudster always came last to the canteen, always after visiting the lavatories, trembling-scared. At the end of the queue there was no one behind him.

Sharing a cell was itself a sentence. Blessedly, Peter's only companion - for his last two weeks – proved to be a West Country man called Francis, who spoke little and seemed to pose no threat of violence. When asked what his offence had been he mumbled something about things being best kept private. It was only two days before Peter's release that, apropos of nothing and without previous conversation, some need to confess seemed to come to him. He glanced at the door, then moved with his usual lurching gait over towards Peter and spoke in lowered tones, yet smiling.

'Right good bint, she were.'

'Sorry?'

'That got me sent here. Only thirteen.'

'But it were her that asked for it. No one'd say no to that.' He glanced again at the door, the cat-flap on its spy-hole closed, the small grill bared like the teeth of some rattling, steel monster. 'Won't tell on me, will you?'

'No. No.'

But from then on, the amiable smile took on in Peter's mind a touch of idiocy. Its hint of ingratiation became sinister, a threat to the harmless and meek.

*

He hadn't expected a posse of pressmen to surround him at the prison gate, though the odd fantasised headline had filmed in his mind: *Author Released Early; Burlington Creator Serves His Time.* Yet the eal world beyond bars came as a vacuum, a dilution of the fug of human contact. He imagined it as the thinness of British air to someone returning from the tropics, the lostness of a man demobbed after a Far Eastern war.

He walked round the city until dusk in vague distress, bewildered by the number of people, so many thousands each hurrying on his way with his own intentions unknown to others. How could they live those cold, atomistic lives? How could their own tiny purposes be sufficient to carry them forward?

He'd forfeited all chance of going back to Penny. There was only Havana House, none of whose occupants had visited him in Manchester, thank God. He'd have to go there. A line Margery had once recited hovered in memory: *Home is somewhere where, if you have to go there, they have to take you in.*

He delayed the return until dusk. That way he could slip in unnoticed, avoiding confrontations. The key was still in his pocket; he'd kept it safe during the long age of incarceration. And they couldn't, surely, have given his old room to anyone else; it had been vacant when he last visited.

Perhaps, if he delayed meeting any of them long enough, when they did meet he could make the encounter seem ordinary, a boring routine event, and so avoid a scene. *Never apologise, never explain,* Nobby Styles had said in the prison yard one day. There'd been wisdom in that clink.

He stole across the hall and up the stairs. Setting his hand on the doorknob was like arresting an old friend. The shiny porcelain bulb revolved, the door began its slow lunge. He peered inside.

Everything was as he'd last seen it. The desk, the typewriter, its mouth half-open to devour or extrude Burlington's latest adventure, a confetti of betting slips, a letter from some girl – he couldn't remember who. On the shelf behind his chair a photo of Penny and Joni. He walked across and with the reverence of a priest kissed the little girl. It seemed so long. Would he still recognise her?

But either a qualm about meeting her mother or the magnetic corridor of habit deflected him. He went to and picked up the telephone, installed – he believed without evidence - as a secret present from Aunt Flo on his twenty-first birthday (Why secret? Had she feared she'd arouse Margery's jealousy or hatred of her sister's interference? Or had she hoped he would ring her to talk in the evenings without treading the hallway where others might see him? Surely not to deliver her tirades at will and often? What a tangle this family was.)

'Hello, Red. Yeh, I'm out. Not that bad - I suppose. Okay. Okay. The racecourse, tomorrow, eleven.'

*

The racecourse was closed except to what the signs called 'Authorised Vehicles' – officials and employees. It wouldn't be open to the public again until the next meeting in a month's time. Peter and Red stood on a nearby hill and cast their eyes round the loop of fenced-off ground following the curve of the river. The talk was tinged with despondency.

'So what you planning now?'

Peter sucked his teeth. 'Dunno. You going to stay with what you're doing?'

Red had a temporary job with the Farm Census. Visiting local farms equipped with a spindle attached to a wheel, he pushed it round the borders of fields to measure their boundaries. A small dial on the spindle clocked up the distances. Unfortunately, at the end of his first week in the job he'd left the wheel lying on a farm track while he ate his sandwiches and a tractor had run over it, mangling it irreparably. As a result his wages had been docked. So far the job had earned him nothing.

'There's selling encyclopedias.'

'Nah. You're not intellectual.'

Upon reflection Red agreed.

'I wondered about…a bit of excitement.'

'Like what?'

'Dunno. Films. Television.'

Images flickered to mind: Kirk Douglas soiled and bloodied from D-Day combat embracing the spotless and silk-clad form of Bo Derek; Tom Cruse in Lincoln green swinging down on a forty-foot liana to carry away his bride-to-be; Clint Eastwood fearlessly confronting Chicago gangsters.

'Forget it. There's no way you'd get in.'

A pang of annoyance at Red's negativity touched him. They gazed across the half-sodden grassland in disaffected silence.

'I gather they've been having a spot of trouble here.' Peter decided against conflict. He nodded towards the racecourse pavilion. Bright after recent painting, its two storeys and timbered grandstand afforded a sweeping view of the course. 'That fellow Nash got the sack.'

'I saw that in the *Clarion*. Funny that, one of the high-ups getting fired for breaking the rules. Usually, it's just ordinary poor sods like us who never harmed anyone.'

'Mm.' The show of solidarity appeased somewhat. But in a moment memory jogged. 'No, he didn't break the rules. He split on the others who was breaking them.'

Slowly the story came back; even into Walton some news had percolated. Nash, responsible as Racecourse Steward for security and legal compliance, had been sacked after a dispute with the Directors. The source of the dispute was never admitted but according to the tabloids arose from a claim he'd made that racing law was being violated. What law they didn't say but around the clubhouse and bar there were rumours of race-fixing, bribes to jockeys to lose.

Yes, that was it. Nash had tried to make the Directors clean things up; but that wasn't their way. Peter had thought of raising the issue with Nash's successor, a former brigadier called Fox-Bewley whom he'd met in the racecourse bar but the man's brusque manner had put him off. All you could do with a martinet like that was keep him sweet.

'Be nice to get real evidence of what was going on, wouldn't it?'

'They hush it up.' Red turned his lips down. 'Scared of libel. No way you'd get proof.'

'Not even if you talked to Fox-Bewley, friendly-like – over a pint, say?'

'Friendly? You and Fox-Bewley friendly?' Red's laughter dismissed the idea. Adding satire to scorn, he added, 'Well, he's always in the racecourse bar after Board meetings.'

But Peter didn't laugh. 'Really. That snooty creep actually is? Now that's interesting. Really interesting.'

*

'Sorry, you can't come in here. It's only people who work here. Or get invited.'

The janitor at the Television Centre's reception desk was an overweight man with white hair, almost certainly a stand-in while the usual dollybird went for coffee. Peter decided on boldness.

'I am invited. Jim Gregson said to come round. He wants to do a report that includes me.'

'What, for *The Hidden World*?' The man blinked, uncertain. He looked round as if for help but no one was about. 'What's your line, then? I mean, what's this report about?'

Throat-clearing supplied vital seconds for thought. 'Crime. The one up North. The horrible one.'

'You mean...that little girl in the council house?'

The sweat of relief beaded Peter's neck. ''Course, what else? High time the TV companies got on to investigating that.'

'They say it could have been her father.'

Peter donned the knowing face of non-divulgence. 'You'd be surprised. You - would – be - surprised. So, where shall I find him? He said it was urgent.'

The janitor fumbled at his telephone. 'Hello, Cathy? It's a gentleman here, says Mr Gregson invited him to come and provide material for *The Hidden World*. About that crime up North...the little girl. Okay, I'll hold.' The man stared down across the atrium, avoiding distraction. His face paled with tension. 'Oh, Mr Gregson. There's a gentleman here.'

It took the presenter some time to remember. Occasional words were audible: 'When d'you say? I meet so many...' But mention of the crime up North brought decision. 'Yeh, I expect I did. All right, send him up. What's his name?'

The janitor looked up enquiringly. Peter leaned forward across the desk. For some reason an impulse of secrecy made him whisper. 'Paul Finchley. He won't regret asking me.'

As he entered the lift he wasn't sure why invention had taken over. Was it the civil servant's deep unease lest any information he released might be secret? Or, as with politicians, did evasion become a habit, even when the truth was sure to come out?

*

'But the man at reception – he said it was about some crime up North.'

'Nah, nah.' Peter put on the indulgent smile of one understanding a subordinate's mistake. He scanned the big studio, its ceiling gantried with lights, metal-boxed cameras, suspended microphones. Its size half-concealed the number of people it held, technicians with and without headphones, a man at a multi-dialled

144

console, a shirtsleeved man centre-stage, a dazzling platinum blonde dispensing coffee in paper cups. 'He must have got the wrong end of the stick. It's about this skulduggery on the racetracks. It's a national scandal. Just the sort of thing we ought to expose.'

Jim Gregson pulled a wry face, a thing Peter had never seen him do on television. His violet shirt with its frilly cuffs and pattern of pink flamingoes were faintly dizzying. Peter noticed that the heels of his handmade shoes were built up to augment his short stature. He reached up to accept a cup of coffee handed to him by a second girl, this one familiar from the small screen and it occurred to Peter that all the women on Gregson's programme were tall and glamorous, while all the men were short. He fought down the inward murmur, *Tell me more about zese dreams.*

'No, we haven't time to go into race-fixing. Time's so –'

'You wouldn't have to. I'll do it.'

Gregson halted. Peter searched his face. With a jolt he recognised fear, the fear of a rival in the programme-making stakes. Peter put on humility.

'Sorry, don't get me wrong. You'd present the programme. But I'd do the donkey work. Do the interview, get the evidence, like. Then you'd introduce and discuss it.'

'Have you any experience of interviewing?'

Peter assumed his *Is-the-Pope-a-Catholic?* smile. Experience of interviewing? Well, there'd been his interviews with Charles Scrimgeour. And didn't being hauled over the coals by old Purlock count? He gave a laugh. 'You could say that. You-jolly-well-might-say-that. Just give me a chance and you'll see.'

He'd feared further questions. But the pre-invented story about part-time interviewing for local radio in the West Country– *Radio Haywain*, he'd decided to call it – proved unnecessary. The presenter threw a harassed glance at his watch. It was the time to strike.

'All I need is a hidden camera. I'll deliver the goods, trust me.'

A tall, dandified man with distinguished-looking, silvery side-locks, one of several such men standing round the studio, was gesturing Gregson away. Gregson made a movement of flustered indecision.

'All right, we'll try it. Celandine,' he summoned the girl with platinum hair, 'would you see that this man is provided with one of the concealed cameras? And told how to use it. Take his name and details, we don't want to lose the equipment.'

He flounced across to the silvery man, casting Peter adrift like unsavoury flotsam.

'This way, please.' The girl moved towards the studio door, her rear swaying absorbingly over stiletto heels.

'I'd be delighted.' Peter lurched into motion. But though Celandine slowed to accommodate his pace he still failed to catch up.

*

'Oh, good evening. Mind if I join you?'

Peter put his briefcase on a vacant chair and settled his pint on the table at which Fox-Bewley was sitting. The bar was empty at this time of day. And Red Thomas was right. After an afternoon Board meeting when the Directors had dispersed, the Steward always stayed on to check the gates and lights before he went home. It was the ideal time to catch him.

'Let me get you another. What are you having?'

'That's very decent of you. I'll have another G and T, thanks.'

The drink bought, Peter felt he could stretch friendship further. 'Sorry, I haven't introduced myself. Paul Finchley's the name – not that it'll mean anything to you. Always been a keen racegoer. Like a flutter now and then.'

'I thought I'd seen you around.'

'Heavens yes, I've a great affection for the course. Splendid place, splendid fellows in charge. How about you? Enjoying your new job? Must be quite a change.'

With relief he watched as the brigadier launched into retrospection. A faint unease at calling himself Paul Finchley – the same name he'd given the television man – slowly subsided. Fox-Bewley would forget it anyway. So, possibly, would Jim Gregson: people seldom remembered a name at one hearing. And he'd struck lucky with Fox-Bewley's character, gruff and no-nonsense, not over-bright. He'd forget, too. As the reminiscences of foreign wars – the confrontation in Borneo, the reinforcement mission to Belize – emerged in staccato phrases it became clear that further enquiry about Peter's own history was unlikely. What interested Fox-Bewley wasn't Peter. It was himself. It was worth remembering: if you want to pass incognito, stick with the egotists.

With a quick glance he checked the briefcase but it was well-positioned, the camera's pinhole pointing at its prey. Yes. A bit odd, perhaps, set on an empty chair like that, but never mind. It was doing its work. He'd pressed the switch the minute he'd arrived.

''Course, there's bound to be aspects of your work here that'll be a bit frustrating.' Fox-Bewley's pause for a sip of gin and tonic gave the next opportunity. 'I know Carlton Nash got fed up when they wouldn't do anything to stop the – you know – the hanky panky, the backhanders and so on.' He said the last words with lowered voice, smiling. He reached for his drink. Under lowered eyebrows he watched his companion. Fox-Bewley returned the smile but said nothing.

They'd reached the moment. Peter breathed deep. His tone became ultra-casual.

'Do you think they care about it? I mean, when someone's paid to lose a race?'

This was it – the ultimate test. Peter straightened his face to moderate the grin. Don't be too complicit. Keep it cool. Stop holding your breath.

But the brigadier, too, was relaxing. He gave the tousled grey of his head a slow shake, grinning back. 'No, they don't give a damn.'

The camera was still there. Silent. At work.

'I presume after Nash's demise you won't be calling attention to the fiddles?'

Another grin, another shake of the head.

They discussed the coming season, the likely lads for the Gold Cup. There were even shared chortles at the foibles of various Directors. All on camera, recorded, incriminating. By the time Fox-Bewley's glance at his watch indicated locking-up time and they rose to leave, there wasn't much going on around the course that hadn't been mentioned, dissected, chuckled over. Not much Jim Gregson and *The Hidden World* wouldn't pay good money for.

Maybe even a career start for the interviewer.

The trouble, Peter reflected as he walked to the station, was that in a bar lulled by afternoon sun, canopied by the aromatic and mellow haze of gin, he'd rather grown to like Fox-Bewley.

*

'But you put the programme out. And it aroused interest.'

'Yes, yes. You did well.' Jim Gregson had seemed harassed on Peter's first visit. Now he seemed manic. Other staff shuffled into far corners of the studio. Celandine was nowhere to be seen. 'But it was a one-off. Permanent employment's another thing.'

'There was comment in the national press. The Steward's in deep trouble.'

'I'm sure he is.' Under his breath Gregson muttered a further phrase. Was it *Not the only one?*

'They surely can't fire him, can they – not for exposing crime, even theirs? That'd look even worse.'

Gregson's last tie of restraint seemed to snap. 'Look, I haven't the faintest what they do to the Steward. I don't know and I don't care. It's not my headache. So if you don't mind –' He tugged at the open neck of his shirt. A button broke free and skittered to the floor. 'Oh damn.' He stamped his foot, a petulant twelve-year-old.

'I can let you have lots more footage just as good as that.'

Gregson heaved a huge sigh. For the third time, he looked at his watch. Its hands seemed to be in the same place as they had the last time and Peter realised with a faint shock of absurdity that the watch had stopped. 'I'm sure you can but – let me speak frankly – I'm *not interested*. Do I make myself clear?'

'But why? Seeing it was such a success?'

This time the sigh was seismic. 'Let me tell you, then.' He spoke quickly, his words stabbed out in monotones. 'Your programme provoked fury from a multitude of viewers. They wrote in by the hundred and by the thousand. We asked you for evidence, actual concrete evidence, of - of the offence you charge people with and you provided nothing.'

'The video-recording itself –'

'- proved nothing. The idle gossip of an old buffer new to his job and a feckless youth –'

'He as good as admitted –'

'You caused me an untold, immeasurable amount of trouble and we couldn't defend it.'

'But your company's independent. You're supposed to speak the truth even if its's not popular.'

Gregson threw back his head, a cormorant swallowing. 'Ha!' He lowered it again. 'Now I have to ask you to go. I've more important things to do. Good bye. That's the way out.'

There was no Celandine to lead him out this time. Peter found his way to Reception where, surprisingly, the white-haired man was again on duty. Peter paused for the comfort of conversation. The janitor seemed sympathetic.

'You had a rough time?'

'I have. I got thrown out.'

'Who threw you, then?'

'Jim Gregson. *The Hidden World.*'

'How come?'

'They didn't like what I exposed. Wanted to keep it hidden.'

'Caused a fuss, did it?'

'But they shouldn't care about that. They're TV journalists.'

'You can't be too forthright on the box.'

'But it's an investigative programme.'

'They don't like investigations.'

The janitor nodded. 'Nah, they wouldn't. Nor would he - Mr Gregson.'

Peter halted. 'How do you mean?'

'His programme's being chopped, you know.'

'Not- not because of my piece?'

'Unlikely. Still, he wouldn't want any more trouble. He's got enough of that with the Chairman's daughter.' With one hand he made convex gestures in front of his belly.

Slowly, Peter nodded. 'I see. I didn't know that. They fire you for that, do they?'

'Can happen. If the Chairman takes offence. And has friends on the Board of Governors.'

'Even if the matter of his daughter's a private matter and he produces good programmes? Balanced, discreet, responsible?'

The janitor stroked a finger down the side of his nose. 'It's a different sort of discretion you need here. Be careful who you sleep with.'

At the door Peter paused again. 'Just out of interest, what was the young lady's name?'

The janitor chuckled. 'Unusual name it is. Celandine.'

Chapter 31
1982

'It's called solipsism,' he announced to Red Thomas one afternoon when his housemate came in from what Peter calculated ~restored~ must be his fifth recent job – as sole proprietor of the You Auto Learn driving school. 'It means you think only you exist.'

'Yeah?' Red took time to offer analysis.

'Yeah. I reckon it's what she' - he broke off, ashamed of coming so close to Margery's name –'it's what some people have.'

'Yeah?'

'It's like narcissism, only more so.'

Red moved his lips but this time the Yeah wasn't audible. He changed a losing game. 'I met Bob Tommelty in town. He's been doing an evening job, teaching English to foreign students at the College. He can't get on Tuesday, though. Wants someone to stand in.'

Peter gnawed his pencil. An evening out of the mill and out of the ordinary attracted him.

'Who are they, then, the students?'

'German mainly. Some Italian.'

'What's it pay?'

'Dunno. Don't matter to you, does it? You get enough from your books. Then there's the benefits.'

'Benefits aren't the same though. Not like doing a job.'

'You can ring and ask.' Red indicated the antique payphone Iolo Roberts had fitted at some date in the remote past. 'Why're you interested?'

Peter took another bite at the pencil. 'I could do with a night out.'

*

Peter had felt confident a writer would be able to teach English, even to foreigners. Especially to foreigners. For heaven's sake, didn't we all speak, read and write the stuff?

Even so, it wasn't easy.

'What does it make difference,' the young German with steel glasses wanted to know, '*among* and *amongst*? How do we tell?'

'Yes.' Peter took out his handkerchief, unfolded it, then refolded it, playing for time. He couldn't say it didn't matter; he'd said that twice already in response to enquiries about split infinitives and the use of *hopefully*. If he went on saying it these students would get the impression that the English spoke their language sloppily. He wasn't going to let that happen. Hopefully.

'*Amongst* is more sort of poetic.' He waited, aware of his pulse. Would a glare put this character off? No, it didn't.

'You have said *sort of*. What does it mean, this *sort of*?'

'Well, it's sort of *in general*. Not always, but by and large.'

At once he wished he hadn't said it. Oh God, *by and large.* Why did he *ask* for trouble?

The gaunt face furrowed as if affronted. Thoughts of war films and Gestapo officers swam through Peter's head. He tried the glare again. Again, no good.

'This means *near to*, this *by*. But near to what? And why *large?* Here have we one preposition and one adjective together. But how are they used? In the grammar book at the page one hundred and two we can read...'

The post mortem looked set to run and run. Sweat coated Peter's neck. What to do? Throw a fainting fit? He dismissed the idea at once. This Gestapo youth, Reinhard, might turn out to be a medical student during the day. He could turn the evening class into an anatomy or physiology session. How to manage the situation, then? Rush to the loo? Too much like a retreat. And attracting too much attention. Crabtree, the College Principal, might learn of it. Bob Tommelty had warned, students were interrogated about their classes afterwards. But what, then? The situation was desperate.

Blessedly, a voice intervened.

'It is only an idiom. So we don't need to know.'

Peter turned to the desk at the side of the front row. The girl who'd spoken – she'd answered to the roll-call as Francesca, an *au pair* from Milan - sat there, dark and beautiful. Equally welcome, a murmur of agreement with her ran round the class. The other students seemed as fed up with Reinhard as Peter was, even though they'd asked especially to be drilled in idioms. Peter felt confidence rebound.

'That's right. I don't think it's worth going into details like that. Now, the next exercise. Page a hundred and ten: idioms using the word 'it'.'

The remainder of the hour passed without major incident. Reinhard, of course, wanted to know what 'it' was. Was it the 'it' that attractive girls were said to have? Or the 'it' that went without saying? Or the 'it' that you hammed up when you overacted? With the class on his side, Peter replied yes to every question. Gestapo

Reinhard's face told him volumes: there'd be a complaint to Crabtree, a post mortem, lectures about the desperate need to come out well in the next inspectors' report. But Peter wouldn't be here by then. He'd have handed the class back to Bob Tommelty. The thought gave him intense pleasure. Tommelty in the brown stuff. And he himself would have got away. With *it*.

It was a pure bonus when, as the other students dispersed at the end of the class, he looked up from assembling his papers to find Francesca standing before him.

'Hello? What can I' – an unintended interpretation of the question made him falter – 'what can I do for you?'

'You are very kind to come when Mr Tommelty cannot. I would like to thank you.'

'I see. That's very nice of you.'

'I would like to go and buy you a cup of coffee.'

'Oh, I see.'

'In the coffee bar.'

'I see.' It was her eyes that took away speech. And, if you could take yours away and look lower... 'That's very nice of you.'

'No, it is you who are nice. Very nice.'

*

So late in the evening the coffee bar was sparsely peopled as they took a table Francesca chose in a corner away from the remaining customers. Relief at finishing the class inoculated Peter against other feelings. Even the vague consciousness that his companion had sat gazing at him from her front seat throughout the class scarcely registered. Returning from the counter she set down the cafeteria's statutory cups of murky brown liquid with the reverence of a priest administering communion.

'Sugar?'

Francesca shook her head with solemnity. A feeling of impropriety entered him, as if he'd been trying some inappropriate advance. As was not a bad idea. In connection with which, what *were* the rules about teachers and students in this place?

'You enjoying your stay in England?'

'Yes, I enjoy it very much.'

There seemed little else to say on the subject. 'Good.'

Francesca leaned forward. In sympathy, feeling something confidential afoot, Peter followed suit.

'You are married, someone has told me?'

God, it was getting intimate. 'Well er, yes, in a way. I mean I am but I haven't lived with my wife for a long time now.'

152

'You have a daughter?'

'Er yes. She's at school. Doing well. A clever girl. But I mean…I appreciate your interest but…I don't quite see…'

The dark locks fell about her cheeks as she strained further forward. Her lips, red and luscious, approached his own. At first drawing back, he checked himself, then resumed a reciprocal position. Francesca lowered her voice.

'In the newspapers we read that many men don't know who is the real father of their children.'

'I suppose not. So what..?'

'But you must be sure about yours?'

'Sure? Of course. I mean… You're suggesting Joni..?'

'You should not believe rumours. They are not always true.'

'Rumours? What rumours. What do you mean?'

'It is just what I hear.'

'What do you mean? You think another man –'

'Is what people say.'

Too many thoughts struggled to be heard. A logjam coagulated in him. Part of him wanted to say, it's utter rubbish, the worst sort of idle gossip, there's not a word of truth, while another part teetered on the brink of shouting, *What's it got to do with you?* But something silenced both. This girl, Francesca, had been gazing at him from her place at the side of the front row of desks all evening. Why hadn't he realised it? She might think this had everything to do with her. She could be motivated by jealousy or some sort of bid for his affections, a romance, an affair. Who could blame her, really? With a man like himself.

Still, mightn't what she said have some grain of..? There came back to him, as if retrieved from the memory of some computer, the day – the only day – he'd visited Penny's house. The day when, in response to Mrs Green's rebukes, he'd agreed to the wedding. With Penny, throughout the whole interview, not there. Only when he'd closed the front door did he look up and see her face at the bedroom window. And not alone. Didn't he remember sounds from upstairs that he at first hadn't registered? Hadn't a deep voice been one of them?

'You look so sad.'

He started, looked up. Oh, good Lord yes, the girl. Francesca. 'No. I'm all right.'

What on earth did she expect? That he'd be all right after being told a rumour like that? A rumour there was no way of checking and which, if there had been, would have been a degradation to Penny, a putting of her on trial, a shame that would destroy any remaining love of theirs even if the rumour later proved untrue.

'I think you don't live any more with your wife.'

'No.'

'It must be so lonely, just you alone.'

He nodded, barely hearing.

'Maybe you need some company, someone to make you happy.'

Another nod. It was like those days at school when he would come home in the deepest anger or disgust with what Purlock of Midge Sprewls or one of his classmates had done and then, the next morning, with every objective fact unchanged, had felt quite different about them. Perhaps, in the morning...

'Why don't we go and have dinner at a restaurant together?'

He found himself looking at her as if for the first time. Francesca. It was another turn of the leaf of how he saw things. She was beautiful. And young. And like the flicking-through of one of those booklets of cine-type pictures that used to circulate at school, many gradually changing photographs glimpsed at speed making a kind of motion picture, her image brought to mind other days, other girls. The girl in the Paris hotel who'd promised no strings, no ties, if he would make her pregnant. The girl at the Inverary summer school with its chalets on the hillside who'd whispered, so low it had taken him a moment to distinguish the words: 'My friend and I both sleep in big beds. There's plenty of room. For one more.'

And now Francesca.

'Who told you,' he said, 'about my daughter?'

She coloured, embarrassed. Even the armour of shamelessness had chinks. 'Herself,' she said. 'Penny tells me.'

He stared at her without expression.

'Is true. We have met at Bob Tommelty's party for end of term.'

'Oh. I didn't know about that.'

'It is just for Bob's class and our friends.'

'And you believe this rumour about Penny?'

'I think it is true.'

Loss rose in him, anger both at the imputation and at its unprovability, the frustration of a charge he couldn't rebut. He wanted to shout, 'I don't care what all of you do or say or think. I want to live my life my way. I hate you all.' But there was no audience in the empty canteen save this beautiful tale-bearer he

154

scarcely knew and the sales girl leaning mindless behind the counter as the clock ticked towards ten.

Like the grappling roots of a tree tossed by storm, anger gripped his belly. Desire and revenge coalesced as he moulded a smile on his face.

'Okay,' he said. 'Let's go and have dinner. Then back to your place.'

Chapter 32
1982

'There was people came round for you.'

Red Thomas displayed his usual elegance of expression. *Came round for you?* Peter could see it: policemen with truncheons, Inland Revenue snoopers, bailiffs. But for which offence? Imagination failed.

'What sort of people?'

'A bird. With long black hair, bit of a dish.'

'Italian? Called Francesca?' A mistake. Never tell Red a bint's name. It could set him investigating.

'That's her. You been...you know?'

'No. Well, yes. But I didn't tell her where I lived.' It had been at her place, not his, after the evening class and the meal.

'She was with a fellow. He's coming back later.'

'What sort of fellow?'

'Said he was an art dealer.'

'An art dealer?'

'Yeh, said he had some deal for you. Too good to turn down.'

'But who is he? And why me? I don't know any art dealers.'

'Said something about you creatives having to stick together.'

'Creatives? Like in advertising?'

The man must have meant Burlington. Peter was puzzled. He'd never thought of his fiction as creative. It was simply writing down facts - what he'd do if he got the chance. 'So the girl put him on to me?'

'Dunno.'

'And she got my address from – yes, that'll be it – her night-class tutor, Bob Tommelty. What the hell's it all about?'

Red shrugged, unhelpful to the last. 'Hang around and see. He'll be back at eight.'

*

'Yes, Tommelty. He said you knew a lot of arty crafty people.'

The man at the door of the mill had a faintly derisive manner. He looked about thirty, with a Lenin beard and a neckerchief. While he spoke his eyes pried over Peter's shoulder into the mill. The phrase 'too clever by half' came to mind.

'Arty-craf-? No. Hardly any.'

156

'You're a writer, aren't you?'

'That doesn't mean –'

'But you're a writer?'

The man made as if to step into the doorway but Peter didn't move. 'Well, I write.'

'What?'

'Novels.'

'Mm. Your mother's something in the art world, isn't she?'

The third degree had gone on long enough. 'Look, who are you?'

The question fetched a metallic but genuine-sounding laugh. 'I'm Nigel Crean, the art dealer. I'm looking for some help placing sales.' The eyes still wandering.

'Sorry. Can't help.'

Peter stepped back half a pace, then reversed the movement when Nigel Crean again started forward as if to enter the mill. They came to rest a foot apart - almost a confrontation.

The newcomer's manner changed. 'Look, old man. If your old lady's in the art world she's bound to know some buyers. Patrons, collectors, you know, the sort who'd be interested in newly-discovered works – some of them old masters and the like. After all, there's money in it.'

Peter halted. The new, glutinous approach was no more likeable than the earlier, aggressive one; but the word *money* had been used.

'You've discovered some old masters?'

Crean examined the polish of his brogues. 'Look, if you know anything about the art world you'll know that in World War Two the Nazis looted hundreds of art treasures. A lot of them are still missing. I travel round hunting them down. With, I may say, some success.'

'Why don't you sell them yourself?'

'No time, old boy. I do the hunting. I need someone else to do the selling. Someone with art connections. At three per cent commission.'

'Three per cent of..?'

'Of the sale price. Which could be a hundred thousand, a million. Could be more.' For the first time the man looked at Peter directly. He knew interest when he saw it. He edged forward again. 'You up for it?'

Peter battled with confusion. He had no connections with the art world at all. Well, almost none. But Margery was always eager to introduce anyone who showed interest in her circle. She scattered the names of arty friends like confetti. And at the moment Burlington had hit the rocks, becalmed and out of ideas. Nigel Crean might be a prune but it would be a new adventure - what Red Thomas, in words used to describe his shelfstacking job, might call 'better than a kick in the pants.' Peter surveyed the hacking jacket and anorexic trousers.

'When?'

'Eleven tomorrow? Number 20a, Melbourne Place off Cranston Street.'

'And your phone number?'

'Don't have one, old man. Can't be at any hanger-on's beck and call. See you tomorrow, then.'

Hands thrust into side-pockets, his thumbs hooked outside, Crean turned and strolled off down the hill. On the road below a glint caught Peter's eyes. Peering down, he made out a car waiting, a two-seater sports model, its long silver bonnet gleaming. The fruits of selling others' pictures.

The encounter had ended abruptly and yet the man had seemed, somehow, the sort you couldn't shake off, a clinger. A strange thought arose: the only way to rid yourself of someone like Crean was to promise to see him again.

*

'Excuse me. Can you tell me where Melbourne Place is?'

The passer-by, the fourth Peter had accosted, looked as puzzled as the first three. Then his face broke into a grin. 'Oh, that. Yes, you can't see the street-sign. It's behind a pile of rubbish. You go down that alley there and it's fourth on the left. Looks like a dustbin zone but some people still live there, so they say. Good luck.'

'Do I need luck?'

'Well, there are streetfights there, the occasional murder. It's known for druggies.'

'I see.'

'Don't worry. Just walk quickly and leave soon. Have a nice day.'

*

There were no house numbers. The term 'dustbin zone' seemed accurate. Two cats stood in mutual suspicion among the plastic rubbish-bags, then moved on. Over the corpse of another creature – curiously, it seemed to be a badger – a multitude of maggots milled like the shimmer of silver-foil on a dancer's dress.

The decaying flesh emitted a sweet, sickly smell that followed him down the cobblestone alley, sticky on mouth and clothes.

Yet it had been a superior area in its day, a sidestreet of stables for the prosperous merchants of Liverpool and Wirral. Above and between the big wooden doors that had once sheltered gigs and traps, landaus and hansoms, he peered into tiny windows now graced by curtains of green mould and the lace handiwork of spiders. Why were there no numbers? Was it that in the days of the place's glory the numbers had been screwed in brass only on the front doors lining the next street? Or did everyone in those days know precisely who lived where? Or – the belated thought brought less comfort – did the present residents prefer a street with no name, no pack-drill? He paused in unease.

There were houses only on one side of the street. Opposite them, the back walls of other, anonymous buildings, possibly warehouses, presented a blank brick face. Well, if there was a 20a, and therefore presumably a 20, all the houses must have even numbers. Taking a chance, he made the assumption that the house nearest to Cranston Street was number 2. He walked along, counting. Ten, twelve – a good many of the houses might be divided, if the appearance of bottles of washing-up liquid in more than one window of the same dwelling afforded any guide – sixteen, eighteen, twenty. But no door. His eye scouted the garage with its poky windows without success. He hammered on the door.

There was no reply. If Nigel Crean really wanted a salesman for his art treasures why hadn't he given clearer instructions on how to find him? Or would that have shown too much respect? Peter picked up a small piece of slate seemingly dislodged from the higgledy piggledy ranks lining the roof and, aiming with care, directed it at an upstairs window. No response. He tried again.

The game was to attract attention without breaking anything. He'd played it before, at one of Red Thomas's numerous former residences. It was easier here in the silence of the sidestreet. The loudness of the impact gave a guide to the right amount of force to use. And it was quite fun, if you didn't run out of slate.

The proviso mattered. At his fourth attempt he was obliged to use an entire slate, having run out of smaller pieces. Resting one end of it against a wall he trod on the sloping surface in an attempt to break it in two. But it was surprisingly resistant. He gave up. He would throw it whole.

The enterprise required something of the skill of ducks and drakes; you had to hurl the slate flat, spinning it as it flew. He swung

159

and released. The slate soared over the lean-to garage and with an exactitude that aroused his pride struck the window end-on. There was a squeal as from a tortured cat and at the same time a low, hollow crack. A crack appeared across the window as, in a long descent, the slate clattered down the stable roof and jangled to the ground.

Peter stared at the outcome of his endeavours. By rote his face adjusted to an expression of pained innocence. When a face appeared at the window he thought of running. But it was Crean, wasn't it, the man he'd come to see? For money. He brought out a smile and waved. The man's own wave – more with a fist than a hand – faltered as he lowered hands on hips, akimbo. He raised the cracked window's sash.

'It's me, Peter Munnerly. Can I come in?'

Crean's face, puckered with annoyance at the breakage, vanished and only after several minutes reappeared, sauntering out of an unnoticed side door. Wearily he gestured Peter in.

*

'My studio.' Nigel Crean threw a hand offhandedly round the attic room. 'You should have rung first.'

'You didn't give me your number. There could be a dozen Creans.'

'Unlikely. I'd be the only Nigel. Sit.'

The studio's contents consisted largely of two large and one smaller table on which rested a variety of prints – old masters, most of them seemed – among an exploded cluster-bomb of bottles and jars. Beneath a skylight set into the sloping ceiling, an easel and chair stood facing a dais on which a couch rested. It seemed more the habitat of a practising artist than of a collector.

'Do you paint, yourself?'

'Have to. No one else would dream of painting me.'

Peter made a show of laughing but the joke, though in a way witty, somehow wasn't funny. Because of its teller? As if remembering something, Crean circumnavigated the room, tidying away what looked like a cocoa tin, a jam jar and a setsquare. Peter thought he glimpsed a roll of toilet paper being thrust behind some bare canvases. Something about the scene seemed odd. The languor of his acquaintance's stroll didn't fit the abruptness of his movements. There came to mind Peter's own hurried hiding of *Playboy* magazine under a cushion when Aunt Flo paid a visit. Margery didn't seemed to mind.

160

'So you've looked out some active collectors of art works?'

'Yeh.' It wasn't true but he would do it the next time he saw Margery.

'Well then, it's just a question of selling.'

'Selling the ones you find.'

'Yip.' Crean pointed his toe, this time clad in a trainer, to flick along the floor an invisible piece of detritus. He twisted his gaze out of the skylight. 'They may have doubts, some of them. In which case...'

'I just mention you. A reliable source.'

Again the hesitation. 'Yes. Well... Who exactly are you going to approach?'

'I haven't brought the list. It's at home.'

'Tristan Wenscombe's a good one to try. He took a Renoir I unearthed. He has a place near Hamilton Square.'

'Can you recommend anyone else?' The onus of finding outlets seemed to have shifted.

'There's Sep Taylor. The Galaxy Gallery's worth an approach – Merlyn Stell. But it's best if you find your own buyers.' In subdued staccato he added, 'Don't go to Heneage.'

'No, of course not.' Whoever Heneage was. 'Haggles too much, does he?'

'He's a bloody snooper.' Crean checked himself. The vulpine smile returned. 'Yes, yes. A bit cheese-paring. Best not to bother him. Hold on, there are a few suggestions I jotted down.'

He walked with unusual haste out of the studio into a side-room. While he waited Peter's gaze wandered round the nearer of the big tables. It supported a tin marked *Woodstain*, a packet of Gillette razor blades and, most curious of all, a shining, new tin of Cherry Blossom black shoe polish. Well, he supposed it was important to look smart when you dealt in art works. But why the razor blades and shoe polish? *Black* shoe polish. Hadn't Crean's shoes been brown?

*

The Galaxy Gallery stood in a sidestreet off the Wallasey sea front. Drawing up on the double yellow line along the kerb, Peter craned sideways to view it before venturing in. Someone – presumably the proprietor, Merlyn Stell – had fitted a broad plateglass window into its narrow frontage. Past the modernist paintings on display there, it seemed to go far back, deep into the Victorian block. Along the resulting tunnel-like room trendily-

161

placed ceiling and floor lights cast their beams at a variety of angles, recalling photographs of the London sky in the Blitz.

The pictures, though, were distinctly end-of-century. Whorls of vivid purple spiralled on white and yellow backgrounds. What might be the black and violet leaves of environmentally distressed water lilies coagulated on a pond of blood. A naked woman's ear seemed to have become attached to a huge, dropsical thigh, not obviously her own. The prospect of selling Nigel Crean's newly-discovered van Ruisdael here seemed remote. But at Tristan Wenscombe's place, and before that at Sep Taylor's, the prospect had seemed no better but had proved wrong: both had bought with some enthusiasm. Success bred confidence.

Sep, he'd discovered, was short for Septimus. Tristan, Septimus and now Merlyn. You had to be christened into the art game. Peter tightened the knot of the tie Red Thomas had lent him, part of Red's uniform during six weeks of unsuccessful employment as a meter-reader for British Gas, and rubbed his shoes to a faint shine on the back of his trouser legs. Time for the lion's den.

He was about to park where he'd stopped but the sight of a traffic warden's wasp-coloured uniform brought a change of plans. Learner drivers were supposed to be supervised. And to show L plates. Edging the car into motion, he gave a wave of heartwarming friendliness to the warden as the man approached, notepad at the ready, peering down at the car's number plates. Luckily, Peter reflected, he'd rubbed mud on them to ensure illegibility. Showiness wasn't his style. Not that it mattered, anyway. It was Bob Tommelty's car.

After ten minutes' search for a parking place he set out again for the gallery on foot, carrying the padded picture-case that contained his offering with extreme care. He pushed open the shining tubular door handle and went in. The silence of the place, smooth and beautiful, resembled Meissen porcelain. The room was totally empty.

'Ehem, good morning.'

A minute's silence. Then a tall man appeared from nowhere. Merlyn Stell, presumably. He, too, was smooth and beautiful. The maroon cravat set off his mauve suit to perfection. The taper of his trousers brought to mind a languid secretary bird. Peter cleared his throat again.

'Mr Stell?

'Hm, yes.' The tone suggested a distaste for the familiarity of names.

'I spoke on the phone to your assistant last week. About this.' He tapped the van Ruisdael under his arm.

'Mm. That was my wife.'

'Ah.' Merlyn was married. Nature was a marvellous thing. 'She took a photograph of it. Said she'd consult you before making an offer.'

'Ye-es.'

'I expect you'd like to see the picture yourself. It's from his later period. Mr Crean bought it from a Paris art dealer, along with the authenticating papers. It was quite a find. A treasure trove.'

'Ye-es. Perhaps if we...'

Launching again into a repeat of Nigel Crean's sales talk, Peter opened the case. Its display position - propped up, still in its case, against a wall on whose upper reaches a Lowry showed matchstick men milling across a vista of factory chimneys - was less than ideal. But it would make Merlyn Stell stoop, which would be fun.

But no, the exhibitor wasn't going to be demeaned. 'Yes.' He dismissed the artwork with the petulant gesture of a testy aunt. 'My wife's photograph of it was sent down to London, to Millington's, and they compared it with other van Ruisdaels for style and so on. We shall need to have one of their valuers up for verification, of course, but the provisional verdict is that it's, well' - he seemed reluctant to use the language of commitment – 'probably genuine. If you could leave it here for a week I may have a client.'

'Are you adequately insured? It could be worth – seven figures.' Peter revelled in the prepared vagueness as much as in the claim itself. Nigel Crean had given him a kind of power.

The petulance returned. 'I think you can trust us to see to that.' Stell snapped his fingers. It seemed the equivalent of stamping his foot. 'What sort of, er, what sort of price were you thinking?'

Time to play canny. 'Won't your man from Millington's give us a guide?'

'I suppose so.' He added, 'My clients don't have infinite resources.'

'Van Ruisdaels don't come cheap.'

*

There were two more sales the following month: a Braque and a Corot both fetched six-figure sums, both certified genuine by the experts from Millington's. Even with royalties from the

Burlington novels now beginning to flow more fully, the prices struck Peter as staggering. Becoming rich was so easy! A world he'd only read of in the tabloids, the world of filmstars and footballers on half a million a year, of yachts off Cannes and villas in Moustique, suddenly began to feel real, within grasp. Unbalanced by the suddenness of the change, he bought a five-year-old Ford as a first taste of opulence and enrolled with the local Here-We-Go driving school. At the end of his test he sat with open mouth, awaiting the examiner's verdict.

'You didn't signal when you were turning right at The Three Stags.'

Peter made a gesture as if to say, *Come on, we don't bother about minutiae.*

'You broke the speed limit twice along Telegraph Road. Fifty in a thirty-mile-an-hour zone.' This time it was more *Oh look, don't let's quibble.*

'And you were slow with the emergency stop. In a real emergency you could have mowed down a dozen pedestrians.'

'Aw, shit.'

Rejected, he decided to try again – some time. But the episode left its lesson. Getting money was easy, dead easy. Learning the commonplace skills that a million ordinary punters could manage was hard. How, for instance, had Charles Scrimgeour and the other directors at Atlantic Finance and Shipping made their pile? Not by hard work. Not by possessing unusual skills or understanding the money-market gambles that juniors like himself had undertaken. Partly, maybe, by inheritance – another sleight-of-hand – but partly by getting in on the right racket at the right time, in their case the manipulation of pieces of paper for profit, for enormous profit. Come to that, it had been the secret of the Munnerlys' success. The source of their pride.

All in all, he preferred the world of financiers and filmstars and footballers, the illusory world of dreams. The world of Cannes and Moustique, fast cars – chauffeur-driven, they'd have to be – and yachts and helicopters. That was his kind of world. Why not? That was where Burlington lived.

Yet as the weeks of work for Nigel Crean turned into months what puzzled him most was where, between the two worlds, Crean should be placed. Each time he called on Crean to report successes the routine was fixed. On his pressing a half-concealed bell beside the mews' unobtrusive side-door he waited, sometimes five minutes, for Crean to let him in.

'Good, so you've made a sale,' Crean would say, not looking at him. 'Right. You'll get your commission at the month's end. Beginning to like it, are you?'

Although Peter grunted assent the oddness of the whole process lodged in his mind and grew. Where did Crean find this steady flow of undiscovered old masters? He didn't seem to travel much; he was always in when Peter called without warning. Why did it always take him so long to answer the door? And, even granted that he was an artist in his own right, what did he do in his studio all day? When Peter arrived there were no new paintings on display. The easel always stood empty.

At first he tried asking.

Crean began to smile, then checked himself. 'Oh, I get around. Not recently perhaps.'

'But you've come up with several big finds recently.'

Again mirth was at once reined in by evasiveness. 'Yes, well, not exactly. There are others. Agents.'

'You have agents working for you?'

A new, dismissive tone. 'I shall be going down to London a week on Wednesday. There are still a lot of interesting works to examine down there.'

'From World War Two?'

'That...and other things. Now, let's get the finances of these last transactions sorted.'

With finality he strode over to one of the tables that stood laden with blank canvases and jars. And it was then that, reaching down to open a drawer under the freight of assorted containers, that he paused to remove a tin perched on the edge. As he shuffled it at speed behind what looked curiously like a camera and a stack of acetate sheets, Peter noticed the label: *Nestle's Condensed Milk*. For his morning coffee break? No. Peter had seen him make his coffee using ordinary milk. As an occasional change? Unlikely. The stack of empty wine bottles under another table showed his preferred variant. The feeling of oddity returned. There was something weird about this whole business.

As Peter took the commission, a wad of banknotes neat in the grip of a rubber band, his newfound source of income seemed sufficient to afford a rail fare to London. A week on Wednesday.

*

Crean would surely arrive at the station by taxi. Unused to extravagance, Peter took an early bus. His ticket bought, he waited at the end of the central platform, concealed in a gap between the station buildings. The eight twenty, the main train to Euston, would be the one. If he hadn't miscalculated.

And no, he hadn't. There he was, Crean, smart in short raincoat, carrying one of those new capacious briefcases with a slide-sneck lock. Why should he need one that big? He didn't look natty, not like Merlyn Stell or the other gallery-owners. Only an air of casual brass nerve, an aura of cocky self-assurance, picked him out from the other commuting passengers, the businessmen making visits to the firm's head office, the town hall officials bound for meetings at the Ministry. As the train drew up Crean sprang into a first-class coach at the front. Peter slid behind his newspaper in a rearward coach. He'd have to keep his eyes open in the Euston crowds. He mustn't lose sight of his prey.

*

If the building had a name he didn't see it. A public building, anyway, rather like a library or reference room, not the private gallery or art collector's den Peter had imagined. At a wary distance he followed Crean in.

Through the dark wood of the swing door he entered a large hall, its entrance dominated by a reception desk at which two women sat: one middle-aged and bespectacled, the other young with a good bust. Neither stirred as Peter, with restrained haste, pushed past.

The walls on all sides were lined with books, many of them large, the sort in which maps or more likely prints of paintings might be kept. Below and around, under a ceiling heavy with plaster casts of cherubs and seraphs, a scattering of people sat at wide shining tables, reading or studying pictures.

For a moment he thought he'd lost sight of Crean. Then he saw him again, in a recess, reaching for a large volume on a shelf. Where to sit and watch unseen? Peter spotted the ideal place, a long table divided lengthways into two separate rows of study places by a wooden partition. Heart jumping, he hurried to an end seat on the side away from Crean. Round the partition he could peer to see what Crean was doing. A book someone had been reading lay open on the table. He pulled it towards him and feigned absorption.

Neither librarian moved. The silence of the place made any movement conspicuous but only he, Peter, seemed to feel the tension. In a moment he poked his head round the wooden panel.

Crean had taken the volume from the shelf and spread it open on his table. Open but not flat. The part of the book nearest to Peter was propped up by something – some papers, perhaps, from the briefcase he'd brought in – so that it was impossible to see at what page the book was open. But in any case Crean wasn't reading. Instead he seemed to be carrying out some operation on it, using both hands, the left one holding something in a fixed position while the right one drew a line or manipulated an instrument, like a draftsman preparing a blueprint.

Peter couldn't look for long; it might attract attention. He was on the point of withdrawing his head when the hiss of someone expelling breath deflected his eyes to the seat at the other side of the partition. There, a woman with her hair in a bun was glaring at him.

'What do you want?'

'Oh, sorry. I didn't realise –' A gold filling lent one of her front teeth a demonic look. It glinted in the light from Victorian chandeliers overhead.

'Well, you realise now. Kindly mind your own business.'

'I wasn't trying –'

A sardonic snort. 'Oh no. I've heard that one before.'

'Sorry.' Peter withdrew his head. Abashed, he lounged back in his chair, extending his feet. They came into contact with something, something soft and mobile. The bun-wearing woman's feet. Quickly, he withdrew them. The last thing he wanted was to be reported to the librarian.

But he was forgetting Crean, the whole purpose of his trek to London. Keeping well back from the partition, knees tucked well in, in desperation he leaned sideways, straining to see Crean's table. But it was empty. Crean had gone.

Peter stood up, just in time to see a man who might be Crean vanish through the turnstile and swing door. He felt an impulse to run after him but it would have been fatal. The librarians, at least the middle-aged one without the bust, would sense something awry and stop him. His manner was bound to betray agitation. All he could do was go to the shelf where Crean had sat and try to find the volume.

Sweating, he rose and tiptoed with concealed speed, first backwards to get away from the bun woman, then by a circuitous route round the hall to Crean's recess. He sensed the bun woman's glare following him as he moved but kept his eyes fixed ahead. They'd done that leaving Hitler's bunker, the Chancellery staff, as they passed through the western troops who stood surrounding it. 'Stare straight in front,' they'd been told. 'Avoid eye contact at any price.' The advice held just as true with bun women. Or bust-free librarians.

It took him several minutes to find the right volume. Whichever it was, it stood exactly aligned with the others, hiding any sign of extraction. Only one clue told which it was – a disturbance of the fine dust coating the top of its closed pages. Where its neighbours stood immaculate, the crucial one carried the prints of fingers. Peter took it down and let it fall open on the table. He knew at once he'd found the right page: *Monet: Cornfield near Argenteuil*. On one of his visits to Crean's place he'd spotted a book of Monets open on a table. This was it, all right.

But why had Crean examined this particular painting? And why had he tilted the book so no one could see what he was doing? What *had* he been doing? Peter examined the picture. There was nothing unusual, nothing suspect about it. Except –

He leaned forward. Breathing more heavily than usual from the strain of his encounter with the bun woman, he'd blown two tiny specks on to the table. They stood out, minute but clear, contrasting with the polished dark mahogany. Specks of the superior paper the book was made of. As if it had been…cut? He pressed the pages apart where they joined the spine. Crean couldn't have…?

But he had. Yes! Peter pressed the join wider. Just at its side, a bare millimetre up the page of Monet's *Cornfield*, ran a precise, finely-cut line. It was where the specks of paper had come from. It had been severed. With some precise, surgical instrument. The old page taken out and a new one stuck in. A tiny bubble of adhesive stood out, the merest pimple, sole evidence of the deft, secret operation of fraud.

But why? Why doctor a picture in this public building, and with such care?

Like the collapse of a house, it became clear. This must be where Crean's London contacts, the men from the galleries, from Millington's, came to check on a picture's authenticity. It could only be used when the picture Crean produced was known to exist, a work gone missing during the War. Most of his finds were unknown, merely recognised by their style and technique. But for the others, this was the checking-place. And so – yes, the camera, the tripod and lighting equipment in Crean's studio - he'd photographed a picture in his possession, then come here to substitute his photo for the genuine one in the book. That way, anyone checking would find an exact likeness. He'd be comparing a fake with the photograph of a fake. Snap!

And for six months – no, more, eight or nine – Peter had been implicated in this trickery. A criminal fraud.

*

'So what you going to do?' Red Thomas emphasised the question by hammering the marmalade jar on the table. Peter wished he'd cut down on questions and give some answers.

'Dunno. If I'd got wise to this before I started…'

'But you didn't.'

'All right, all right, I didn't. But I do now.'

'So what you going to do?'

Peter wondered if it was shelf-stacking that made you like this. No, Red had been the same when he'd worked as a storeman at Argos and as invoice-checker at Redcliffe's, the builder. He'd be quite good at that. He should have stayed there.

'I could just quit and say nothing.

'And let him go on getting away with it?'

He meant Crean. 'Or I could tell him he's rumbled and try to get him to stop.'

'He wouldn't like that. He wouldn't stop.'

'I'm just going through possibilities.' The sheer negativity was maddening. 'Or I could report him to the police.'

'They'd get you as well, then.'

'I know. Not that I knew Crean's game till now.'

'They won't believe that.'

'And they might want to refund my share of the loot to the guys he's swindled. The experts.'

He spat the word with contempt. Old Purlock, so proud of his headmastership, had been an expert. Midge Sprewls. Charles Scrimgeour, the high financier. All the high-up guys in the news, politicians and businessmen, weather forecasters, economists. What a fraud eminence was.

And, to tell the truth, he had some sympathy with Crean. After all, if his pictures were as good as Monet's, wasn't it fair to charge art dealers the full price for them? Come to that, if these guys were experts oughtn't they to spot the fraud? Recollections of Crean's studio came back to him: the tin of condensed milk, the Nescafe jar, another jar of what looked like ground-up old brick, some soap powder. *That* was what they were – all constituents in Crean's forgeries. And the experts certified them genuine. Even the canvases the fakes were painted on can't have been manufactured in Monet's time. It was all so preposterous. These guys got what they deserved.

'I think I'll just get quietly out of the racket.' He raised a hand to make himself some coffee but the label, Nescafe, brought a change of mind. He turned to the tea caddy. 'Or I could warn Millington's. Anonymously.'

fact

*

In either course of action was a starter. Unwilling to run the risk of having to repay large sums of commission he'd already spent, he couldn't go to the police. Equally, if it was shady for him to sell fake pictures as genuine, it would be no better if done by someone else, his replacement if he resigned. He didn't decide to confront Crean with his skullduggery. But as it happened the charge came out unplanned.

'So you've sold nothing since last time?' Crean's voice had a built-in sardonic tone.

'No.' A gulp of breath. 'Matter of fact, I didn't do the rounds this week.'

'Too much like work?'

'I decided to find out more about these pictures before I tried again.'

'Oh yes? Like what?'

'Like where exactly they come from. There seem to be an awful lot of them. And yet you don't travel much. Hardly at all.'

'You don't know. You only call in now and then.'

'But you're always here.'

'Not always. I wasn't that time after Easter.'

The smart answers, the truths told with intent to deceive, roused irritation. Peter marched to a tall cupboard in the corner of the room, a cupboard never once opened during his visits, and threw open the door.

'Hey.'

But Crean's shout of objection was ignored. 'There!' Peter pointed up to the crowded shelves. On them stood a pedlar's fair of oddments, many of which he'd seen lying about before: not just the condensed milk and Nescafe but a tin of Lyle's syrup, a wad of putty, some Blue-Tac, a ruler, string, a jar full of used paint brushes and below them, where the shelves had been removed, a tottering sheaf of canvases. As one canvas began to fall Peter seized it and held it up.

'Is this where you keep your Monets?'

Crean forced his way between Peter and the cupboard and slammed the door. He grabbed the canvas.

'You mind your own bloody business. Get away from my property. And keep your nosing to yourself. Bloody creep.' He shouldered Peter away, towards the door.

170

He'd never been like this on any previous visit, furious, deeply rattled. And it was that, the venom and muttered vitriol, that told the whole story. Peter lolled against a table.

'How long does it take you, Nigel?'

'Never you -. What do you mean, you prying shit?'

'How long does it take you to knock off a Monet? Using the condensed milk and instant coffee, a touch of putty or Blue-Tac? An hour? Two?'

The sour turn of lip persisted but slowly composure returned. Crean gave a grudging smirk. 'Depends. If it's a repro it can take days. If it's a new find, twenty minutes.'

'That's for a Monet. What about, say, a Van Gogh, or a Vermeer?'

'About the same for Vincent. I don't do Vermeers. They're too rare.' The smirk had become ingratiatory now, a complicity. 'You're going to have to keep your lips sealed tight from now on.' He watched, the eyes narrow as needles.

The thrill of power rose in Peter as if from the Ecstasy tablets he'd once taken at a party. It was an experience wholly new to him. He had this man at his mercy. But the memory of others with power jostled his elbow, jockeying the pleasure aside. He didn't want to be like Midge Sprewls and Scrimgeour and those old figures in the dark pictures on the stairs at Havana House, George Munnerly and Rosina and Amos, people congealed with pride and power. True, you weren't supposed to look down on people but if it stopped you being like them..?

Crean misinterpreted the hiatus.

'All right. I'll raise what you get to five per cent. We'll get it back through higher prices. The experts'll still buy. Now that we're well known. Respected.'

But Peter shook his head. 'No. You won't raise it to anything. You'll stop painting fakes. Or I'll drop a line to Millington's.'

His footsteps padded in the ensuing silence. At the door he paused to look back. Crean was standing stock-still, the look of a man grievously wronged on his face, a man who'd made a fortune only by milking those whose expertise, like his own, was fake, who valued not beauty, only profit.

For a moment Peter thought: in a world like this how do you tell crookery from best practice?

Nor was the thought displaced when two burly men in police uniform brushed passed him on the steps, making their way through the door he'd opened, up to Nigel Crean's studio.

Chapter 33
1981

Inside the door of the mill a red and black mat inherited from previous occupants served to absorb soil, grass and gravel brought in on Peter and Red's boots. En route for the lidless dustbins outside, Peter noticed a worm squirming in the mud that encased the mat and, from some vague thought of cleanliness mixed with an impulse of kindness, picked it up and returned it to the thistles and nettles outside. As he stepped back over the threshold his foot caught on the mat, dislodging it from its dugout. Caked earth crumbled from its fibres and was blown by an incoming gust of wind across the floor. A colony of ants and stag beetles scuttled for cover.

But the wildlife was too commonplace in the mill to retain his attention. Instead his eye glimpsed an envelope, dirty and crumpled. He picked it up and read the writing.

To: Peter Munnerly
The Old Mill,
Wirral

What was it? How could any communication so vaguely addressed have reached him? And how long had it been lying there?

He looked for the postmark, then realised there was no stamp. It had been delivered by hand, pushed under the door past the decaying and rat-gnawed rubber flange with which some former tenant had tried, with spectacular lack of success, to exclude draughts. But the writing was vaguely familiar. Round and florid. A woman's. He tore it open.

Ms Margery Munnerly
invites Mr Peter Munnerly to dinner
at Havana House, Rock Park
at 8.0 pm on Saturday 31 May
RSVP

As a mother's invitation to her son it seemed rather formal. But that was Margery. He liked the *Ms*, too – a flourish of defiance, a reminder that there'd been no archaic ceremonies and legal shackles where she was concerned, and never would be. Never would be! He pondered. The thought that Margery might still take – *might already have taken* – another lover came to him with breathtaking force. But who would have the nerve to take Margery on? There were animals, weren't there, where the female ate the male during mating? Dancing with death. Maybe, translated to some oriental souk or bazarre, it was an adventure Burlington might like to embark on..? Peter halted. Yes, that was a thought. The germ of a thrilling chapter began to sprout. And the dinner party might yield material.

Hold on, though, the date. 'Red, what's today's date?'

'Twentieth, I think. Or twenty-first.'

'Of May?'

'No, April.'

'Great. There's still time to accept. If I want to go.'

*

It was a big if. The precondition brought troubling thoughts. In a way he wanted to see Margery again; in a way the invitation could be seen as a peace offering, an attempt at reconciliation. He supposed. And how else could he ever pin her down long enough to hear what she was doing, how the literary world was treating her, what her old friends from Cambridge were doing – no, on second thoughts he didn't want to hear about them – or whether she proposed to set off on her foreign travels again, a thing she'd often talked of.

On the other hand, who else would be there? Not Red Thomas, anyway. No, Margery didn't like Red, although you'd have thought he was just her sort of nonconformist. Maybe she could visualise him staring at her with disbelief, casting an air of vague disapproval over the proceedings while she held forth about poetry and did her ballerina swirl – what was it called, a pirouette? Or maybe this was some sort of family gathering? In which case he'd have the pleasure of meeting Georgina and Flo and heaven knows who else. A jolly evening. Though it would be fun to see Hazel and Caroline again. Perhaps, before answering, he ought he to find out?

On an evening later that week, after work but with sufficient delay for darkness to be gathering, he tapped on a window on the ground floor of Havana House. He waited, then tapped again. This time he thought there were sounds and in a moment Flo's face appeared through the pane, its expression one of stern enquiry. Seeing Peter, she raised her eyes to heaven. He made gestures as of someone lifting the sash window and with a sigh of resigned desperation Flo obliged.

'Oh yes. And what is it now?'

'Can I come in?'

'Not this way you can't. There are things called doors.'

'I don't want to be seen.' Silently, he mouthed *by-you-know-who* and, as if humouring a dangerous lunatic, Flo heaved at the sash window until with sudden force it shot upward and he was able to throw a leg, followed by the rest of him, through the opening. Flo fetched a duster and cleaned the bootmarks from the sill.

'And to what do I owe this unforeseen intrusion?'

'This.' He produced the invitation from a pocket, uncrumpled it and held it out. 'What's it all about? Why's she doing it and ought I to come?'

'My dear idiot boy.' Flo spread her hands as if shaking a tablecloth. 'Your mother invites you to dinner and you ask me if you ought to accept. Of course you ought.' She raised her head and addressed the ceiling. 'Otherwise, think what you may be missing. Ecuadorean hotpot or Bolivian paella. Roast Tanganyikan babies.'

'Who else is invited? Are you?'

Initially she seemed to baulk at answering the personal question, but at last she relented. 'The whole family, such as remain, I believe. Throw in, possibly, some of Margery's literary friends, those she doesn't at the moment consider dreadful phonies and pains in the neck – there won't be many of those – plus Hazel and Caroline, and that's about it.'

'None of Arthur's old friends from Atlantic Finance and Shipping?'

'Even Margery would surely have more sense than to lure your former employers into the same room, or house, or county, as you. This is a dinner party, not a dockers' brawl.'

'And no one to do with the racecourse?' Hastily, to clear all avenues, he added, 'Or the army or the police?'

'Young man, you are asking me to prognosticate your mother's intentions in far too much detail. I am a retired gentlewoman, not a psychiatrist.'

And with a stab of the arm she pointed to the still-open sash window, indicating beyond doubt that the interview was at an end.

*

In fact, the gathering consisted largely of family members. Those literati who were present congregated at one end of Margery's living room, looking with eagerness through an open door down to the Great Hall, its shining mahogany table heavy with their hostess's best silverware and damask napkins, but talking exclusively among themselves as if fearful of being stained by the outside world. Margery had hired a catering firm to provide dinner and a selection of leggy, bosomy girls were visible below, carrying from the kitchen

175

to the table dishes that included carrot-cream soup, Dover sole and *steak tartare a la bourgognais*. Disappointingly, they seemed too busy to engage in much conversation as they tripped back and forward but at least they had the advantage of freeing Annie from heavy duties. In defensive mode and in need of a shield against expected disapproval from other members of the family, Peter coralled her into a corner, his back half-turned on the gathering.

'Quite an event, isn't it?' He kept his voice low: Georgina had been eyeing him with what he took to be disfavour. 'What's come over the old girl?'

Annie stifled a guffaw under pretence of disapproval. 'You shouldn't talk about your mother like that. Maybe it's an olive branch.'

'Do you think so? That thought did cross my mind.' He turned as the shrill voice of one of the writers reached the climax of a joke he was telling. 'You don't suppose I was invited because I'm a writer, do you? I mean, the other writers didn't ask to meet me?'

It was Annie's turn to burst into laughter. 'Good heavens no. None of them would be seen dead with the man who created Burlington.'

'No, I suppose not.'

'They certainly wouldn't. I've heard them talking.'

The rejection hurt. It wasn't that he'd entertained any hopes of acclaim for his writing; but stray ideas had flitted through his mind: the Booker Prize; that award they gave for the best first novel; the arrival of a package postmarked Hollywood and heavy with what must surely be a contract; the voice of someone summoning at the telephone: *'It's for you. From Stockholm.'*

'I'm sorry you think that.' With studied nonchalance he added, 'It takes time for a writer to become known.'

Annie seized a wine bottle from a passing waitress and refilled his glass.

Strangely, though, he seemed to be wrong. As Margery rang a handbell and he followed the others down to the hall hoping to take a seat next to someone innocuous – Hazel or Caroline would be ideal if Georgina hadn't declared him a no-go zone – he found himself accompanied by one of the literati, a man with black, wavy hair and rather thick lips whom he seemed to remember meeting before. Hazel and Caroline, he noticed, had settled at the other end of the long table: the no-go theory could be right.

'Hello.' The wavy-haired man smiled. He seemed eager for conversation. 'We've met before. Norton Waybridge. The poet.'

'Ah, yes.' Peter shook the proffered hand. The poet. For a second he wondered, *Is there only one?* But it wasn't true. A glance down the table confirmed that.

'Er, I gather you've been having considerable success with your books. Financially, I mean.'

'Oh, I see. Yes. They're selling well.'

'Very good.' A chuckle. 'So you'll be well in with the publishing world, I expect.'

'Well, I don't know. The publishing world's a big one.' And when he'd sent his first Burlington book in they'd all rejected it. He'd had to publish it himself. It was different later, of course. Once an unknown firm had taken it on and the money began to flow there'd been headed letters in the post, soignee female agents immune from all literary taste or skill, wearing sheath dresses and prodding their stilettos with distaste into the mud round the mill door.

'Of course, what writers need before they hit the big time like you've done is a bit of help from those on the ladder.'

'Ye-es, I see what you mean. What sort of – help had you in mind?' Peter paused for Norton Waybridge's slight snigger to break the pause. 'Financial?'

'Oh, good heavens, no. Well, that as well, of course. But mainly... It's so important to know the right people in this game, isn't it?'

So that was it. The Burlington they mocked, the novels their sort had turned down, the ones Annie had heard them talking about with derision, were what brought him the company of Norton Waybridge, the poet. And – but to his surprise a woman on his left, another writer, was also starting to engage him in conversation. Peter sighed: he'd been ambushed. The recollection of a schoolroom poem faltered to mind: *They flee from me that sometime did me seek.* How strange to find the opposite also true.

*

It wasn't in Peter's nature to reflect on, or even to remember, things that had happened the night before. Yet the dinner party, with Margery reciting her verses to the accompaniment of dramatic gestures and the guests applauding, stayed in his mind as a fixture. She'd given him time, breaking away from her friends in a way she'd never done before, wanting to talk about old times, his schooldays, infancy.

'You were always a maverick,' she said. 'At nursery school, you were always happy playing on your own. Or leading, being the boss. Never following.'

He'd grinned, touched by what seemed her sudden, urgent desire for a truce. It was what he'd long wanted. Was it possible that now at last, at her age, she could make real contact with him, realise he existed?

'People say there are leaders and followers,' he told her. 'What they forget is that there's a third category: loners.'

He knew from the way her face lit up that he'd created, for the first time he could remember, a bond.

*

He and Red had just finished breakfast, sitting at the rough kitchen table with empty coffee mugs the following morning, when the boy arrived. Peter went down the ladder to let him in.

'Hello, Jemmy Galston. What on earth are you doing here?'

The boy from the house at Rock Park next door to Havana said nothing, merely handed over a note. It was in Flo's hand.

> *Peter, would you come at once. Your mother has had⟶ a stroke and it's unlikely she will live. Please drop everything and come. Flo*

But by the time the Sunday bus service had delivered him to the mansions of Rock Ferry, Margery was dead.

As if she had held out a little longer, just for that last conversation with her only son.

Chapter 34
1983

The death is announced of Miss Margery Munnerly of Havana House, Rock Park. The funeral will be held in St Bartholomew's Church at 3 p.m. on Saturday 24th April. No flowers please. Donations to the Margery Munnerly Fund for Young Writers.

*

After Margery's death there were no more girls. It was as if, suffering one loss, he inflicted upon himself a second. The life had gone out of him.

He couldn't understand how he felt such loneliness at losing someone who for years he'd so seldom seen, someone who, in his whole life, had never focussed her attention on him for more than a few fleeting moments, who greeted him like a long-lost relation or presented him to guests like a prize bloom at a flower show but then, with the mayoral speech of pride and celebration over, unfailingly flitted to other things: her friends, poetry, travels, her time at Cambridge. Friends, did he say? Had Margery really had any friends? Weren't the people she called friends, like himself, kaleidoscopic images cast on to a screen forever flickering onward to new cartoons of experience?

There stayed with Peter, too, the way she'd invited him round for dinner on that last night of her life.

'She knew she was going.' Flo said when he ventured to remark how strange the invitation had seemed, unprecedented and unforeseen. 'The quacks had told her. It was her curtain call.'

The more he thought of it the more he felt what he inwardly longed to believe: that belatedly she'd realised what really mattered to her - the son she'd always neglected. Suddenly, at the last, her values had tilted, shifted like bedrock cleft by some earth tremor. Weren't there theorists who said people always acted so as to maximise their happiness? They had forgotten the people who never discovered where their happiness lay.

Sitting in the mill at his writing each day, another parallel arose. Dimly he'd often realised that Burlington was not only the self he himself would have liked to be, the life he'd have liked to live, but in a hologrammatic twist also a hero to worship, a father who'd not been present for him to admire and love, whose very name Margery's cruel whimsy had never allowed him to know. But weren't the girls he'd known also in some weird way substitutes for

179

a missing mother, always bringing hope and always disappointing? Prizes, flower-show blossoms, on whom he smiled brightly and fleetingly and then, like Margery, moved on? Where did the world of symbols and images, surrogates and revenants end? Where did reality begin?

Chapter 35
1983

The solicitor, Mr Hargreaves, had arranged the chairs in a loose arc in front of his desk. They took their seats, Nancy flanked by Flo and Georgina in the centre with Tom and Peter at either wing. On two chairs behind, alongside Hazel and Caroline, sat Joni and Annie Smith, whom Nancy had instructed to attend on the ground that the will was certain to affect her. For Nancy, Peter reflected, everything was certain. Doubt wasn't his own strong suit. But he wished he was as sure of anything as Nancy was of everything.

Mr Hargreaves cleared his throat. 'The reason I have brought you all together here is so that no one can claim their interest was neglected in the matter of Miss Margery Munnerly's will.'

He raised his eyebrows above bifocal spectacles. The finely-shaved skin bordering his sideburns crinkled, drawing attention away from the bald crown. 'Before I read the will, since it may prove contentious – though I hope it will not – I want to emphasise a number of points of law. A will may be contested on a number of different grounds...'

As the modulated voice droned on Peter carried out a survey of the audience. Nancy sat stone-jawed, clearly impatient with all this flimflam. Flo and Georgina had their hands crossed in their laps, waiting with patience for the substance. Tom's face held a slight grin, abstracted by some humorous thought unrelated to the solicitor's spiel. Joni and Annie had switched off.

It seemed to be the words that did it. *Testamentary capacity, codicil, nuncupative will, natural claims to provision.* What a load of bogus technicality. You could allot a measure of pretension and phoniness – there would be a posh name for it, yes, a *soporific coefficient* – to each phrase. The same way he and Red Thomas, down at the local, used to allot millihelens to the birds that came in. Helen's face launched a thousand ships; a millihelen was enough sexiness to launch one ship. 'Course, if you looked round a room like this - his eye fell on Joni. Yes, Joni could launch a few ships. Oh yes. If she hadn't been his daughter...

'Does anyone have any questions so far? In that case I will now read Miss Munnerly's will.'

Pencil and notepad at the ready, Peter took down the list.

To the horses of the Animal Sanctuary at Lache Lane

Chester I leave £1000. To my lifelong friend Ena Sophie
Gardner of 11 Dixon Avenue Prenton I leave £4000.
The remainder of my estate I leave to The North West
Poetry Society except that if my estate is of a value
equal to or greater than six thousand pounds one
thousand pounds shall be left to my son Peter Munnerly.
I also wish that Peter Munnerly shall meet my funeral
and testamentary expenses.

The silence that followed was so palpable that even the sound of his pencil's pressure became unbearable. Peter raised it from the paper and waited.

It was Nancy who spoke first.

'Does she leave nothing to me, then?'

Nor to Flo or Georgina, Tom nor Joni. Nor to Annie Smith. At least he, Peter, had done better than them. Though it hurt that his mother should, in the last reckoning of her life, value him less than horses.

Chapter 36
1984

All the time he was searching for a parking space Margery sat silent at his elbow. As he at last found a gap between two vehicles, climbed out and locked the car, her memory blanked the noticeboard with its warning of car thieves, anaesthetised his ears against the tussocks' rustle on the sandbanks rearing from Thurstaston beach. Abstraction bore him on a stormcloud of unreality. Someone else, some stranger, wore his sandals as he slithered down the shore, stripped to his swimshorts and, leaving his clothes in a neat heap at the high-tide mark, waded into the estuary. Bereavement numbed sensation.

Parallels with the loss of Penny kept flashing back like late flares from a spent rocket. He'd felt bereavement then but, as now, only after she'd stormed out and left him. Was there something wrong in him that he valued people only after they'd gone? Was he crippled, incapacitated by nature to face real people rather than just his dreams? Or did debility somehow spring from fatherlessness, the ceaseless irk of wanting to know, the unforgiven cruelty of Margery for making light of his demands, brushing his pleas aside? Arthur, the nearest he'd come to finding a father, had years ago left on his own long, private journey. *There* was loss. Perhaps that journey, an embrace of death, was what he, Peter, should seize as well?

But the delusion was never watertight. True suicides, he'd heard, felt that some outer power took control of him, directing them, guiding their feet and hands to self-destruction. His abstraction had none of that. Always the demon of presentness and calculation, always the pursuit of advantage snuggled, smart and devious, in his bloodstream.

Further along the coast, the sands were empty. The holiday crowds hadn't the energy or desire to stray far from their cars or to carry deckchairs and infants a mile up the narrowing throat of the Dee. A hundred yards out, swimming gently to avoid any white splash, he turned upstream and with slow breast-strokes, his head an invisible dot in the choppy tide, edged towards the deserted beach.

The water was cold but not killing. It stung in a way that exhilarated, a brash march at the onset of adventure. No, suicide wasn't Peter's style. Murder – that was different. When the art scam had been exposed, the judge at Chester Crown Court with his Welsh name and sly anglicised voice had been criticised in the press for his leniency in letting Peter off with a £2000 fine while the forger Nigel

Crean was given a stretch. But Griffiths had been right on that: Crean was the real crook, Peter merely a sucker drawn along by the devious underwater current.

Griffiths had been satirical and mocking. *Smart enough at selling fake pictures to expert buyers but not smart enough to realise they were fakes? Is that your story, then?* Oh yes, he was good on cynicism. But cynics never realised how various the world is, in what different accents it accosts different people. It had been beyond Griffiths to feel any twinge of sympathy for the entrepreneurs of art who sold pictures exactly like the originals they claimed to be. If the buyers cared only for art and beauty, weren't identical pictures just as good? And if they didn't, if they claimed the title of experts solely in pursuit of money, didn't they deserve to come to grief when they failed to detect paint and canvases manufactured long after the dates of the supposed masterpieces? But you couldn't expect Griffiths to see that. The old fool hadn't even known about the best-selling Burlington novels or that the revenue from them would pay off £2000 in a month or two. Yes, murder was possible.

But that wasn't what galled Peter most. Something else far outweighed the blindness of a clownish judge. Nancy's death not so many years ago had left him cold, relieved. But the loss of Margery wept like fresh-cut birchwood. The Margery he'd never possessed.

Approaching his goal, he reflected how irrational emotions were. One could envy others for owning things one didn't want. One could grieve at losing what one never had.

*

The escape went better than he'd hoped. Flurries of triumph and amazement assailed him at how smoothly the whole enterprise worked. Timed to synchronise with his swim from Thurstaston, the incoming tide bore him upstream faster than he'd calculated. The tiny sheltered shore he'd chosen for landing was deserted, his cache of newly-bought clothes still in their hidden plastic bag, intact. With deft, hurried movements he dried himself on the towel they were wrapped in, then slipped into the waiting suit, weirdly alien in its conservative cut and the light-grey material tailored for a hot climate. There followed an old-school-looking tie and natty brogue shoes. He'd studied himself in the mirror at home: slick but plausible. He made a good businessman.

For a moment he hesitated, holding in his hands the horn-rimmed spectacles he'd bought in a theatrical properties shop in Liverpool. They added to his disguise, concealing his eyes, matching more closely the

184

photograph in Mr Siddiqui's expensively supplied passport. But viewed in the mirror, they'd looked odd and stagey. The last thing he wanted. With a quick shove he thrust them into the side pocket of his suit. Maybe later, if necessary.

But necessity didn't arise. The bus that wove its way across the Wirral to Bebington station arrived on time, undelayed by holiday crowds. On the train to James Street, and after that on the airport coach, no one who knew him appeared. He needn't have worried. An actress he'd once met – she'd been 'resting' at the time, he remembered, (resting in his bed if the truth were told) – had once told him how precious anonymity, the fact of not being recognised, was. Most of all to successful actors such as she planned to become. All the way to the airport Peter cherished her wisdom. Hard as he tried to remember, her name still escaped him.

*

Singapore was safe, too. In this curious Mussolinian democracy they might jail you for failing to flush a public lavatory, or hang you for carrying hash, but they let bogus businessmen in easily enough. Commerce cancelled sin.

Lying under a single sheet in his room at the Asia Hotel where he'd chosen to break the journey, he saw his life silhouetted against the ceiling's cracks by light cast from musty uplighter-bulbs. Why was he here?

An interesting question. He must have known the answer at home before he set out. But bygone reasoning had died with the Merseyside drizzle. He wasn't in debt. Far from it, with luck when he reached Sydney there'd be a hefty few thousand pounds, already translated into Australian dollars, waiting in the bank. Account 00296306, Mr Piers Maudsley: he must remember that. Always choose a name with the same initials, and which sounds vaguely like your real name, in case you should forget and blurt it out. Oh yes. Follow Burlington's example.

It hadn't come cheap, the transition to businessman. He'd had to leave a painful amount in the bank at home so as not to arouse suspicion. Even the Australian money had had to be transferred piecemeal, bit by bit, circuitously via snakes and ladders of intermediaries. But there'd still be enough. No, debt wasn't why he'd faked death.

Was it the feeling of being robbed by the deaths of Arthur and Margery and by Penny's walkout? They came into it but taking on a new persona wouldn't dissolve that grief. If he was found out, the fact of faking his death would alone convince the world – *them*, the ones against him, the lot he couldn't stand - that he'd been up to no good. Oh, how they'd love raking out what they considered disreputable incidents in his life, inventing shady reasons for his quitting. There'd be some – Nigel Crean, the old farts at the racecourse, Charlie Scrimgeour – who'd feel it an affront that he'd gone without their permission. In their eyes his flight would prove him a ne'er-do-well. The tabloids would show no mercy.

Whereas in fact..?

In fact, he himself hardly knew. It was just that he longed for a fresh start. He was sick of them all, the people, the actual individual people, not simply the rackets by which they made their piles – slavery or lending money at extortionate rates of interest or turning a blind eye to fraud on the racecourse or faking pictures. He wanted rid of all of them, to begin again in a new country with a new name and a new personality and...

A new personality. Was that it, then – a desire to change himself? Utterly and totally?

It was the first time he'd ever thought it: *I'm a racketeer as well.*

*

He put a hand to his left ear, muffling it. The hemispherical hood of the phone booth scraped his head but he ignored it. Other hostellers staying at The Billabong thumped by on thinly carpeted floor. A smell of chlorine drifted down the open stairway that led to the rooftop swimming pool.

'Hello. Red?'

But the silence of non-response slept on.

He walked up the stairs into open air. A man with an Irish accent was holding forth on some political subject to a group of other hostellers, some in swimwear dripping from recent immersion.

'It's the only way you'll ever break loose from Britain. Psychologically, I mean.'

'We've broke loose years ago,' a cobber voice called out. 'You're an immigrant, you don't understand. Irish is half Pommie.'

'Not at all, I understand only too well. I get half the backwash against the Brits that they themselves get, even though I migrated here from a different country. What you need is to do what Ireland's done. Become a republic.'

Peter left the debate and moved to the railed edge of the roof. Sydney lay sprawling below him, a city such as he imagined Los Angeles to be, stretching in an infinite host of houses as far as the eye could see to the Blue Mountains and beyond that the dusty unending outback. A man could start a new life here.

He raised his mobile and phoned again.

'Come on, Red.'

But this time, though there was a signal, he received no answer. He wondered where Red was. Still out at his latest workplace on the hot dog stall? No, of course not. It would be night-time in England.

'Nar, we sure wanna republic but not so's to rid ourselves of the Poms. That's already done.'

Isolation draped itself over his shoulders. The dampness of a spider's web on a wet morning. He was alone here. It was what he'd wanted and yet somehow not welcome. Perhaps he should buy a paper. They wouldn't fly the *Echo* out here but his disappearance might be in the national broadsheets when they arrived on the stalls a day late.

'It's not just me that's of this opinion. It's on a plaque in the Parliament Building. Some Australian prime minister years ago said it. It's your only way of ditching the inferiority complex.'

'Inferiority! Mind what you're saying, mate!'

Peter edged still further from the group, now growing in number and excitability. That was it: he'd get a Pommie paper at the store and bring it back here to read.

Under plain cover, of course.

*

The Telegraph, 5 September

WIRRAL MAN DISAPPEARS

Clothing including a T-shirt, jeans, trainers and underwear found abandoned on the beach at Thurstaston, Wirral on the afternoon of 31 August is believed to have belonged to a local man, Mr Peter Munnerly of Rock Park. Mr Munnerly was recognised by a passer-by as he entered the sea in bathing shorts soon after low tide. He has not been seen since. His car was parked in a nearby car park.

Speaking of the dangers of bathing in the Dee Estuary, Inspector Joe Brearley of the Cheshire Constabulary emphasised the treacherous nature of the tides and the strength of the currents off Thurstaston. He appealed to all holidaymakers to take extreme care when swimming and not to go beyond their depth. The search for the missing man continues.

*

187

8 September
MYSTERY OF MISSING SWIMMER
Cheshire police are pursuing enquiries concerning the disappearance while swimming in the Dee estuary of Mr Peter Munnerly, whose clothes were found abandoned on Thurstaston beach on 31 August. The missing man, who was identified by a scrap of paper found in the wallet inside his trouser pocket, was the son of the late Mr Arthur Munnerly, a director of the Atlantic Finance and Shipping Company, and was recently fined £2000 for his role in an art scam for which the forger Nigel Crean was sentenced to a term of imprisonment.

In response to questions concerning Peter Munnerly's whereabouts Inspector Joe Brearley in charge of the investigation said it was most unusual for the body of anyone drowning in the Estuary not to be washed up within a short time. He stressed that Mr Munnerly, who had no fixed career and at the time of his disappearance seems to have been unemployed, was likely to have been put under severe pressure by the fine imposed on him and may have been in shock as a result. Enquiries had revealed that his bank account contained a good deal less money than usual at the time of his assumed drowning. Suicide could not be ruled out.

*

16 September
FOUL PLAY SUSPECTED IN MUNNERLY CASE
Cheshire police yesterday refused to rule out the possibility of foul play in the case of Mr Peter Munnerly, who went missing while swimming off the Wirral last month. The case involves a number of unusual features, in the view of Chief Inspector Brian Ledsham, recently placed in charge of the investigation.

First, the wallet which led to Mr Munnerly's identification was almost empty when found on Thurstaston beach, a possible indication that Mr Munnerly was robbed before his disappearance. A second bizarre feature is that his bank account had been largely emptied by withdrawals in cash not long before. Friends and relatives report no signs of undue stress or depression on the part of the missing man but blackmail remains a possibility. The non-reappearance of his body may be a sign that it was removed from the scene of the accident or crime, or possibly weighed down by heavy objects of some kind so that it sank. Police are dredging the Dee Estuary near the site of the abandoned clothes.

*

23 September

MISSING WIRRAL MAN SIGHTED

Cheshire Missing Persons police are following up a report made to their Australian counterparts by a recent British visitor to New South Wales. Mr Merlyn Stell of Wirral was on holiday staying with his son in the Sydney suburb of Mascot when, while spending a day on the beach, he saw and recognised Peter Munnerly, the swimmer who went missing on Thurstaston beach in August. Mr Stell knew Munnerly in connection with his work as an art dealer and gallery proprietor. Chief Inspector Brian Ledsham of Cheshire Constabulary warned, however, that many sightings prove on closer investigation to be mistaken. The search continues.

The question, *what am I doing here*, came to Peter again through the weeks but less as a serious resident of the mind than as the across-the-street quip of someone he'd met and joked with in the pub last night. Life was so comfortable. Day after day of warm spring sunshine; a city that, for all the gruesome motor-ridden backstreets, wore regally its fine avenues and huge park, the cool spacious marble of its art gallery, the men playing chess with huge plastic men under towering trees.

He swanned around. A trip by rail up the coast to Queensland, returning in falling dusk through woods in which nestled the lights of a thousand homes. A four-day visit to Canberra with its variegated modern embassies, the clean-cut Parliament Building, the great Lake around which joggers puffed and pistoned. He wondered if he might not stay here, idle but happy, forever. The bank held an ample stock of transferred wealth.

Once or twice he tried writing some more Burlington. After all, it was Burlington who'd brought in the money. But somehow, in this new world, history seemed alien, rootless in the sand of a country only two hundred years old. The discovery troubled him. It meant he couldn't, after all, settle here forever without taking employment.

He thought of Margery. Where would her spirit be now? She'd always believed in an afterlife. Was there another vast Australia in the sky where she could perform her poems? He wondered if she would miss him. Somehow the thought seemed unlikely. It wouldn't be Margery.

And himself? Did he miss people? Surprisingly, yes he did. Most of all Joni. He'd seen little of her anyway since she'd gone to work in the Midlands but still it bit deep, the pain of not being able to talk to her, the sole person in the world he'd ever come close to. In a way, that, too, was a fraud. He wasn't close now, hadn't been for years. What he craved was to be with the Joni of the past. He longed to play with her in the nursery, to tease her with funny hats and disguises, sing jingles that made her laugh. Growing up had taken all that away: she was lost to him before she left. The thought was too painful. He stamped it from his mind.

He missed, too, Red Thomas and the two now also-grown-up little girls, Caroline and Hazel. The comradeship with them, created in nursery days, still stood, a temple seldom entered but enduring and sound, a home for his affection. It would be a blow when those little girls found husbands: another theft of what he'd never owned, except in his inmost heart.

He even, in a way, missed Flo for all her forbidding ways. Ah yes, perhaps that was it. *The Telegraph* had said in one of its snippets that Flo had paid his £2000 fine. How kind of her. He thought he'd paid it himself. But with the Burlington money coming in thick and fast through concealed channels he was never sure about things like that. Flo's generosity was unfortunate in a way. The fine had seemed a plausible reason for his 'suicide'. He didn't want Chief Inspector Ledsham to be deprived of a plausible theory. Especially since it was completely wrong.

Merlyn Stell's meddling, though, was another matter. Damn the man. He wished he'd sold him more fake pictures.

*

Another snippet in *The Telegraph* caught his eye. There was in the art world, it seemed, a market for known fakes. Your real Renoir might sell for, say, a million; a fake of the same picture would fetch six hundred thousand.

Peter fondled the information like a baby. What if you faked a fake? It might mean offering the genuine one as if it were fake. But no, more likely it would mean selling a brand new picture that was a replica of a fake. A kind of faked fake. Could the market put a higher value on a fake than on the authentic article? What fun! What side-splitting fun!

But in a way, no different from anything else. Charles Scrimgeour, a fake financier, was paid far more than he, Peter, had been paid for playing the markets, doing the work. Old Purlock, the school Beak - a fake educator if ever there was one - was highly paid for it. There was Fox-Bewley and Septimus Whatsit and the other one, Tristan, and all the other bogus experts of the art market. An old song came to mind.

Putting on the agony,
Putting on the style,
That's what all the fine folk
Are doing all the while
And as I look around me
I'm very apt to smile
To see so many people
Putting on the style.

It's not what you know, it's who. He'd often thought it, but never said so; it would have sounded like sour grapes. But now that he saw the falsity of success exposed in reality, he felt surprise. It could have only one meaning. He hadn't really believed his cynicism. In all those years when he'd said, 'I'm getting too cynical', the truth was, he hadn't been cynical enough.

Oscar Wilde breathed in his ear: *Never tell the truth; you're bound to be found out.*

*

'Excuse me, sir, we'd like to take a few minutes to ask you some questions.' The incomer, short for a policeman and with a blotchy complexion, thrust forward a plastic identification card like a stocktrader signalling 'Buy'. 'If you'd care to follow us downstairs. The manager said we could use the television room.'

At this hour of the morning the room contained only two viewers. The short officer's skin-headed colleague ushered them out. The policemen swivelled easy chairs to face Peter.

'We understand you've only recently arrived from England?'

'Yes.'

'With the intention of becoming permanently resident in Australia?'

'I've been given immigrant permission. What's all this about?'

Shortie exchanged glances with Skinhead. A decision to answer seemed agreed. Shortie heaved a mini-sigh.

'We've had a communication from the police in Cheshire, England. They're trying to trace a Mr Peter Munnerly who's said to have disappeared in mysterious circumstances. You wouldn't happen to know anything about Mr Munnerly's disappearance?'

'No. Nothing. Look, you don't imagine he's me? It's absurd. The names must have got mixed up. I'm Piers Maudsley. What makes you think I might be -?'

Shortie coughed. The act reddened the carbuncles on his cheek as if with defensiveness. 'We further understand that Mr Munnerly had recently been fined two thousand British pounds for taking part in an art fraud. You wouldn't know anything about that, I suppose?'

'How could I?' One evasion deserved another. 'Look, what's the evidence for all this? Who put you on to me?'

'It's a routine check. A disappeared person.'

'But what's he done wrong? The fine's been paid –'

Peter halted. Shortie raised an eyebrow. It was Skinhead who spoke.

'Mr Munnerly didn't pay the fine.'

'Didn't pay -? But I – ' Peter halted in fear. The smell of self-incrimination rose from his pores. Any question risked admission.

'You seem surprised to hear that.'

'I don't understand. I'm not Munnerly. I don't owe the police anything. Or anyone else.'

'It was Mr Munnerly's aunt who paid the fine for him.'

Exuberance rose in Peter's chest. Skinhead had given his case away. He'd revealed what Peter wouldn't otherwise have known. 'There you are, then. So what's the offence supposed to be? Am I supposed to have murdered this disappeared man, whoever he is? Did I rob him? Assault him? Am I supposed to be fleeing from some crime? What?'

Shortie held out an arm to restrain his junior, a referee stopping play.

'That remains to be seen, sir. Meanwhile, could we please see the passport on which you entered Australia?'

'It's a perfectly good one. I'd no reason to run away from England. I'd done nothing wrong.'

'If that's so there'll be no problem. Now, if we could just go back to Reception where we understand you left your passport for safekeeping.'

'How do you know that?'

'We took the precaution of looking at it before we came to see you.'

'You -? So you've been prying into my affairs already? And for nothing! I've committed no offence.'

'That hasn't yet been established. In our experience people don't flee from a country unless they've something pretty serious to hide.'

'But I've broken no law.'

'That could be going a bit too far, Mr Munnerly. Entering this country by means of a false passport is itself an offence.'

*

He'd thought they would simply put him on a plane at Mascot and that he'd be met by British police at Heathrow. But absurdly, a burly man in a mohair suit accompanied him all the way. Someone in risk assessment had allotted the case a wrong rating.

There was no introduction or arrest, no handcuffs. But there could be no doubt. The muscle-bound man in plain clothes, possibly an officer already booked for London on some other duty, followed him through the various hurdles – baggage and ticket check-in, passport desk (hilariously, they still let him keep and use the forged Maudsley document, surely a unique case of one government service deceiving another), the body search and boarding card display. At Brisbane the passengers had to change planes and in an almost empty Boeing the sleuth's elephantine step took him to a seat in the row behind Peter. Occasional glances showed him watchful in case his prey attempted further felonies.

The Boeing shuddered in the indignation of engine-testing, then lumbered to a canter and raced to take-off. The plane tilted and strained. In an hour or so the brown dust of the outback blew away and they soared over tropical islands, green oases encircled by golden sand, set in a sapphire sea.

A blonde stewardess, starved of customers, brought repeated trays of food and drink. At her third approach Peter recovered presence of mind.

'Take a seat. You've no one else to attend to.'

The upholstery of seat and anatomy, both rounded and generous, lured to close contact. 'Where you headed for?'

'England. You like a quiet flight like this?'

And as if at the opening of a spigot her life and loves poured out: the Malaysian businessman who'd bought her fashion tops, rubies, a gold-wired bra; the Mexican who only through the misfortunes of trade had been prevented from taking her to his villa in the hills; the captain who during weekends of passion in the Hong Kong Empire Hotel had carried her to a different, breathless world,

193

then vanished back to his wife leaving her in a stratospheric void of bliss. Behind the trolley bearing tea, coffee and wine bottles, memory was her aphrodisiac.

'You'll be around Heathrow quite often, I guess,' she said, head tilted girl-like, as he edged past her at the exit, their fronts brushing together.

'Not really. I may have a long stay with the Cheshire police.'

*

'So the clothes left lying on the beach were yours, Mr Munnerly?'

'Well, er, yes.'

'Why did you leave them there?'

'I wanted people to think I'd drowned.'

The sergeant raised eyebrows. He hadn't expected truth. 'Why did you want that?'

'I wanted to start again. A new identity.'

'Was that in order to conceal something you'd done?'

'No. Just to start my life over again. I felt I had the potential to be a new, really good person but old ties and my reputation with other people bogged me down. It was a fresh start.'

The word *reputation* made the sergeant perk up. Here was familiar ground. 'What would you say this reputation was, that you wanted to escape from.'

'When you're young you're bound to make mistakes. Do things you regret afterwards.'

'What things in your case exactly?'

They were trained to do it, these rozzers. Like tabloid reporters, they ferreted for muck, ignoring any good you ever did. Sinking experiences came back from the past like a bad fairy's curse. The departure from Atlantic Finance for an offence his superiors got away with. The time a drunken driver dinted Peter's bonnet and the copper who turned up arrested him after finding he had a worn tyre-tread and a light over the number plate not functioning. Grillings before the school beak, Purlock, and the final punishment for cheating he hadn't done. People saw what they expected, not what was there.

'Just general dissatisfaction with myself.' Before the sergeant could bounce back the inevitable question Peter added, 'Some people have higher standards than others.'

194

The policeman narrowed his gaze. The hint of an insult hadn't helped. 'I gather you have a criminal conviction on your record.'

'Oh?' Innocence: he was good at that.

'For operating a betting business without a licence.'

'It was years ago. I took the rap for that long ago.'

A studied silence allowed the full enormity of the crime to sink in.

'And now, according to the Australian police, you were fined for entering the country on a false passport.'

'So? I've paid the fine. I've done nothing else wrong.'

'I just wonder why you were so keen to hide your true identity. What drove you to fake your own death? ' But at the last word a new thought inflated the buttoned collar and dark uniform. On the complacent face a smile formed, grateful for discovered guilt. 'And by denying your guilt obstructed the police in the execution of their duties.'

Anger seized Peter by the throat. 'If you're going to find me guilty of something I haven't already paid for, tell me what it is. Otherwise let me go. The Aussies said it's no crime, here or there, to change your name unless you do it to practise deception. Well? Who have I deceived? What have I done that breaks the law?'

But the sergeant's only response was a fulfilled nod. As if anger and the loss of self-control were themselves a sufficient proof of guilt.

Chapter 37
1985

It wasn't like Peter to feel awkward; but turning up at The Swan after the well-publicised Australian debacle required brass nerve. To go late would involve appearing before a full house, the centre of a drama. To go early would mean repeating his misadventures to successive latecomers. In the end he chose the mid-point of the evening. Going with Red Thomas, his appearance would be diluted, not the focus of attention.

'It was in the paper,' Red told him when he called at his friend's place. Left alone during Peter's travels, Red had moved to a hired room in Woodchurch. 'You got arrested for faking your death.'

'Yeh.'

'Was it for the insurance?'

'I'm not insured. Never was.'

'Debts?'

'There's always money from Burlington.'

'Why, then?'

Peter pulled a face. It sounded too Sunday-school-like. 'I just wanted to start again. A new leaf.'

Red laughed. Pull the other one. 'Did you get some bird in the club?'

'Nah. Like I said.' He eyed the smile of scepticism 'Don't believe me, do you?'

'You've had plenty of fresh starts. Atlantic Finance; the racecourse; Burlington; the art racket. You could just as well have found another.'

'It's not the same. I wanted to *be* someone else.'

'Anyway, they let you off in the end?'

'Who?'

'The Ozzie cops.'

'It wasn't a question of letting me off. I'd done nothing wrong. Using a false passport was the best they could think of.'

'You saying it's not illegal to fake your death and change your name?'

'Only if you do it to defraud.'

'And you didn't?'

'You don't believe a word I say, do you?'

'What about the British cops?'

'They couldn't pin anything on me, either. But I've got to see them again.'

'Aha! When?'
'In the morning.'

*

'So you say your only reason for pretending to drown was to make a new start in life? Take on a new identity?' The inspector's face was thickset and square with black bristles already appearing at mid-morning. A blustery voice mingled aggression with the nerviness of a man demoralised by being out of his depth.

'Right enough.'

A pause. 'And you removed most of the money from your bank account and sent it to Australia in advance of your arrival?'

'I needed something to live on. There's nothing illegal about that.'

'Hm. I gather you're divorced with one daughter.'

'The alimony was paid off years ago.'

'You didn't realise people would be bound to think you were trying to cheat someone when you cleared off with a faked suicide like that?'

So now it was what people might think. They couldn't find anything he'd done wrong, so they fell back on what people might think. 'It wouldn't have worried me.'

The policeman lurched forward stabbing the air. 'So you don't care what people think?'

The violence was disequilibrating. Peter took a while to steady himself. 'What I mean is, I wouldn't have worried even if I'd thought – what other people might think.'

'Hm.' The policeman seemed to feel he'd scored a point, like a lawyer who repeats something a witness has said in court, making insignificance momentous. The theatricals of it all. Charles Scrimgeour. Merlyn Stell. Putting on the style.

'You left your car parked on the clifftop near the beach where you staged your disappearance. Did it occur to you that, left overnight there, the car might create an obstacle and public nuisance?'

'It was legally parked.'

'That's not the point. It was left there without an owner, blocking the space it occupied. You didn't take due care on that account, did you?'

'I wasn't breaking the law.'

Then it came, expected after the Australian arrest but still unbelievable: recourse to the one thing they could pin on him.

'There's another thing. How much time do you think the police force has had to spend tracing you and investigating this case, Mr Munnerly? Did you ever think how serious it is, the offence of wasting police time?'

Peter's eyes took on the glaze of weariness and depression. Crystalline truths fell one by one into the deep pit of his consciousness, heavy as drops of mercury. These men, here and now, were wasting an hour they could have spent in pursuit of lawbreakers. But of course, that didn't matter, what *they* did didn't count. Nudging that thought from behind came the realisation that for a man in love with himself the emptiest of points scored brings bliss. But the third and last was saddest of all: a man can never escape his past.

Margery had once recited a poem:

> *The moving finger writes and having writ*
> *Moves on. Not all thy vanity nor wit*
> *Can lure it back to cancel half a line*
> *Nor all thy tears wash out a word of it.*

Chapter 38
2006

'And it was while you were in jail on this trumped-up charge and the resulting, as you say, dubious conviction that you began writing the Burlington stories seriously?'

'I'd published a few before but that was my breakthrough.'

'Most of the stories are set well in the past, before you were born - in Britains's later colonial period and in the Second World War, for example. What drew you to go back to historical times like that?'

'I'm not sure. The romance of the past. An interest in history.'

'You've read a lot of history?'

Peter breathed relief. History was safe. There'd been no avoiding the questions about Walton and his unlicensed bookmaking but at least the rest of his career seemed to have eluded the BBC researchers. There'd been nothing about insider dealing or faked Old Masters..

Most of all, nothing about Australia. Here at least, he'd escaped the dire character stain of his attempt to begin a fresh life. For a moment he could forget the horrible, ensnaring truth that you could never extricate yourself from people's addiction to gossip, never start again.

'I do. I research all my stories thoroughly.'

'And the result has been that they've sold well. Thirteen million copies in twenty seven languages.'

'They've even been translated into American.'

Natalie Springdale laughed, a bell-like chime. As he launched into an account of his historical reading the sense of reprieve freed him to look at her for the first time. Ambitious, that was obvious. And not a bad-looker when you got down to it. Well-sparkled teeth, hair bouncing nicely round her cheeks. Well-upholstered where it mattered.

Pity about the ring. But it mightn't count, not with a career girl. After all, this was the new millenium.

'What would you like for your next record?'

He hadn't memorised the reply. There was no need. The list he'd posted in – the very list which, newly typed, she'd set on the table before him as an aide-memoire at the start of the programme - had been clear enough:

Number 5: My Old Man's A Dustman
Number6:Burl Ives
– The Big Rock Candy Mountains
But the desire to tease tickled his lips, inassuageable.

'I'd like Phil Harris singing *Somebody Stole My Girl.*'

He watched closely, trying not to laugh. The interviewer was disconcerted. She reached over and pulled his list to her.

'There seems to be some confusion. I've got you down for –'

'No. I'd like Phil Harris.'

She raised her shoulders, pulling her slim frame together as if to make the idiom literal. She smiled, the pearly teeth shining. 'Well, just let's see what we've got.'

Cheese, her smile reiterated in the seconds that elapsed until the folk singer's voice came through the air:

> *In the Big Rock Candy Mountains*
> *You never change your socks*
> *And the little streams of alcihol*
> *Come a-trickling down the rocks.*

But from then on until the cry of gulls and the harmonies of tropical romance unfurled the programme's end her smile nurtured a tiny twist of hatred, a minuscule capsule of cyanide nestling between snow-white teeth.

*

'Mr Munnerly, could you wait a second. There's a message for you.'

The girl at Reception ran across the lobby holding out a white, unstamped envelope. The same girl who'd showed him where to go when he first arrived.

'I think it's rather urgent but I couldn't give it you earlier. It only arrived after your programme had begun.'

Puzzled, he tore the envelope open. There was no address, no signature, only the message.

> *Your aunt Florence was taken seriously ill last night. Her*
> *sisters weren't able to contact you. She has been rushed*
> *to the Countess Hospital, Chester.*

A shaky blankness drained him of feeling. Last night? Yes, he'd been at The Wheatsheaf with Red. Hadn't checked the ansaphone when he came in.

But just a minute, there was another chit. He slit its covering.

Aunt Florence died at the Countess at breakfast time today.

Bewilderment became disbelief. But how could he not believe, he wondered, grief prickling his eyes. One couldn't disbelieve what one could only have expected, what one must have *known* would soon come.

'Who gave you these?'

'One of the girls. They were written by Natalie. Natalie Springdale.'

'But she was interviewing me.'

'She sent them through separately, first one then the other, beforehand. Before she went into the studio. We were to hand them to you when you left.'

'She delayed telling me?'

'I - I don't know. Yes, I suppose so. Is it – something serious?'

'So as not to spoil the programme. So I didn't rush off to the Countess.'

'I'm sorry, I don't under-'

'Of course. So as not to cancel. So her career...'

Other memories, a cataract of career-seekers and power-brokers, self-publicists and intrigue-addicts, cascaded over him, a Niagara of bitterness. And yet, the men in Walton – they were the ones locked up.

'Don't worry. It's not your fault.'

But as he pushed open the tubular doors he wondered: wouldn't I, given the chance, also be guilty of this?

Chapter 39
2006

The moment she entered the bar Peter knew it was her. The tailored suit, the expensive material. And about time. He couldn't have kept off the whisky much longer.

He lurched to his feet, guyroped a smile to his face. Bloated cheeks and the onset of strawberry pores on nose and forehead dampened the morning's talcum.

'Mrs Lascelles?'

She fluttered to a halt.

'Oh, yes. Are you Mr Munnerly? I'm sorry. I'm not used to finding my way, I didn't quite...'

'That's all right. I knew it was you from your letter.'

He pulled back her chair. Always a good wheeze, that - *noblesse oblige,* like they say. Not that he ever would say it. He hoped the received pronunciation was working this time, varnishing the Scouser accent he'd rebelliously cultivated since youth. 'Like a suit that don't fit,' Nobby Barnes had called it in Walton. Cheeky bugger.

A white-jacketed waiter appeared. 'Gin and tonic?' Peter suggested when she hesitated, and she seemed relieved to be provided with an answer.

'I'm glad you liked my book that you read. Which one was it?'

'Oh it's not just one. I've read them all. *Burlington and the Kosovo Campaign. Saddam's Nemesis. Burlington at Port Stanley. The Houris of Baghdad.* All of them.'

'That's great. Which one did you like best?'

She lowered her eyes. A faint blush coloured her cheeks. The pearl necklace – pretty certainly real - quivered. He felt a jet of elation, almost endearment. How old, though? His own age, he'd guess – maybe a bit more, pushing fifty-five. But good on maintenance. Figure a bit overblown but that was the sort he went for. And so innocent-like. Naïve. He waited.

'Well, to tell the truth, Mr Munnerly -'

'Call me Vince. Vince Munnerly-Smythe it is, actually. I change it for the books.' He wasn't sure where the lie came from. The assumed names arose on impulse, taking even himself by surprise. 'And your first name -?'

'Lavinia. Yes, do let's be friends.'

She'd wanted to be friends in the letter. There'd been a variegated landslide of mail ever since the Burlington stories hit the big time – fan-mail missives drooling with admiration, approaches from film companies wanting the rights, requests for money from charities. There'd been some from American academics who assumed the stories were true, impressed by the façade of scholarship – the footnotes and copious bibliography, most of all the preface setting out how Burlington's memoirs had been discovered in the old vicarage belonging to the author's family and used to construct Vince Munnerly-Smythe's stories. Some of the academics were writing critical studies of the Burlington novels, others planning biographies. The boost to Peter's morale was explosive.

Then there'd been the letters from women. Variously, they'd proposed meeting, an affair, marriage. Peter struggled to believe them real. But the one from this classy bird, Lavinia Lascelles, stood out from the rest. Partly, it was the address – 5 Clifford Mews, Kensington SW10 , partly the air of loneliness sent out by a widow still grieving for her husband. But most of all it was the sheer childlike simplicity, the hint of someone whose marriage had shielded her totally from real-life decisions and the need to be streetwise. Striking an ore of shyness like that, he'd have been a fool not to take up her hint of a meeting. You got a nose for women.

'Yes, 'course we'll be friends. I was just going to say that myself.'

'Mr Munn – I mean, Vince. I hope you don't mind my asking, but Burlington – he's really you, isn't he? You've just changed the name. I mean, how else could you know so much...?'

Peter hesitated. The shelves of his work-room at Havana House came to mind, the row upon row of volumes on past centuries' wars, conflicts, social conditions: *Ungovernable Britain 1900-1950, Victoria's Profligate Aristocracy, From the Dockers' Tanner to Jarrow*. That sort of history was the passion of his life, always had been. Only whisky hooked him more.

He took a breath and smiled. 'You're real smart, a real lady,' he said. 'I've just been thinking. With so much in common we ought to see more of each other.'

Her lips barely moved. 'I'd love that.'

'I know, why don't I take you out to dinner? It's past seven, so why not now?'

'Oh!' She was adither with happiness.

'Come on, then. Here, I'll get your coat.'

At the door, mouselike, she ventured a query. 'You didn't really answer. You are Burlington, aren't you?'

Peter chuckled. 'I can see there's no way of fooling you.'

Chapter 40
2008

They parked the car and followed the narrow road towards the ravine.

'This is it,' Peter said. 'Llewellyn's Leap, they call it. Where the Welsh chief, fleeing from his enemies, took a flying leap, right the way across.'

'He can't have.' The woman - Dilys, she was called - wasn't impressed. You had to be careful with smartypants like this one. 'It's too wide.'

Peter surveyed the gorge. Sixty feet down, water gathered in a deep black pool before pouring down towards the North Welsh coast with its far glimpse of Liverpool's towers speckling the sea-mist. Above the pool, the single-lane road writhed across an iron bridge crowded with people. 'It's just a legend,' he said. Clutching for extenuation, he added, 'The battle was real, though.'

'Who was he fighting?'

Peter cleared his throat. 'Dunno. Some enemy.'

'But who were they?'

'English, probably. After the battle of –' His tongue faltered, unsteadied by the double whiskies he'd had for lunch. What did it matter? 'Way back. Edward, wasn't it? Or thereabouts.'

'You don't seem very sure.'

'I'm not. It's not my day. Look,' his voice took on haste, 'I've got to go and get harnessed. You stay here and watch. Enjoy it.' He stooped and pecked her on the cheek. Never go too fast with this sort of bint.

'You sure you really want to? Above all that?'

'Yeh, no problem. I'm not scared.'

He'd always wanted to do it, bungee jumping. Partly, it was to prove his courage, the way he'd always had more guts than most men. That and wanting to strip to the waist in front of a crowd of women and show his muscular body – still pretty good if he held his belly in. It was only after he'd invited Dilys to the event and couldn't get out of it without loss of face that he realised you made the jump fully clothed. The water below was no more than a safety net if things went wrong. Which they wouldn't.

There was no queue for harnessing. Not many people fancied a free fall, more a topple than a jump, so you fell straight down without slewing around. Not many people had the bottle for that. They didn't get the kick.

He wondered if the organisers picked the right rope for the jumpers' weights, like for a hanging. While two men attached the rope at ankles and trunk, his heart pounded. He felt a faint stir in his bowels and checked his belly against risk of accidents. In a way it helped, took your mind off the jump.

But there was a pleasurable tremor in watching the man in front climb over the handrail to the ledge, then, with arms clasped across his chest and his back towards the drop, plunge like a falling matchstick. The spectacle had an unreality, even something of the humour of an animated film. At the low point of the fall there was an element of surprise in the bounce and rebound and then the way the man, with a kind of joggling motion, went into a second, lesser fall. After that, the upside-down dangle, the slow haul back to the bridge. It was all over in five minutes.

The need for action calmed. As with everything, the waiting was worst. At least it would win his bet with Red. A hundred quid, if he paid. Worth it for that, never mind Dilys.

'Okay, go ahead.'

He climbed on to the ledge. He breathed deep. Keeping his body straight as instructed, he leaned back. For an instant he felt fear, electrifying but at once doused by the knowledge that there was nothing he could do. Then the void of falling, with no time to think, the up-rush of trees, bridge, water as he twirled and turned, then straightened out, the rope beginning to tighten, to decelerate. At the expected yet still startling rebound he rose only halfway back to the bridge but the rope jumped higher, snaking into a loop, then falling in a noose about his chest, his neck. He raised his hands to grip it, to loosen, but it was no use, he couldn't throw it off.

There were shouts. 'His neck! God! Stop him!'

But by the time he was hauled in, there was no breath in the man whose last sight had encompassed, beyond river and hills, the city that had been his family's livelihood and their life.

Printed in the United Kingdom by
Lightning Source UK Ltd., Milton Keynes
138988UK00001B/42/P